Copyright

All

The characters and events portrayed in this book are fictitious. Any similarity to real persons, living or dead, is coincidental and not intended by the author.

No part of this book may be reproduced, or stored in a retrieval system, or transmitted in any form or by any means, electronic, mechanical, photocopying, recording, or otherwise, without express written permission of the publisher.

ISBN: 9798288313493

Cover design by: Art Painter
Library of Congress Control Number: 2018675309
Printed in the United States of America

For Dad.

*My consistent source of inspiration,
encouragement and guidance.*

CONTENTS

Copyright

Dedication

BEFORE 2

Chapter 1 3

Chapter 2 8

FRIDAY 10

Chapter 3 11

Chapter 4 19

Chapter 5 31

Chapter 6 39

Chapter 7 56

Chapter 8 63

BEFORE 84

Chapter 9 85

Chapter 10 95

SATURDAY 99

Chapter 11	100
Chapter 12	112
Chapter 13	123
Chapter 14	136
Chapter 15	145
Chapter 16	152
Chapter 17	167
Chapter 18	171
Chapter 19	177
Chapter 20	183
Chapter 21	195
Chapter 22	206
Chapter 23	222
Chapter 24	229
BEFORE	236
Chapter 25	237
Chapter 26	241
SUNDAY	246
Chapter 27	247
Chapter 28	261
Chapter 29	262
Chapter 30	268
Chapter 31	283
Chapter 32	293

BEFORE	301
Chapter 33	302
Chapter 34	308
TWO MONTHS LATER	311
Chapter 35	312
Chapter 36	322
Chapter 37	330

THIS TOO SHALL PASS
By Emma Browne

BEFORE

CHAPTER 1

'This won't last much longer.' Was that the phrase? When she read it, she'd found the words to be profound - calming and comforting. They spoke directly to her, and she was filled with a sense of tranquillity; a belief that everything would be okay.

Now, as she scrabbled to find the same phrase that might still her thoughts, the words refused to come to her.

'This will be over soon.'

Too formal.

'This is not forever.'

Perhaps.

If she couldn't remember the mantra, how could she use it to get through the next few minutes?

She needed to breathe, to quiet her mind and the words would find her.

She could already feel the weight of him crushing against her chest, restricting her breath and bringing her back into the reality of the room.

Breathe.

Breathe.

The room was dark, but she could see his face clearly - a wash of tension as he pulsated back and forth. His eyes were closed, scrunched together tightly, focusing hard on the task at hand. His mouth was terse and rigid, slightly open and revealing his bright white teeth - clenched shut. The stubble of the day covered his chin, but his strawberry birth-mark endeavoured to peek through, barely visible below the bristles. She found herself wondering why he insisted on the stubble. She loved him clean shaven; loved the mark that made him unique. It reminded her of the day they met and the comfort she felt in uncovering its beauty beneath the shards of hair, as she ran her fingers across his face during their first kiss. He always chose to keep it covered.

Why did he pull that face? Why did he keep his eyes closed? Did he even enjoy this?

This was so unlike their regular love-making: calm, soft and gentle. She knew he loved her, yet when this demon ritual reared its ugly head, she succumbed to the fact that this was just a part of their lives. A sordid secret that only they knew.

Close your eyes and repeat the phrase. Focus on the words and believe in them... This too shall pass.

That was it!

The stale stench of alcohol was hard to avoid, but the words would keep her focused for the next three minutes.

This too shall pass.

She had, long ago, learned that saying 'no' was futile. Trying to wriggle free or cry out only made him bear down on her with more force. He needed the power and the control.

He was always apologetic afterwards - not with words of course - but with gifts and tenderness in the coming days. She knew he meant her no harm. He loved her dearly and she loved him too. This had just become a part of their world and she was letting it happen. It was just a blip. Just a vice. Every couple had their problems. Every relationship held secrets.

This too shall pass.

She closed her eyes and repeated the phrase, as he pulsated harder within her. The force was strong and she could feel her insides begin to ache. Two more minutes or so and it would be over, but she knew this time would leave blood and bruising. More than last time. The last few incidents had been a little rougher than the ones before - a little harder, a little more aggressive. The sheets would be stained again - bright and vibrant red that was hard to scrub off. She'd change them tomorrow, without him noticing, to avoid any acknowledgement of the act.

Suddenly, he grabbed her arms and shoved them above her head, pinning them down with his own. This was new.

Another grunt, louder now. She knew this meant he was nearing the end. She clenched her eyes closed - the black emptiness - a welcome escape from the room. She repeated the words, over and over again in her mind: *This too shall pass. This too shall pass.*

His hands around her arms grew tighter and she could feel her wrists being squeezed against his grip. Would they be bruised in the morning as well? External bruising would be harder to hide.

'You fucking slut!'

His words startled her.

The pressure was stronger now. The thrusting was harder. Any second and it would be over. Should she try to count down from ten? No, she couldn't bear the thought of reaching one and him not being finished. She'd stick to the mantra.

This too shall pass.

His clench on her wrists was tightening as he groaned louder. She could feel pressure in her hands as the blood flow continued to be restricted. One final thrust, one final groan, and, with a sigh of relief, he finally collapsed on top of her.

His sticky skin clung to hers and his warm, stale breath panted hard upon her cheek, making her stomach churn.

He slid off of her and exhaled loudly.

With any luck he'd be asleep in seconds, so she'd lay still, rigid and quiet. Soon, she would hear his breathing change - from hard and fast to slow and rhythmic - the sign she would need to know it was safe. Once his breathing had changed, she would be able to clamber softly out of bed, making her escape to the safety of the en suite. Once on the other side of the locked door, she could begin to clean herself up and wipe away her humiliation.

She took a deep breath and began to slide the covers away, slowly and silently so as not to disturb him, preparing herself for the retreat of the bathroom.

He shuffled again.

She paused, held her breath, and closed her eyes tight.

He breathed deeply before sidling back across the bed, stalking his way towards her once more.

Oh God, please no! she thought. *Please, not again.*

He leaned over, his head just inches above hers, still and silent but for the inhale and exhale of his breath on her face, close enough to smell the whiskey.

Time stood still.

What was he doing? Why was he back above her, but this time, not moving?

She forced one of her eyelids to peel open. As her eyes adjusted to the face, so close to hers, she braced herself for more, embarrassed by the assumption that it was over for tonight.

His eyes were hard and cold, his mouth still and harsh.

This wasn't the man she knew.

She blinked, and when her eyes opened again, his expression had changed. Like the swift shift from night to day when the sunrise begins to creep over the horizon, his eyes were back. The corners of his mouth rose as a welcoming smile spread across his face. His soft blue eyes looked lovingly into her own and he saw her now, not through the lens of lust or longing, but with earnestness and respect.

'Goodnight my darling,' he whispered, and he landed a soft, delicate kiss on her cheek, before sliding off of her and turning his back to her once more.

The shock of the exchange left her motionless. She could no longer bring herself to get up and move to the bathroom, even once she heard his breathing change and the snoring ensue. Instead, she slid slowly onto her side, facing away from him and staring directly at the wall. A single teardrop fell from her eye and trickled down the pillow, warm and wet.

'This too shall pass,' she whispered, as she closed her eyes once more, inviting the night to grab hold of her.

Sleep would be her salvation.

For the next six hours, she would flee her reality and disappear into the safety and solitude of her own subconscious.

Tomorrow's a new day.

CHAPTER 2

The phone in her hand turned to black as the screen locked automatically.

She continued to stare straight ahead, her eyes fixed firmly on the wall where their picture hung, hopelessly. The couple staring back at her from within the frame was fraudulent; she could see that now.

How had she missed it before?

She closed one eye, so as to only see half of the picture - his half. When isolated from her, she could suddenly make out the stare of uncertainty in his eye, the glint that was missing, the spark that had fizzled. A cursory glance would have missed it. In passing, people would have glimpsed up at its counterfeit beauty and the forgery would have continued to go unnoticed. But today, her gaze allowed time for scrutiny and the truth hit her flat in the face.

She peeled her eyes away from the picture and encouraged them to travel back down to her lap, where the phone lay helpless and exposed in the fabric of her crossed legs. The tiled floor below her was hard and cold and the rawness of it felt fitting. She swept her thumb back across the screen with urgency and punched in the code. He never went far without his phone, so she knew he could arrive back any moment.

The screen illuminated itself once more and the messages presented themselves again, lording their conceit over her. The words that remained were fragments of a larger story. That much was clear:

I'll pick you up at 4

Can't wait!

See you soon x

xx

Who was the unknown woman? The unknown number, unsaved in his phone?

She felt a flush of humiliation strike warm in the pit of her stomach.

How had she allowed this to happen? She had her flaws, but she'd been so good to him. She'd trusted him and he had let her down.

Rage boiled up through her as she steadied herself to stand. Placing her hand firmly on the cabinet, she tried to take a gulp of air and buy herself some time to think. Her chest pounded uncontrollably and she felt a tightness as her muscles constricted across her back. She needed a plan, but her mind would not slow down to allow for controlled thought.

A sound, and her eyes darted towards the front door.

The key clinked firmly in the hole before turning forcefully in the lock. The door clattered open against its hinges and the sunlight flooded its way through the opening, illuminating and exposing her, catching her red-handed.

'I think I forgot my phone,' he announced.

FRIDAY

CHAPTER 3
SARAH

Beep Beep.

The phone vibrated in the pocket of Sarah's denim shorts, sending shivers up through her side. She had debated her outfit choice for a good five minutes this morning, switching her weight from leg to leg in the mirror, swishing her body back and forth, judging each angle in detail, before settling on the denim shorts, paired with a white, cropped jumper and some Birkenstocks. But now, standing in the late afternoon, September air, she was beginning to regret her decision.

The promise of an Indian summer hadn't quite come to fruition. Instead, today felt fresh and brisk - a warning of autumn's imminent arrival.

Her parents' sleepy village was awash with pensioners, but they tended to reserve their activities for the morning. Afternoons were spent at home, presumably to rest and recuperate, before going again the following morning. Any potential rebels who might otherwise have toyed with the idea of a light afternoon stroll today were clearly repelled by the weather.

There was a serenity about this place that Sarah admired. She'd known the village all her life - her parents having never moved out of the family home - and after spending her late teens studying in the big city, there came a yearning to return back to this space. The village was home to a sense of nostalgia, wistfulness and remembrance that made Sarah feel warm and at peace.

The wind gushed past her again, shattering the feeling of warmth and bringing her crashing back to reality. The sound of the tennis ball smacking back and forth was punctuated only by the grunt of Sarah's father, who was trying his hardest to keep up with the pace of his, much younger, future son-in-law. Another ball swept past Greg and landed just inside the baseline, before flying on and smashing into the fence.

'Game!' Simon called out, unable to control his competitive nature.

'Great shot,' Greg threw back, attempting to control his breathing and sound nonchalant. Despite his efforts, the redness in his face and the pouring of sweat betrayed him, broadcasting his fatigue for all to see. Sarah was sure that, at times, Simon forgot that he was thirty five years Greg's junior.

Beep Beep.

Her mother threw a terse scowl towards Sarah's pocket - the source of the noise - before rolling her eyes up Sarah's body and settling them disapprovingly on her face.

Judy was the embodiment of 'keeping up appearances'. It didn't matter that this playful Friday afternoon knockabout was just a bit of fun in an, otherwise empty, park. To Judy, a tennis match was a silent affair and there should be no noise distractions. Perhaps she liked to imagine that Simon was, in fact, playing in the finals at Wimbledon. Sarah could envisage her mother obligingly stepping in to play the role of Simon's own mother, wiping a salty tear from her eye as the camera got the perfect shot of her gazing lovingly and proudly towards 'her Simon'. That's what

Judy had taken to calling him, since he became engaged to her daughter, last month: 'My Simon'. Sarah had not yet broached the issue of explaining to her mother that if Simon were, in fact, belonging to anyone, it would be to her, not to her mother.

Sarah could feel her mother's eyes burning through her, but when she turned to look, the eyes were no longer fixed on her pocket. Instead, they had crept down Sarah's leg, and rested themselves judgmentally on her footwear. Judy's head was cocked sideways with a disapproving grimace.

Despite never directly commenting on her general appearance, it was clear to Sarah that her mother disapproved of how she carried herself. Sarah defied the more reserved millennial stereotypes that she assumed Judy felt she should embrace. Instead, she identified more as a Gen Z: body confidence and positivity.

She'd worked hard to maintain her figure; why shouldn't she show it off?

Sarah had spent thirty five years on this earth, but her fellow gym buddies often remarked that she could easily have passed for being in her late twenties. She was popular at the gym, a regular attendee who dedicated hours every day to a mix of cardio and strength training. The rest of her style was more fraudulent; not garish *Barbie*, more subtle *Beauty*.

Unwanted hairs were hard to come by, her forehead barely moved when she smiled, and her eyelashes were long enough to curl round and touch her eyebrows. Her real hair was hidden between the thick and flowing, brunette extensions that engulfed her head and the lips she was born with had been altered more than any lipstick would manage, yet she still held an air of class and natural beauty.

Beep Beep.

Sarah quickly patted down her body, trying to figure out where she'd stashed her phone. The last thing she needed was her mother announcing that she was having to call this Wimbledon final to a halt, while the noisy idiot in the crowd was removed by security.

She knew exactly who would be messaging her and she knew the messages would keep on coming.

Why did Katie refuse to write just one bloody message? Her texts were a reflection of her personality: constantly desiring attention and refusing to say in one word, what could be said in twenty.

Finally, Sarah located the source of the noise and fished her phone out from her skin tight denim pocket. She held it high in the air.

'It's off now, guys! So sorry,' she announced in apology.

'No problem,' Her father called back to her. 'We're taking a break anyway. Poor Simon needs a breather before I break his next serve!' he jested between laboured breaths.

Simon strolled his way across the court, winking back at Greg, before arriving at Sarah's side and planting a gentle kiss on her cheek. Greg followed behind before collapsing into the chair which had been strategically placed courtside by his future son-in-law. Greg wiped his glistening brow with his towel, before taking a large glug of water.

'Katie again?' Simon presumed, pointing towards Sarah's phone. 'What's the drama today?'

Sarah shot him a warning stare, but it was too late. Judy's ears had pricked up.

'Drama?' Judy questioned. 'What is it now?'

In the six months since her retirement, Judy had made it her mission to become more learned about the village folk than anyone else in the neighbourhood. Sarah was convinced that Judy lived in an egocentric bubble of superiority over her pensioner pals: she and her family had never been the subject of any real drama themselves. (If you exclude the time that Greg got drunk and peed on the neighbour's carnations.) So it seemed that Judy now busied most of her days by researching the intricate details of her so-called friends' private lives. That is, when she wasn't fulfilling her babysitting duties.

Although Abbie's children were no longer babies, Sarah felt that her mother was seemingly babysitting them all the time! It wasn't that Sarah was jealous, as such - she certainly didn't resent her niece and nephew - she just didn't understand why her mother had to have them quite so often. Abbie lent on their mother too much, that's what it was. The woman had just retired, for goodness sake. Why was she now Abbie's full time nanny? Sarah barely asked for favours, so why did Abbie always get what she wanted? Perfect Abbie. With her perfect job, her perfect house and her perfect family. She didn't deserve favours - she already had enough.

'Is it her and Rob? Have they been arguing again?' Judy enquired. 'Jenny said she saw them arguing in the street last week. The street! Can you believe it? What an embarrassment. Poor Lisa. She wasn't at the parish council meeting last week. Probably didn't want to show her face for fear of the questions, poor love.' Judy patronised.

Katie's mother, Lisa had been everything Sarah

had ever wanted in a mother. As a child, Sarah would spend most of her evenings at Katie's house after school and she developed a wonderful relationship with Lisa from there. Lisa would bring them healthy, but tasty snacks; she would tell jokes and listen closely to their predicaments; she would always have a mature and helpful piece of advice to offer to their teenage dilemmas.

Lisa did not judge, and she had a way of connecting with people that Sarah had never experienced before. Lisa was kind and considerate, mature and wise, yet she was still so fun!

Sarah knew that her mother was envious of her relationship with Lisa, though she would never have admitted it. Instead, Sarah witnessed Judy take it upon herself to belittle Lisa at any given moment. She would criticise her dress sense, her car and her life choices. And now that her daughter's marriage was on the rocks, Judy took it as another reason to swipe at Lisa's 'failures'.

'I must say,' Simon commented, turning towards Judy with a scandalous eye, 'Katie did seem upset last night. She was having a drink with Sarah but she left not long after I got home. Sarah's being coy - as ever - about it though,' he remarked, rolling his eyes. 'You know what she's like.'

'Okay, now.' Greg interjected. 'Let's get you back on this court and leave the gossip to the ladies, shall we Simon?'

Sarah sucked a gulp of relief. *Good old dad,* she thought as he slipped her a wink and walked back to the baseline with his singles partner.

Poor Katie, thought Sarah. She had no idea that she was the centre of the village's gossip (or her mother's, at least) and she didn't deserve it either. Yes, Sarah was becoming tired of hearing the same old dramas, but that's what friends did, right? She would listen to Katie's woes and continue to offer the same supportive and loving advice, even if Katie never took it. Lisa had taught her these skills and she was determined to fight against her biological influences, continuing to be the good friend she'd learned to be.

Realising that she would be receiving no gossip, Judy began to saunter back towards the clubhouse. Finally, Sarah could check her phone. She was already preparing her stock reply in her head:

I know, hun. I'm so sorry you're going through this. Come round later…I've got a bottle of Savvy B chilling in the fridge! Xx

But the pre prepared script was not needed.

Sarah unlocked her phone and recoiled in surprise.

It was Katie, but she wasn't messaging about her disastrous marriage. She wasn't flooding Sarah's Whatsapp with messages about her own dramas. This was something else.

Sarah read the messages again, and felt a flood of panic surge through her.

The wind had died down and the sun was discovering its way past the clouds, heating up the ground below. The shiver from before had been replaced with a sweaty, clammy feeling. Sarah adjusted her stance and felt the denim stick to her upper thigh. She peeled it away and glanced around to see if anyone was watching her lose her cool. She swayed from side to side, but not with the confidence she'd had in the mirror earlier. Now, the sway was one of concern and anxiety.

Sarah peered back at her phone and tried to decode the messages:
OMG Sarah...
I've just seen Abbie at the school gates!
What the actual FUCK is your sister doing???

CHAPTER 4
ABBIE

The low murmurings of the children was unsettling to Abbie. The essay was supposed to be written in silence, but at 3pm on a Friday afternoon, how on earth was she supposed to encourage concentration? She could barely concentrate herself - her mind wandering back to this morning's disastrous school run.

'Shh please,' she echoed softly into the abyss. She knew, full well, that the children would take no note of her plea, but at least this way, she could pretend that she was attempting some kind of behaviour management.

Out of the corner of her eye, Abbie noticed a hand rising at the back of the classroom. She took a deep breath in and kept her eyes fixed tightly on her computer screen. If she didn't acknowledge the hand, she wouldn't have to get up and deal with the query. And if she didn't get up to deal with the query, she wouldn't have to notice Tia texting on her phone. And if she didn't notice Tia texting, she wouldn't have to deal with the fallout. A Tia Tantrum on a Friday afternoon was the last thing she needed. She had enough of those at home, these days.

Abbie's mind flashed back to this morning and her heart sank, once more…

'Hurry up!' she shouted. 'We are going to be late to your Nan's house. Again!' She hovered by the front door, pacing back and forth impatiently, while George stood patiently by her side.

From above her, she could hear the floorboards creaking and she knew exactly what Lucy was doing: brushing her hair. That girl could spend hours in front of the mirror, brushing her hair, over and over. Abbie had tried to tell her that it would get greasy if she brushed it so much and that there really was no need to go over the same strands twenty times, but Lucy refused to listen.

'For God's sake child!' Abbie yelled. 'Your brother and I are literally waiting by the front door. I'm going to be late for work and you'll be late for school. HURRY UP!'

George's head brushed against her waist, and she had a startling feeling that he suddenly looked so much older than he had done yesterday. Ian had helped him gel his hair to the side, and his school tie made him come across more mature than his eight years really required. *Stop growing up*, she wished, silently.

There was no reply from Lucy, but the floorboards creaked again, louder now, so at least she was moving along the landing and towards the stairs.

'Are you coming, or what?!' Abbie bellowed, but still no reply came from her daughter. Abbie was sure that the silent treatment was a deliberate tactic used to punish her. She knew it was the worst pain Abbie could endure.

The thought was interrupted by shoes clonking down the stairs.

'Finally!' Abbie sighed. 'Why does it take you so long? Oh, let me guess, the bloody hair brushing!' she snarled.

Lucy responded, not with words, but with a huff and an eye roll, before walking off to the kitchen.

'Are you kidding me child?' Abbie scoffed. 'Where the hell are you going now?'

'Bottle,' Lucy replied.

'Bottle?' snarked Abbie. 'Do you mean, *'To get your water bottle'*? Why can't you speak in full sentences, child?!'

'Chill,' breathed Lucy, returning from the kitchen - bottle in hand - before brushing straight past her mother and back towards the stairs again.

'Chill?' Abbie echoed, before swinging open the front door - a little too hard - and leaving a dent in the newly whitewashed hallway wall. ' Don't you dare tell me to chill!' she screamed. 'And where the hell are you heading now?'

'Phone,' she exhaled, before pacing back up the stairs again.

'You are driving me mad!' Abbie continued. 'You have no regard for any of us. There's no urgency at all. All you care about is your bloody hair and your God-damn phone. And, I tell you what - we are all fed up with it. Fed up of you. Living with you makes us all bloody miserable!'

Abbie shuffled uncomfortably in her chair.

Had she really said that?

She was supposed to be the grown up, the adult, the one who had the maturity to cope in these moments of stress.

She knew exactly what it was like to be a teenage girl - she remembered it all so clearly: the confusion, the insecurity, the knowledge that no one quite understands you. She got it! She really did. So why could she not connect with Lucy, anymore?

Abbie had sworn, at the age of fourteen, that she would never forget what it was like to be a teenage girl.

When she had her own children, she would learn from the mistakes her mother had made. She'd be a patient mother, a kind and understanding mother, the kind of mother that you would want to talk to about your deepest fears and darkest worries. Yet here she was, twenty years on and completely unable to connect.

Lucy was her first born child, and since the moment she was born, Abbie knew that there was something different about her. Somehow, Abbie had managed to create the perfect person.

She didn't know how it had happened, or why they were blessed with this gift, but the child they bore was remarkable.

Abbie did not feel that she was particularly remarkable herself, and God knows Ian wasn't! But together they had created this gem. This precious bundle of joy and fulfilment, that encased her heart in wonder and brought a new realm of happiness to her life.

Abbie decided, there and then, that she would never be able to have a second child - the poor thing would never be able to compare. No child would. Besides, Abbie would have no love left in her heart for a second child; everything she had was being used up on adoring this little person she now owned.

Lucy was a good sleeper, a solid ten hours from six weeks old. She lapped up the pureed mush that was prepared for her meals, with glee. When the time for teething ticked round, there were no dramas - Lucy would settle with a simple dose of calpol and a warm hug.

Abbie knew that her child was brighter than the other children too. She smiled after only a few weeks and began crawling at just five months old.

Her first words were more advanced than baby babble - choosing 'dog' as her third word, while the other children at playgroup were still making grunts and squeals.

As she grew older, Lucy advanced in other areas too. She was academically advanced, learning to read fluently by age four, but she was also a talented dancer and musician. Lucy made friends easily at school and was invited to all the birthday parties. She was polite and respectful to the adults she met, she was empathetic and gentle when other children got upset. It was obvious: Lucy was perfect.

Abbie couldn't put her finger on when things had changed, or even how they had changed, but changed, they had. The aching love she felt for her daughter was still there, but something else was missing, like a huge void that had developed between them, made up of white noise and static. She had tried to wade through it, to grab hold of her daughter and pull her back in, tight to her embrace, but she couldn't quite reach. It was like one of those dreams, where your arm is outstretched, desperate to grab hold of something, but as you inch close to it, it shoots away.

Abbie was tired too, and she knew that didn't help. Their pace of life had become too fast. She needed things to slow down a little. If only she knew what might enable that to happen. She had been working twelve hour days; George was trying out for the football team, which meant more training sessions at the weekend; and Ian had a new client to take care of so he had his head permanently in a laptop or a phone. She just needed a break.

'Miss!' Came the shrill cry from the raised hand and Abbie was jolted back into the room.

She glanced at the clock. Four minutes past three.

She took a deep breath and stood up.

'I'm coming, Jack,' Abbie replied, while trying to prepare for her next move. She would have to walk past Tia to get to the back of the room, so dealing with the situation was unavoidable. However, with only six minutes left of the lesson, she was pretty sure that Tia would agree to the very brief confiscation, before being reunited with her addiction at the end of the day.

Abbie took three steps forward, her heels tapping gently on the carpeted floor, before pausing next to Tia's desk. She peered down at the child and coughed, expectantly.

'Thank you,' Abbie motioned with an outstretched hand and a head tilt. Her face fixed its expression to one that she'd practised for years - sullen with disappointment. It often forced children into such guilt that they obligingly handed things over with a dejected apology.

'I'm texting my mum,' Tia argued, her face still and unwavering. 'It's important'.

This was just what Abbie needed: another grumpy teenager!

'Important as it might be, Tia, we can't have phones out in class,' Abbie scripted. 'Just pass it over and you can have it back at the end of the lesson.'

Tia stared directly at her teacher, unmoving and unrelenting. She kept Abbie's eye, refusing to glance away, despite the discomfort it was creating.

The murmurs of the room softened to a silence. The other children's ears pricked up as they sensed that something was about to unfold.

Tia relented first, breaking her stare away from Abbie's and back towards her phone.

'I'm nearly finished,' she grunted.

Abbie was surprised, but unshaken. She was generally liked at Longleaf Secondary School - by the students and the staff. Being disrespected like this would not do.

'Hand it over, please, Tia. I shan't ask again,' she continued, the mock confidence escaping from her voice.

Tia did not move.

'Thank you,' encouraged Abbie, her voice breaking slightly as she fixed herself to the ground, her arm still outstretched.

Tia did not move.

Whispers picked up around the room, and Abbie felt a hot flush swipe through her cheeks. Her heartbeat quickened as she tried to plan her escape. The students were waiting, an audience of year elevens, watching eagerly, with bated breath, to see who would win this battle: Tia or Teacher.

Abbie saw her moment to pounce. Without hesitation, she snatched at the phone in Tia's hand, and scooped it into her own.

A mass intake of breath was audible, as the room seemed to physically recoil in shock.

'Give it back!' shouted Tia, jumping from her chair with such force that it crashed to the ground behind her.

Abbie turned her back and walked onwards to Jack, trying her hardest to ignore the thirty pairs of eyes fixed solely on her. If she could regain her cool, the situation could still be pacified.

'Give it back!' screamed Tia, now standing tall

and stamping her foot, hard on the ground, like a toddler.

Abbie arrived at Jack's desk and halted, ignoring the warfare kicking off just ten paces behind. 'How can I help you, Jack?' she asked with an air of serenity.

'Um,' mumbled Jack. 'Um, um,' he continued, his eyes darting back and forth between Tia and Abbie, unsure if the saga had finished or if it was about to erupt further. 'I actually can't remember now,' he squeaked.

'You BITCH!' screamed Tia. She ran to the door and yanked it open, rattling the hinges in the frame, before slamming it closed behind her with one final crash.

The room froze, holding its breath in the deafening silence.

Abbie paused, momentarily, before spinning on her heels and trotting back towards her desk. 'Well,' she sighed, 'Good work today, everybody. Now, let's pack our things away, shall we?'

#

After the students had exited the room, Abbie collected her things and threw them into her bag: her leatherbound notebook, pencil case and travel mug - which still housed the cold remains of this morning's coffee. She placed Tia's phone carefully in her jacket pocket, and slinked off outside.

She would normally stay behind after school - there was always more work to be done - but she had had quite enough of today. Besides, she would need to deposit this bloody phone somewhere. She had never confiscated a phone overnight before, let alone over the weekend. She'd leave it at reception on her way out and email home to make Tia's mother aware.

Hopefully she'd understand.

Abbie walked briskly across the courtyard, weaving in and out of students as they rushed towards the car park, which was packed full of parents eagerly awaiting their little darlings' return.

The wind had picked up since this morning and it felt fresh and autumnal. The clouds were collecting swiftly and Abbie prayed the rain would stay away. The last thing they needed was rain this weekend.

There were teachers dotted around, some eyeing their peers to see if it was an acceptable time to rush off for the weekend, and others supporting the students with their exit - making sure they really did leave school for the day, please, and quickly. Abbie gave a courtesy wave to her colleague and kept moving, head down (she liked to keep to herself these days), when she heard a yell.

'Mrs Hart!' came the call.

Abbie peered up to see a woman walking hurriedly her way. *What now?* She thought. Parents were the worst. They always wanted more and they always expected to get their own way. Did these people not realise that this was now her weekend too? She needed a break.

'Hello,' Abbie responded, cheerily. 'How can I help?'

Despite her disappointment at being spotted, Abbie always remained professional. She prided herself on it. Fifteen years in teaching and she had never had so much as one parental complaint.

'Who the hell do you think you are, abusing children like that!' Came the shrill shriek from the woman, now only a few yards from her, yet still gaining pace. 'Who the hell snatches things from a child?'

The unexpected noise attracted some onlookers. Most noticeably, Mr Winterton. That's just what she needed: a scene in front of the headteacher.

'Good afternoon. Mrs White, is it?'

Abbie spoke calmly. She was sure she could defuse the situation, she just needed a moment to explain.

'You bully!' squealed the woman, as she moved closer still. She was dressed in gym gear - a Lycra top, leggings, socks and trainers - yet she wore a full face of makeup and a barnet sprayed to perfection, with not a single hair out of place. 'I had an emergency,' she continued, 'and I needed to speak to Tia. She was clearly upset and you prevented her from messaging me. Who the hell do you think you are?'

'Mrs White,' Abbie repeated, 'I am terribly sorry if you...'

'You will be sorry, you snobby bitch,' the woman warned.

Abbie recoiled in shock, as the woman halted, just inches from her face. She had dealt with difficult parents before but this was something else. She was aware of needing support, when she felt the weight of Mr Winterton by her side. For a large man, he sure could move fast. She sucked in some air, and realised that she'd been holding her breath.

'What seems to be the problem?' Joe asked.

'The problem, Mr Winterton, is that your staff are abusing children in the classroom!' the incessant mother shouted.

That was the second time she'd used that word. Abuse! How absurd. How dare she say something like that. And in front of all these people.

The scene had now formed a crowd and she was aware that people could hear. This kind of hearsay could ruin her career, her life in fact. Abbie felt the anger start to rise within her. She didn't deserve this.

'Oh now I'm sure we can sort this out, Mrs White, if you'd like to come with me,' Mr Winterton said as he gestured his arm around her and motioned towards reception. He really was a charmer - so good at getting his own way.

But something was rising within Abbie that she couldn't suppress. This woman had verbally attacked her, in public. And for what? For doing her job! It was her job. She was upholding the school standards. She was teaching these little maggots day in, day out. She was trying her hardest, putting up with their back chat and their defiance, their entitlement and their arrogance. And then she was being accosted for it, in public.

The injustice rose further within her as she called out, 'Hold on a minute.'

When Mrs White turned around, Abbie didn't know what her next move was going to be, but her body took over, working faster than her mind could catch up with.

Abbie felt her hand reach into her pocket and grab the phone. She squeezed it tight and pulled it from its cocoon. She lifted the phone high before pulling her arm back and, in one catapulting stretch, she launched it straight at her enemy.

'There's her fucking phone back!'

The words came out in a gush, flying up into the air around her, before floating back down and resting in her ears, where she heard them back.

The phone flew through the air, twirling in

slow motion alongside the words she'd screamed. It reached its target, cracking against Mrs White's nose, before tumbling to the ground and shattering in pieces.

As her brain attempted to make sense of what she had done, she saw the blur of the background come back into focus. People. So many people. All with the same expression - sheer disbelief.

She panned back around to face Mr Winterton, who was paralysed, frozen, the same face as all the rest.

Finally, her gaze fell on Mrs White. She had one hand rested on her hip and a superior smirk plastered across her face. The crimson pouring from her nose dripped down her face and landed with a dollop on the ground.

Shit, Abbie thought. *Oh shit.*

CHAPTER 5
SARAH

As the smoke seeped its way through the kitchen doorway and into the front room, Sarah became aware of the, all too familiar, choking smell.

'Everything is okay in there?' she hollered, over the noise of the extractor fan and the clanking of pots. It was 5.58pm and her stomach was already rumbling.

'All under control, darling!' he bellowed back, with a squeak in his voice.

It had been nearly two years since their first date and Simon still insisted upon acting out these courtship rituals. He would never admit to feeling threatened in their relationship - he knew that Sarah loved him - but some hidden insecurity appeared to rear its head in moments of weakness. Tomorrow's party was looming ever closer and Sarah knew he was anxious about it.

Tom would be at the party.

Tom had been Ian's best friend from school, so when Ian and Abbie began dating, he quickly became a part of their lives, and then a part of Sarah's life too. Tom seemed to pop up everywhere that Sarah went - birthday parties, barbecues, he even came to Christmas one year - before she eventually realised the feelings she felt for him were more than just those felt for an annoying big brother; she was in love. But she woke up one morning, five years on, and suddenly realised that Tom didn't love her back. The truth smacked her straight in the face. He couldn't even say the words. How had she missed it before? They'd settled into a life of placid complacency and she knew she needed more. She packed up her things and said goodbye, just like that - mature and respectful. Sarah met Simon two weeks later and the rest was history.

Sarah had never cheated on Simon. She'd never cheated on any of her boyfriends, in fact. She didn't really understand cheating. The lure of the unavailable or untouchable had never tempted her.

Sarah was good at making decisions. So if she wanted something, she would reach out and grab it. Simple as that. Sarah couldn't understand people's animal instincts to toy with their catch and then let it go again. It helped that Sarah didn't feel the urge to succumb to alcohol's sinister pull. She'd never really liked drinking - had barely touched the stuff since that night in January - so the dizzy haze of lust for a married man, or the appeal to hook up with an old flame, had never really affected her.

Sarah made conscious, sober decisions and then she stuck by them. Her mother had once mocked at her 'unusually strict moral compass.' Sarah couldn't understand the insult - wasn't it good to know right from wrong?

So, with Greg's party only twenty three hours away, Simon was beating his chest hard and fanning out his tail feathers. He knew that Tom would be present, so he needed to exert his masculine dominance, ready for the big show off. Even if he was the only one involved in the duel.

'Running slightly behind schedule,' Simon called back again from the cloud of darkness surrounding the room. 'A slight issue with the dauphinoise, but it'll be ready in five, don't fret. It's all under ...'

The shrill shriek of the smoke alarm punctuated his words and Sarah heaved herself off the sofa to quiet the noise, while Simon continued to flap around the kitchen in disarray - an oven glove on his left hand, a blackened pan in his right, and a tea towel flung carelessly over his shoulder.

This could be a long wait.

#

Simon laid the plates on the table, as a patient Sarah sat waiting.

'Voila!' he announced, before leaning down to kiss his fiance, firm and smooth on her plump lips. 'Better late than never,' he smiled.

A glance at the clock showed Sarah that 7pm had just passed, and she knew that her sister would be calling soon. The brief text message earlier had only been a holding note. When Abbie suggested a phone call, Sarah recognised the seriousness of the situation. Abbie suggested 7.15pm, which she assumed would be fine. She'd not foreseen the Gordon Ramsay Soiree that lay ahead.

Sarah swished her steak from side to side, sweeping around her plate, feeling nauseous at the thought of the impending call. Speaking to her sister was never calming. There was always an air of awkwardness in their chatter. Sarah had always been jealous of those sisters who talked for hours about anything and everything; those sisters who could read each other's thoughts and finish each other's sentences. Sarah and Abbie's talks were always stilted. They had a knack of starting their sentences at the same time, followed by them both repeating, 'Sorry,', 'No you go,', 'No you!' in synchronised fractions, until silence ensued.

But Sarah had to talk to her sister today. She was worried about her. Abbie was many things, but she was never one to be involved in drama. She would describe Abbie as understated, innocuous, even invisible at times. So what the hell had happened this afternoon? She'd heard of nervous breakdowns and midlife crises, but there was no way Abbie was having a breakdown! Maybe she'd had an embolism or a moment of madness caused by a tumour pressing too firmly on her brain. Perhaps she had a doppelganger who was impersonating her in an attempt to steal and take over her wonderful life. Perhaps it was all a hoax, an elaborate prank designed for a new reality tv programme. Sarah needed answers.

'Are you feeling unwell, darling?' Simon questioned lovingly, reaching out his hand to stroke across her fingers.

Sarah brushed away his concern. 'I'm fine, Si. Just worried about Abbie.'

'It's only… I couldn't help but notice that you're late.'

Sarah's eyes shot up and rested on Simon's face, which was beaming with expectancy and hope.

The moment paused, while Sarah considered her next move. Was she really going to give this more air time? She hoped that a comical remark would slide the subject off of the table.

'*I'm* late?' Sarah chuckled with a fake smile. 'That's ironic, given how long this meal took.'

She really didn't want to go there again. Not tonight.

Simon brushed away Sarah's attempt at humour and questioned, 'Have you taken a test?'

Here we go, thought Sarah. *Again.*

She took a gulp of air and inhaled deeply.

'No Simon. I don't need to take a test. I'm not pregnant.'

Her words were hard and cold.

The silence hung in the air. Simon continued to saw at his steak and Sarah hoped this was the end of the conversation.

'Maybe you could test in the morning?' he whispered.

The softness in his voice pierced Sarah straight through the chest and down into her gut, reverberating aggressively as it went.

'Simon, please don't do this!' she begged, sliding her chair away with a scraping sound on the tiled floor below, and gently discarding her napkin on the table.

'No pressure, no pressure!' He urged, standing up hastily and following her around the table before pulling her firmly into his hold. 'I shouldn't have said anything,' he apologised. 'I'm an idiot. I know that. I'm sorry.'

Sarah felt his arms surround her. The warmth of his embrace was comforting. She felt safe here, enveloped in his love. His cheek was soft and comforting against her forehead and his biceps around her shoulders made her feel content.

'I can't keep doing this, Simon.'

Simon squeezed her tighter.

'It was just a question,' he resolved. 'I didn't mean anything by it. I just noticed, that was all, so I thought I'd ask.'

'We've done this, Si.' Sarah continued. 'We've had this talk. We've talked it, and talked it, and talked it. There's nothing more to say. I don't want children. And you've said you're okay with that. So why do you keep on asking?' Her voice was getting louder as she shrugged him off and headed towards the sofa. She slumped down and buried her face in a plump pink cushion.

Sarah had never been the maternal type. While the other little girls were playing mummies and daddies in primary school, Sarah was playing hopscotch. In sex ed class during year ten, Sarah announced that not all women should have to have periods if they didn't want to have babies - a comment that flawed Mr Jeffs, her fifty year old substitute teacher. When her friends began to settle down in their late twenties, she was still travelling the world, enjoying her freedom and experiencing things others would only ever read about in their Sunday morning magazines. On her thirty third birthday, two months before Simon entered her life, she made a decision: children were not in her future. The decision wasn't a difficult one. Yet when she voiced this to friends or family, she was always met with the same response. The pitiful head tilt and the condescending tone. People told her that she would miss out on being in *the club* - whatever the hell that meant. Um no, actually, she could spend every weekend clubbing, rather than sitting at home with a screaming baby. Her friends remarked that she'd regret it when she was older. The comments came thick and fast:

'Having a child is like having a best friend that biologically understands you.'

'Who will look after you when you're old and grey?'
'What's the point of life if you leave no legacy?'
'You're missing out on so much!'

But Sarah didn't feel like she was missing out. She had weighed up her options, calculated them to precision, researched her possibilities, and she always came back to the same conclusion: she didn't want children.

When she and Simon met, he was still a dewy eyed thirty year old. When she announced her big secret, he didn't seem phased. Simon had never really been in a long term relationship. He'd spent his early twenties hopping through life, jumping from venture to venture and from job to job. He'd spent his late twenties travelling the world - a surprise afforded to him as a result of a large inheritance sum he acquired after his parents' freak boating accident.

Simon's parents' death affected him, but perhaps not in the same way that it might have affected others. He spoke about how he had loved his parents but they weren't close. He described how his dad had been an investment banker, spending most of Simon's childhood working long hours in the city, earning the big bucks, while his mother spent her days spending it all in designer stores.

Simon left for college, aged eighteen. That same year, his parents retired with their fortune, packed up their things and moved abroad to live the life they'd always felt they missed out on, due to their decision to parent.

They were dead within a month.

Simon resented them for nothing. He admired their decision to uproot their lives and explore the world in their fifties. If anything, he felt guilty that he held them back from doing it sooner. Simon was a free spirit, too. He wanted flexibility, he wanted fun, he wanted freedom. So why was he saying these things now?

'Baby...' he pleaded. 'It was just a comment, I

meant nothing by it.' He continued. 'Let's forget it and sit back down to eat. I've made tiramisu for dessert.' He balanced himself carefully on the edge of the sofa and lifted her chin with his fingertips, urging her head up slowly. She raised her head hesitantly as Simon's face began to merge back into focus, but her stomach lurched again. She hated tiramisu.

Before Sarah could decide how to respond, the ring of her mobile phone saved her.

'That's Abbie,' she announced, beckoning quickly towards the coffee table, 'I'll have to get it.'

Simon watched Sarah's urgent leap for her phone and rejection hit him.

'I'll take my plate upstairs,' he moped, 'Give you two some space to have a talk.'

Sarah tracked Simon's movements as he lifted his plate and plodded towards the door. The ringing noise was intense, but Sarah didn't move. Abbie would have to wait.

Simon slid through the doorway and pulled the door shut behind him. Instantly, Sarah swiped her finger across the phone.

'Abs!' she yelped. 'What the hell is going on with you?'

CHAPTER 6
ABBIE

'Suspension?' Abbie questioned.

She'd heard the headteacher's words several times before in this very room, but it was usually aimed at the defiant child, not the teacher.

'While we conduct an investigation and obtain all the facts,' Mr Winterton continued. His voice was monotonous and his face was still and cold. Instead of looking directly at her, his eyes remained on the paperwork glued in his hands, which rested on the table in front of him.

Abbie had to physically stop herself from snorting a laugh. Surely this was a joke. Joe was an arse but he was also a dumb fool. He strutted around school like a dopey giant. His look consisted of over gelled hair and a crinkled white shirt which always hung loose out the back of his suit trousers. In staff meetings, he would stumble in over his size thirteen shoes and then fumble over his words. He was a guffawing great lump of a man, whose six foot five frame was too big for him. His density was the product of too many after work beers and packets of crisps, rather than too many evenings spent in the gym.

Abbie had saved his neck in the past, too.

In March, when Joe was due to give a speech at the year eleven Awards Evening, Abbie found him in a state of panic as the parents began arriving. He had lost his cue cards and had a 'terrible headache'. (Perhaps brought on by the stress of the evening.)

Abbie had stepped in.

'Don't worry, I can speak this evening.'

'No, I couldn't ask that of you,' he bumbled while searching through stacks of papers for the escaped cards.

'It's no bother,' she continued, feeling a warmth of sympathy as she watched his frantic movements. 'I'd like the opportunity to talk to the parents anyway. To remind them how they can support with revision plans in the run up to their children's exams.'

'Well if you'd *like* the opportunity to talk...' His words were short as he paused his searching and gaped up at her, his pleading eyes were almost watery.

'Yep, all fine,' she continued, 'I'll go and get prepared.' And as she turned to leave the room, she felt the tension release and she knew he was watching her walk away.

The parents didn't notice anything unusual - she was the Head of Year, after all - but she knew she'd saved him. Half way through her speech, she shifted her gaze and spotted Joe off to the side of the stage, staring at her with a glint in his eye and a half smile that crept into one cheek. She wasn't sure quite what the look meant, but she knew he admired her, respected her and maybe something more.

Then there was the summer party incident in July. Joe had arranged an end of term celebration at the local cricket club. It had been a tough year, with Ofsed's arrival, and he wanted the opportunity to thank his staff. The night soon got out of control. Miss Evans threw up in the rose bush, before falling in herself, and Abbie was pretty sure that Mr Jones and Mr Dickens were both snorting cocaine in the toilets. Mrs Rivers fell in the pond - an ironic anecdote that did not escape the rest of the staff - and Mr and Mrs Holey disappeared to the back of the carpark for a curiously long time.

As the evening was winding down, Abbie began clearing up. She had enjoyed a few spritzers, but she was convincingly the most sober one left. She darted her eyes around the room and felt an instant pang of guilt - maybe even embarrassment. The clubhouse staff would have to clear up this drunken rabble's mess! So she grabbed a black bin bag and shuffled over to the buffet table. People had been too concerned with drinking, so had neglected the food on offer.

As she swept the remnants of the hardened crusted sandwiches into the bag, she felt a hand brush the back of her neck. She spun on her heels and saw a staggering Mr Winterton, gazing down at her.

'You're a great girl, Abs,' he spluttered, stumbling over his own feet, while steadying himself with a hand on the table. 'A great help. A great teacher.'

'Just trying to do my bit,' she dismissed, turning back to the tray of food and continuing her sweep. He was drunk and the last thing she needed right now was an awkward encounter that they would both be embarrassed about the next day.

'Such a good girl,' he continued, swaying back and forth behind her as she felt his hand brush the hair on her neck to one side. 'I hope you know how much I appreciate you.'

She knew that she had every right to be appreciated. She worked bloody hard - they all did. Yet Joe was not normally one to air his thanks in such a blatant manner. He chose to write a few praise remarks in the weekly newsletter at a push, never open declarations of thanks. Abbie had once sat in a senior leadership meeting where staff were discussing who to thank in this week's staff notices, when Joe had thrown his papers down on the table, like a child throwing their toys out of the pram, exclaiming that they were all just doing their jobs and thanking them all makes a mockery of the system.

'Next we will be thanking the cleaners for remembering to clean the toilets,' he'd declared. The rest of the room paused, unsure if this was another one of his 'banterous jokes' or whether he was serious.

When no one spoke, he sensed the unease in the room, before switching the subject to who would chair tomorrow's meeting.

Now, the air in the room stilled and Abbie felt the tension tightening within her as his warm breath grazed over her shoulder. She glanced from side to side to check whether anyone could see them. She knew how this would appear to a tipsy onlooker. She could hear tomorrow's rumours.

'All over him, she was.'
'Anything for a payrise.'
'It's embarrassing and desperate.'
'I always took her for a slut.'

The room was empty, but for a barwoman cleaning down the sides, her back towards them. She had hoped that if she could catch the eye of another English teacher, Erica or Chloe perhaps, they would have the sense to see the dred in her eye and save her from this encounter, but they were nowhere to be seen. She was powerless, submissive to his mercy. His hand began to slide from her neck, down her back.

She froze as she considered her options.

His hand continued to slide as his breath got closer to her neck. The stale stench was putrid, its heat penetrating her ear. His hand continued to glide, until it rested on her buttock. She felt a tight squeeze as his lip caressed her ear.

On impulse, Abbie shifted to the side and brushed him off. A stealth glide under his arm allowed her to escape his grasp, before he could even tell she'd evaded him.

She peeked back at his confused stance, before grabbing her bag and slinking out of the room, his surprised and disappointed face watching her go.

'Goodnight Sir,' she called back. 'Get home safely to that lovely wife of yours.'

After that night, Abbie knew she had the upper hand. That night had changed things for the two of them, inextricably. Joe knew it too.

The summer break had followed, during which time Abbie had barely thought of the encounter, let alone discussed it with anyone, but as the start of term rolled around, she began to dread returning to school. She had no idea how he would react to seeing her again. Would his pride and masculinity be dented in such a way that would mean he would make her life hell? Was he angry and filled with rage towards her? Was he embarrassed and regretful over the encounter?

Abbie lay awake the night before Inset Day, tossing and turning as her mind whirred constantly. She was used to 'Sunday Night Dread' but this anxiety was crippling. When 5.15am clicked on the alarm, she'd already been awake for hours, staring at the ceiling and willing a September snow day to materialise. *Had that ever happened before?*

On the drive in, she'd settled on acting nonchalant and walking straight over to the middle leadership table, where he often liked to position himself at these events, acting like one of the 'normal people'. She strutted over and plonked herself next to Chloe, but he was nowhere to be seen. When she eventually spotted him, he was standing in the corner, with the rest of the senior leadership team. He didn't approach Abbie's table once.

That was three weeks ago.

Since then, she could not recall a single time that he had been able to offer her eye contact. He'd deliberately not questioned or challenged her during the Year Eleven Results Meeting, he had rearranged their Line Management Meeting twice, and she had not yet received her SLT drop in. It was clear that he was avoiding her.

Yet now, here he sat, reading from his piece of paper as if he were making a public service announcement.

'Joe,' Abbie pleaded, reaching her hand across the table in an attempt to steal his focus. He had once admired her, fancied her, even. She needed to find a way to reach him. 'This can't be real.'

He pulled his arms back instinctively and placed them by his sides. 'This letter details your suspension period, which commences today.' He continued to stare at the paper, reading the words with a forced sincerity. 'During your suspension, you will receive your normal salary and benefits. You should cooperate with our investigation and should not set foot onto the school site or perform any of your normal duties, until told otherwise.'

Abbie slowly retreated her hand and placed it in her lap. She took a deep breath and exhaled slowly. Her attention was drawn to the flickering light in the top corner of the room - the CCTV cameras were on.

She knew how this would appear. Now she'd been the one making contact with him, holding out a hand to touch him, while he pulled back. It was caught on CCTV. If anyone *had* seen them at the party, this would corroborate any narrative that he might try to spin again.

'They were all her advances.'
'She had been trying it on for months.'
'She was hoping for a leg up.'

She breathed hard again and stood up slowly. Lifting the letter from the desk, she gathered her things together and walked towards the door.

'Thank you,' she whispered. His silence behind her was deafening and she knew in that moment that she was alone, isolated, abandoned. She'd have to deal with this shit show on her own. There would be no support from the school. She'd fucked up and she needed to be scapegoated. Stepping over the threshold, she pulled the door closed behind her, the thud of reality rattling assuredly in her wake.

#

It was 5.15pm when she finally walked through the front door. Barney barked gleefully and ran straight to her, wagging his tail in a frenzied excitement before running back to the lounge to collect his stuffed dinosaur in his mouth. *At least someone was pleased to see her.*

The rest of the house felt eerily quiet. Abbie considered where they could be. Ian was preparing for his presentation next week and needed to work without distractions, so he had planned to be working from home, yet a peek round the office door revealed his empty desk. Her mother was due to drop the kids home by four. She double checked the calendar - no after school clubs today - so Lucy and George should be home by now. Her mother would normally wait for her to arrive home before leaving, but with Ian at home and the big party impending, her mother would have headed home, for sure.

Surely, she thought, *someone would come to say hello.*

Abbie dumped her bag onto the floor, the letter stuffed firmly inside it, and slid out of her heels. She shuffled towards the kitchen and clicked the kettle on. Tea was needed.

As she settled down at the kitchen table, a steaming mug of tea in hand, she attempted to relax into the chair, but her body would not oblige. She stretched out her legs, one at a time and clicked her neck to either side in an attempt to release the tension in her neck, but to no avail. Her body refused to relax. She felt sprung tight, like a jack in the box that had been wound so tight that it might explode free when finally released. She breathed in deeply and attempted to force her shoulder blades to slide down her back on the exhale, but they wouldn't move. Finally, the familiar sound of bickering began to rise from the floor above. The jolt back into reality was almost welcomed.

'Give it back!' George screamed. A large thud followed his yell and she knew what would come next. Just as anticipated, the sobbing ensued, growing louder and louder with each foot that stomped down the stairs. George tumbled into the kitchen, his eyes red and soaked. He dragged himself towards her, feeling sorry for himself with every step, before falling into her embrace.

Abbie spotted the red mark on his arm immediately.

'What happened, sweetheart?' Abbie questioned. Calmly at first. She could guess where it had come from and she already knew where this was going to lead - it was the same story, just another day - but she needed to buy some time and learn the facts of the altercation.

George collected himself together and his sobs subsided. He brushed the back of his sleeve across his face to dry his eyes.

'She smacked my arm and then she pinched me,' he squeaked.

At age eight, George still had the uncharacteristic voice of the 'every child'. The voice did not yet reveal his gender or his personality, it was pure innocence. She was desperate to notice the childlike in him before it escaped him completely. Perhaps Abbie still babied him, but that was her prerogative. Surely every mother wants to capture the youth of their youngest child for as long as they can.

'And what happened before Lucy smacked and pinched you?'

Abbie had practised this interrogation several times before. Remain neutral. Gather the facts.

'Nothing!' he yelled defiantly. 'She just hates me.' He winced, rubbing his hand back and forth over the bruised arm.

'Something must have happened, George. Were you in her room?'

Although Abbie's voice remained clam, she could feel the annoyance building. *George was eight for goodness sake. Why did Lucy have to be such a cow?*

'Well, yes...' admitted George.

'There you go then,' Abbie continued. 'What have we said about going into your sister's room?'

'But I just wanted to show her,' his voice tailed off and his cheeks became moist once more. This time, his sobs were silent, which Abbie knew meant real upset.

'Show her what?' Abbie asked, inquisitive now.

George gulped at the air, in between his sobs. 'My picture,' he whispered, before thrusting his head into Abbie's stomach and crying some more.

'Okay, okay.' Abbie tapped at George's head. 'Lucy!' she yelled.

No reply.

'Lucy, come down here, please.'

Unsurprisingly, Lucy did not reply with words, but Abbie was impressed when she heard her footsteps plod down the stairs within seconds. At least she had listened, this time. Perhaps this negotiation would be amicable and amenable for all.

When Lucy strutted into the kitchen, she held an air of superior nonchalance. Refusing to acknowledge either Abbie or George, she headed straight to the drinks fridge, collecting herself a can of diet coke and teasing it open before glugging down a cool mouthful.

'Lucy,' Abbie began, calmly and in control. 'Did you smack and pinch your brother?' Hopefully this would be a resolvable dispute, not another battle.

'He was in my room!' She snapped back, defensively, with a stare that threatened to harm them both.

'I only wanted to show her!' interjected George.

Lucy rolled her eyes and took another gulp of the fizzy liquid.

'Show her what, darling?' Abbie asked inquisitively.

George pulled his face away from the nook of his mother's side and gawped up at her. His eyes were round and innocent.

Abbie was always shocked at how similar his eyes were to her own - green and dazzling. The kind of eyes that made you take notice. George lifted his hand deep into his trouser pocket and pulled out a crumpled piece of paper. He unfolded it carefully and handed it over to his mother.

Abbie unfolded the paper and her heart sank.

The page was an elaborate design, filled with hearts, stars and patterns. The colours were Lucy's favourite - blue and pink - and in the centre of the page, George had written in his neatest hand: *Lucy Hart, My Best Sister, I Love You!*

Abbie stared at the page and then back at George, his face blotchy and puffy from the tears. She looked up at Lucy, who was leaning against the wall, practising her best carefree stance.

'Can I go now?' Lucy asked, arrogantly.

Abbie felt her heart begin to race.

Did she actually think that she was being respectful by asking for permission to leave? Did she honestly believe that she was in the right here? Who the hell did this girl think she was?

Without waiting for an answer, Lucy turned and began to leave the room.

In a moment of panic, Abbie saw herself losing control.

This girl would not get to just walk away. She was not going to take any more crap. Not from Tia, not from Mrs White, not from Joe and certainly not from Lucy.

Her chest tightened and she felt her face flush. Her arms grew rigid and a thick fog of rage smothered her.

There were no thoughts at that moment; only feelings. When looking back on it later, Abbie would describe it as an out of body experience. She didn't remember moving to the step of her own actions. Instead, when playing it back, she would see the scene unfold in front of her, as if she were merely a voyeur, not the main participant.

Abbie lifted George from her lap and climbed calmly but swiftly from the chair, manoeuvring George down into it. She crossed the kitchen floor at speed and caught up with Lucy as they both approached the door frame. She reached out and grabbed at Lucy's shoulders, pulling at the fabric of her top. She spun her daughter around and pinned her firmly, up against the wall. Her jaw clenched as she pinched her daughter's arm, hard and aggressively, feeling Lucy recoil under her grip.

She stared deep into her eyes and spat the words at her first born:

'You little bitch!'

#

Dinner time passed in silence.

Lucy refused to come down from her room and George was too upset to speak. Ian had chosen the exact moment of the pinching incident to emerge from the toilet and observe the assault. He had vehemently expressed his disgust with her action, exclaiming his unbridled shock and disappointment within earshot of both children, so now, the silence hung between them. What more was there to say?

After ten minutes of food being slipped back

and forth across their plates, Abbie wordlessly declared an end to the meal by standing and carrying her plate to the sink. The evening had escaped them all too fast and without their knowing, darkness had arrived. She placed her plate on the countertop and peered up, expecting to glance out into the escape of the garden, but instead, she caught sight of her reflection in the window. She recoiled in shock at seeing her mother.

She had gotten old. When?

Abbie was thirty seven and had always had anxiety about aging. On her twenty-first birthday, she cried her eyes out. Not from joy or excitement. Not due to the showering of love and gifts that were poured down on her. But because she was distraught. Distraught about the concept of being over that threshold and having to now accept and succumb to real adulthood.

Being an adult was scary.

Abbie couldn't ever quite put her finger on what it was that made her feel this pit of despair, but it was something to do with the passing of time; the fear of things not being relished or enjoyed to their most thoroughness before they were gone. She longed with deep nostalgia for the days gone by. She'd read about mindfulness techniques: practising the art of being in the moment and appreciating the present. But no matter how hard she tried, thoughts of what was to come rushed her brain.

Abbie glanced at the clock - 7pm. Shit. She'd agreed to call Sarah at 7.15pm and she hadn't built herself up for it yet. As soon as Abbie's phone pinged this afternoon, she knew that Sarah would be searching for the drama. That was before the suspension.

Oh fuck, the suspension. The memory hit her like a punch to the gut. *How had this happened?*

She hadn't yet told Ian about any of it. After the Lucy incident, there was no chance she could admit to any more of her failings, and thankfully, Ian had not yet seen any social media or received any text messages. She didn't know how long she had, but she would make the most of his ignorance while she held it.

'Come on sweetie, time for bed.' Abbie gushed, slowly prising George from his chair. 'No need for a shower tonight, let's just get you upstairs and settled.'

Abbie guided George to his room and helped him into his pajamas as she glanced around the room. The dinosaur murals on the wall were beginning to fade and the paper was peeling away from the plaster in the far corner. She made a mental note to stick it back on one of these days.

His bed was tucked neatly in the corner, topped with a mound of teddy bears, all lined up against the wall, expectantly waiting for their master to return. The centre of the room left an open space for his race track rug which was strewn with a mixture of toy cars and figurines. Abbie observed the way the figurines were mainly larger than the cars and wondered at the beauty of a child's imagination, still able to ignore the limitations of reality.

Abbie pulled the curtains closed, enveloping the room in darkness, before the glow-in-the-dark stars on the ceiling came to life.

George had emerged from the bathroom, rubbing at his eyes. She guided him into bed and lent down to tuck him in, pulling the covers up high, securing it tightly.

'Mummy?' George asked softly, his head poking out of the covers.

'Yes sweetie,'

George pulled the covers up over his head and hid himself. 'I'm really sorry,' he mumbled into the darkness.

Abbie peeled the tips of the covers away gently until the top half of his face was once again visible. She focused down at her boy and beheld the fear in his eyes.

'I shouldn't have gone into Lucy's room,' he continued, his voice more audible now. 'I know the rules.'

Abbie lent in and hugged him, throwing her arms around him and gripping him tight, feeling the delicate ribs beneath his cotton top.

'George, my angel,' she started, 'You are a good boy and you did not deserve to get pinched. You have nothing to be sorry about.' She spoke into his neck as she breathed in the faded scent of his cherry shampoo, still present from yesterday's wash.

She loosened her grip and sat back up. 'Now, let's tuck you in and close our eyes, shall we? Tomorrow is a new day.'

Abbie tucked George back in, creasing the sheets carefully around his body. They both knew that he would wriggle free from its grip as soon as she left the room, but they both enjoyed the ritual. She kissed him gently on the cheek and rose to exit.

'Mummy,' she heard George plead. 'Can I read to you?'

Abbie paused at his expectant question and glimpsed down at her watch. She had a decision to make: stop and be in the moment with her boy, or concern herself with what was waiting for her in the moments ahead. It didn't take her long to choose.

'Not tonight,' she apologised. 'Definitely tomorrow.'

She leaned down again and kissed him firmly on his forehead, pressing her lips into him for a second longer this time, an attempt to show how much she loved him.

She started towards the door. 'You're allowed to read quietly to yourself for twenty minutes and then lights out okay? I love you.'

'I love you too mummy,' George echoed back, but before Abbie had left the room, her son had laid himself down and turned to face the wall, pulling the covers up over his head and succumbing to the night.

Abbie crossed the hallway, glancing down towards Lucy's room, before deciding against it. Nothing would be gained from attempting that conversation tonight. Instead, she entered her own bedroom, shut the door softly and leant her back against it in an effort to push the day away from her. She took a deep breath and retrieved her phone from her pocket, opening her recent call list and scrolling down further than she expected to, before being greeted by Sarah's name.

'Sarah Abbingdon'.

Her sister had always mocked her for listing people's full names in her phone. Abbie wasn't sure what she was listed as in Sarah's. 'Drab Ab', probably.

'Here we go,' she sighed, before pressing the green button and raising the phone to her ear.

By the ninth ring, she felt a pang of relief. She could escape the call this evening if her sister didn't pick up. One less person to disappoint. As she removed the phone from her ear, she realised she was a second too late.

'Abs,' she heard through the receiver. 'What the hell is going on with you?'

CHAPTER 7
SARAH

The condensation caused drips of ice cold water to slide onto the table, leaving the base of her glass resting in a puddle. The warmth of the room juxtaposed the coldness of the night outside. The arrival of the autumn air caused a chill that felt biting.

'*Severe rain is heading our way shortly.*' That's what the news had reported in the car on the way over. Sarah had listened eagerly to the details of the weather report. '*A storm blowing in from the east overnight.*'

Mother wouldn't be happy.

Inside the room, Sarah shifted on her stool, her eyes fixated on the woman at the bar, her bulging belly brushing the countertop as she served the raucous men their pre-drinks. She could have been no older than twenty five, yet she commanded her space. Sarah could not hear their conversation, but the woman's comment as she placed the shots down made the men roll back with laughter. She held their gaze, and all of the power, while they followed her movements with their eyes as she strutted back up the bar. These men were enraptured by her. Her glossy hair was the product of her impending arrival, Sarah was sure. She had always heard that pregnancy made one's hair thicker and more luscious.

'Hun?'

Sarah's attention was drawn back to the reason they were here. Katie sat expectantly across from her, her eyes wide and staring, waiting for an answer, an explanation.

'So what's happening then?'

Sarah took a deep breath and prepared for the conversation ahead. Katie was her best friend and she adored her company. God knows, Katie had saved her from some disasters and bad dreams of the past. But Katie was also hard work. She lived for the drama of other people's lives. Perhaps to escape her own.

'I think she just got to the end of her tether.' Sarah suggested.

'What tether, exactly?' scorned Katie. 'She lives the actual dream!'

'I don't know, exactly. She said she just snapped. She couldn't really explain it, but she didn't sound right.'

'Hmm,' judged Katie, as she lifted her glass and downed the final sip of white wine. 'Drink up!' she ushered, nudging Sarah's diet coke towards her. 'Do you want another?'

Sarah ignored the offer.

'I just think she's had enough. I know we judge her. I know we joke, but I'm not sure that she's okay. Her voice was odd. Cold. I've barely even seen her, recently.'

'Ha,' joked Katie. 'That makes a change!'

'I'm serious Kate. She didn't seem right.'

Katie paused and looked closely at her friend. Her face softened and she exhaled, resignedly.

'Okay. I am listening. So, what are you going to do?'

'I don't know, exactly, but I'll see her tomorrow at the party. We can talk then.'

'Do you really think you'll be able to have a heart to heart with your big sister during your dad's seventieth birthday party?'

Katie had a point. The night would be crazy. Sarah's mother had gone over the top. There was a live band coming to perform under the marquee that she had ordered for the garden. The guest list was out of control; she was sure the whole village had been invited. And the pantry was already overflowing with bottles of alcohol and trays of vol-au-vents. The night would be a busy one. Not the ideal time to talk.

There was just no time to talk nowadays. Abbie always had the kids with her and she never wanted to do anything in the evenings. There was always an excuse: she was too tired, she had Parents' Evening, Ian was out so she had to stay in. Abbie had been drifting away from Sarah for a while and she was fed up of always being told no. There was only so much rejection one could take before retreating.

Sarah's stomach lurched again.

'Sure you don't want another?' Katie questioned, rising from her chair.

Sarah shook her head and placed her hand over the top of the glass. 'I'm all good.'

She watched as Katie swaggered to the bar in her mini skirt, strutting in her heels and swishing her hips from side to side, accentuating the roundness of her backside. Immediately, she attracted the gaze of the pre-drink ballers. Katie would be gone a while, as she made the most of the attention.

Sarah lifted her bag onto her lap and reached a hand inside. She pulled out the small cardboard package. It was still sealed. She had hidden it in her bag as soon as it was delivered that morning - she couldn't risk Simon seeing it. Sarah wiped the puddle with a napkin and placed the box on the table.

It was no bigger than a large match box, so the

pills inside must be fairly small. She'd read everything online, so she knew the process: one pill first and then the other four the following day. She wouldn't be able to take them yet anyway; she'd need to be alone when it happened. She'd let the weekend pass and then deal with it on Monday.

A wave of guilt swept through her again but she shrugged it off.

A glance at the bar showed that Katie was now fully engaged in conversation with two of the ballers; swishing her hair back in flirtation; loving every second of the attention.

Sarah's phone vibrated, causing it to slither over the table. She caught it. The banner read *Simon* and she rolled her eyes. *Really? Could he not give her one evening to herself?*

She wouldn't open the message. She didn't want him to see that she'd read it, but a pull down of the banner showed his intent.

Missing you! X

She placed the phone firmly back on the side and sighed deeply.

The phone vibrated again.

Let me know when you'll be home. Xx

The more messages there were, the more she felt inclined to reply, but she held firm. She'd be home in a few hours, he'd be fine without hearing from her until then.

She focused her attention back towards the bar and saw Katie's annoyance. The ballers' attention had diverted again, away from Katie and back to the barmaid who swept past them with a comment and a wink, before continuing on down to the end of the bar. *How did she have this power? Such coolness in her casual indifference.*

Katie readjusted her top - just enough cleavage to entice - and tapped one of the men on the shoulder. The desperate attempt to regain the focus worked and they were chatting once more.

Sarah chuckled to herself and tried to send her friend a telepathic message: *Act aloof.*

Her phone buzzed again.

I'm heading out to grab a few beers. Do you want anything?

Sarah looked back at her, still full, glass of diet coke and shuddered. She was perfectly able to buy her own drink, if she wanted one. He didn't need to message.

Sarah was proud of the life she had built.

Since the age of sixteen, she knew she might have to make it alone. Sarah was an overweight child, but this hadn't held her back yet. She had an expanse of friends. She was 'the funny one'. But on her sixteenth birthday she realised that 'funny' was code for 'never going to get a boyfriend'.

The cake had been cut and she was searching for Jason, two slices in hand, wishing to discuss the dj's awful choice of music, when she heard whispering coming from the downstairs loo. She halted outside the door, her ears pricked.

'Sarah?' She heard Jason joke.

'You're always with her, I assumed you guys were a thing...' Ruby's voice was unmistakable.

'No bloody way!' Jason continued, 'Can you imagine getting in bed with her? I'd likely suffocate!'

Sarah retreated to the upstairs bathroom for the rest of the evening, complaining of a stomach ache, much to her parents' annoyance. They were then left to dismiss the rest of her guests with profuse apologies.

Sarah made her way through her teenage years, popular, but single. She had more friends than anyone she knew - both male and female - but never a boyfriend.

At age seventeen, Sarah lost her virginity to a twenty year old dealer in the village park - a humorous anecdote that continued to circulate for years to come. She wouldn't have sex again until her twenties.

Sarah ploughed herself into work instead. After three years as a junior copywriter, Sarah launched her own editorial business. Her determination came second only to her intelligence and she built herself up from the ground to her six figure salary.

Sarah earned more than anyone else she knew. She owned her own house and drove a Range Rover Sport. Sunrise Copper, they called it in the showroom, but she'd shrugged her shoulders. It was just red to her. Her wardrobe was sprinkled with Chanel, Gucci and Dior. And she'd visited a wealth of tourist hotspots at her leisure. She travelled wherever she wanted and didn't think twice whenever she chose to take a break from work.

Yet there was always something missing...

'Bloody prick,' Katie huffed as she plonked herself back into the chair and shocked Sarah back into the room. 'He's an ugly twat anyway. As if I'd be interested in him!'

Sarah grabbed at the box, but it was too late. She saw Katie's eyes dart towards it and then bolt straight up at Sarah.

'Hey,' she paused. 'What is that?'

'Nothing,' Sarah lied, attempting to shove the

box back down into her bag.

'Sarah?' questioned Katie, reaching out and grabbing the box before Sarah was able to hide it. 'Is that what I think it is?'

It was too late. The information was out and Sarah had no way of erasing it. She shouldn't have been so foolish. Of course Katie would recognise the package.

Sarah took a deep breath and breathed out a slow, audible admission.

'Yes Katie, 'I'm pregnant.'

CHAPTER 8
ABBIE

When Sarah's words echoed down the phone, Abbie headed straight for the bed and cowered beneath the covers. She'd fooled herself into thinking the conversation could be positive, helpful in fact. Sarah was a high powered, successful woman. Maybe she would understand the stress that Abbie was under.

'It's really not that big of a deal, Sarah.'

'Not a big deal, Abs? You had a fight with a parent! Apparently it's all over the class WhatsApp chats already.'

'How did you hear about it?'

'Katie texted me.'

'Ha, of course she did.'

'What does that mean, exactly?'

'These parents are like a gaggle of high school mean-girls. Except now they also have mobile phones, social media and their husband's money.'

The world had evolved from the one she'd grown up in and Abbie wasn't sure how much of it was for the better. Privacy seemed non-existent lately. Perhaps they had failed to enjoy it to its fullest before. At least when she was younger, people could lead elements of their lives in peace without the whole world knowing. But in today's world, one could barely get away with sneezing in public before someone they knew was being warned that they 'probably had Covid'.

'This isn't Katie's fault, Abbie. Honestly, do you

know how embarrassing it is for my friends to contact me about my sister going crazy in public?!'

Abbie had no words. She would have laughed if it wasn't all so depressing. How did Sarah have such a natural way of making everything be about her?

'You just can't behave like that in public, Abbie. What the hell has gotten into you?'

'Sarah, I really don't need to hear your disappointment.'

'Fucking hell, Abbie, take some responsibility. What is wrong with you?'

That was a good question. *What was wrong with her?* She knew that she wasn't behaving in a rational way. She knew she was miserable, overworked and underappreciated, but she also knew that she had a nice house, a family and money in the bank. Yet she could not escape the deep rooted feeling of emptiness - or was it fullness? Was there something missing or too much of something? She couldn't explain it. All she knew was that something was off balance and she had no fucking clue how to level it out again.

What she needed, what she really needed was someone to talk to. Someone she could be open and honest with. Someone who would listen while she described her deepest darkest thoughts. And maybe someone who could actually offer her some helpful advice. But no one had the time for her issues. *Everyone has their own shit, right?*

'Abbie, you just need to apologise. Speak to the Head and find out what you need to do to make it right again, okay? Katie said he seems like a great guy, someone who will be supportive and have your back.'

The silence was uncomfortable.

'Okay, Abbie?'

'Yep. Thanks Sarah.' she replied. Her words were cold and flat.

'You'll be absolutely fine. Things always work out for you - you're the lucky one, remember?'

Abbie had no words. How could her closest living relative be so disconnected from her? The loneliness began to ache.

'Anyway, Abs, I have to shoot. It's been a crazy day and I've got loads to do. I'll see you tomorrow at dad's okay? Just wait til you see my new dress!'

'Can't wait,' Abbie replied.

This time, Sarah felt the icey tone. They both sat silently, the unsaid words floating between them both. Abbie was suddenly startled by the wetness of her cheek. Tears were falling, but she had no recollection of when or how they had started.

The tension between them was still and thick. Abbie knew that this was the moment. If Sarah had reached out and tried a little harder to connect, it would all have come flooding out. A simple question could have released it all: *Are you really okay?* or *How can I help?*

The opportunity was there, waiting for them to choose it and things could have been different; she could have found relief, solace, answers, and some form of hope.

'You'll be okay, Abs.'

She couldn't let her sister hear the pain in her voice. 'Uh huh,' she managed.

'Love you,' Sarah said and the receiver clicked off.

Abbie felt like any energy she had left had escaped her. She pulled the covers over her head and continued to sob.

Twenty minutes later, that's where Ian found her.

#

'Abbie, what are you doing?' Ian questioned, leaning over her, as if he were trying to identify a wild animal in an unusual habitat.

Abbie peaked out of the corner of the covers, her brown, matted hair sticking to the side of her face. She attempted to brush it away but it was glued to her cheek. She was a mess.

She willed for him to sit down, to lean on the side of the bed next to her and reach out an arm, but he remained standing. Her appearance was clearly concerning, as his face crumpled into a disapproving stare and he cocked his head to one side.

At that moment, she felt so vulnerable. She stared up at his intimidating frame and observed him carefully. When was the last time she had really noticed him?

Ian was still dressed in his blue, tailored suit trousers, but his tie had been removed and the top two buttons of his white shirt had been undone. His dark stubble was flecked with white and she noticed new wrinkles around his brown, brooding eyes that she had failed to see before.

He looked handsome.

She looked embarrassing.

How was it fair that, as men age, they get more attractive and more alluring, while women get haggard and old?

'Abigail, what on earth is going on?' he questioned again, with more authority this time.

The shock of his voice made her flinch and she pulled the covers tighter, up around her neck. She closed her eyes and took a few deep breaths, preparing to tell him the truth. But she knew just how this conversation would go and she could not bear it any longer. She could not stand for any more judgement. She could not contend with any more scornful glances or disapproving stares. She knew as soon as she told him that he would instantly wish to go back in time, to before they met, so that he could pick a different suitor. Someone who could be a good mother, a loving wife, a supportive friend and an impressive worker. Someone who wouldn't ruin his life.

She removed the covers and sat up in her bed, staring at her knees. She could feel his eyes burning through her and she knew she needed to get the words out.

'I've done something bad...' she whispered.

#

The evening had morphed into the night. As the sky turned to black and the talking became repetitive, they wordlessly declared an end to the evening. Ian removed his clothes, hung his suit trousers back up in the wardrobe, and slipped into bed. She migrated to the bathroom, brushing her teeth and wiping away the day's mascara, which was now smudged into dark circles around both eyes. By the time she reentered the bedroom, he was fast asleep, and yet here she sat, still very much awake.

As she lay in her bed, she tried to remember the conversation they'd shared, but the details wouldn't come to her. She could barely remember what they'd spoken about. She felt like she'd said a lot, yet she knew she'd omitted the most important parts about how she was truly feeling; the raw honest truth; the ugly truth that is relinquished with vulnerability and total trust in the ears of the listener. She wasn't there yet.

She'd talked through the acts of the day, explained how when she reached her wits end she just snapped. She explained how Joe had invited her into his office and explained the next steps in his cold, harsh monotonous voice. She recounted the facts, listing the issues that had led her here, but she'd kept emotion out of it. She hadn't expressed her remorse, her guilt, her embarrassment. She hadn't admitted the fear she held over what the next steps might be, for her, for Lucy, for their whole family. She hadn't divulged her innate desperation for things to change, for her to escape the facade she was living in.

Ian had listened. He had ummed and arred in the right places. He had stayed in the room and allowed her to talk. But now that she tried to piece the conversation back together in her mind, she couldn't really remember his responses. He had been shocked, that much was for sure. He had failed to even look at her for the majority of her explanation, but he had stayed in the room and he had listened. Or, at least, he had pretended to listen. *Had he offered any answers? Was there a plan for how to move on past this?* She was suddenly filled with the dread of possibility. *What if he was disgusted by her?* Perhaps he was plotting his way out, which would explain why she could barely remember any of the actual words he had muttered. He certainly hadn't embraced her, hadn't held her and rubbed her back, hadn't told her that things would be okay or that he would support her. He laid back against their headboard, legs out before him, crossed at the ankle, and stared straight ahead. *What did he really think of her?*

She rubbed at her eyes with her fingertips until she saw stars. She was exhausted. She needed sleep.

The silence of the night was interrupted by a thunderous intrusion that jolted her. The wind had picked up and now the storm was definitely on its way. The darkness that should have commanded sleep was punctuated with a streak of lightning that pierced its way through the window and into the room. This wouldn't help to induce sleep.

And breathe, she ordered herself, with futility. Abbie had learned long ago that wishing for sleep did not grant it, yet her resolution remained unwavering.

She tried to summon some of the mindfulness, grounding techniques she had read of. How many could she remember?

The five things. Identify five things you can see, four things you can touch... No, this would require her to open her eyes, which would surely take her back a few paces.

Body Scan. Start from her toes and work upwards. What could she pay attention to and how could she force each area to release tension? That might work.

Abbie focused on her right foot. The heels of today had left her arches tender and she focused her attention on releasing the stress. She stretched it down and then up again. She scrunched the toes and released them back out again. Breathing deeply as she went, each exhale released a smidge more tension. One last exhale and move on up towards the ankle and the calf.

As her attention shifted, so did the source of the thunder. Ian flicked out a foot and she felt a snagged toenail scrape down the side of her leg.

Abbie launched herself to sitting, in a fit of frustration. For fuck's sake!

Today had been horrific. All she wanted was the beauty of escape; a few unconscious hours to hide away from her life, yet she couldn't even be afforded that luxury. Someone up there was taking the piss out of her, she just knew it.

Abbie reached for her phone that rested on the nightstand, and the harsh light made her wince, as if it was annoyed at having been woken. Well if she couldn't sleep, why should it? As the thought passed through her, Abbie felt a pang of immaturity.

She glanced over at Ian. He was the one who didn't deserve sleep. The injustice smacked her full force and she began to feel the warmth rise up in her again. Was it anger or jealousy?

She stared at him. He appeared filled with peace, while his snoring filled the room and refused to allow anyone else the pleasure of tranquility. That was Ian all over: pure selfishness.

Abbie considered their lives. How could two people live together, sharing the same spaces, the same people, the same events, yet have such completely different experiences? Her and Ian lived in parallel existences. To the external world, they walked side by side, living in harmony; united in their journey. While, in reality they existed in completely different spheres. Perhaps even different universes.

Sitting up stiffer and arching her back, Abbie took another deep breath and considered what her days tended to look like, now. She couldn't quite face reflecting on today, so she journeyed her mind back to yesterday - Thursday.

She woke at 6am. Six was a pretty typical wake-up hour. Abbie had always been an early riser and there was a lot to do before the day started for anyone else in her family. A hot shower to wake her up, before getting dressed. Abbie laid her work clothes out on the bedroom chair the night before, to avoid a wardrobe mishap. Dressing in the dark could be dangerous, and she'd been known to arrive at work with her top on inside out in the past, so preparation was key. Makeup was harder to do in the dark, so she had recently moved to a new skincare routine - tinted moisturiser and a brush of mascara. Applied in the dull light of the en suite. Natural was fashionable, right? She was sure she'd read that in one of Lucy's magazines recently: *Be Your Natural Self!* was the headline, which introduced a three page spread of different products that would be required to successfully achieve the look. She'd need to read it again and find out what else she could do to remove the eye bags and red patches.

Abbie would tiptoe downstairs and say good morning to Barney. She smiled at the thought. He was always so pleased to see her, wagging his tail and shuffling from side to side in excitement. There was something special about having a dog. While he caused her constant stress, with the incessant barking and growling at strangers, he had an unconditional love for her. He wouldn't judge her for shouting at Lucy or for 'assaulting' Tia. He wouldn't care if she didn't have a face painted to perfection or if she had her shirt on inside out. He didn't mind if she was late or if she hadn't completed her marking on time. He would continue to greet her - no matter what - with pure love, affection and sometimes even a sloppy kiss across her cheek. Suddenly, Abbie felt a lump in the pit of her stomach as she realised that being greeted by Barney could actually be her favourite part of every day. *Was that normal?* She felt the sadness flood her body, but she shrugged it off.

What came next?

Waking the children.

Once, this had been her favourite part of every day. Their groggy eyes opening with confusion and a little wrinkle appearing between their eyebrows. She'd sit still, smiling down at them and waiting. In a matter of seconds, she would notice the wave of adjustment sweep across their faces and their eyes would flicker with recognition. The change would make their eyes light up and their faces would soften. They would hold each other's gaze and they would smile back at her, before blinking away the sleep and reaching out an arm for a warm embrace. Nothing but pure love and happiness.

Yesterday morning, it had taken three gentle attempts at waking George before he eventually got out of bed - not too bad. On the fifth entrance into Lucy's room, Abbie had chosen to pull the curtains open, as the gentle arm stroking and soft 'good mornings' thus far had failed to heave Lucy up from her slumber.

Apparently this was not the correct thing to do.

As the curtains unfurled and the sunlight began to spread its welcome into the room, Lucy shrieked! The noise was so startling that, for a split second, Abbie jumped in fear that her poor child was in pain, before realising that the girl was simply turning into a nocturnal vampire. Lucy proceeded to scream inaudible words at her mother, before Abbie retreated, backing out of the room with her hands held up in surrender.

Ian slept soundly.

By the time Abbie had fought with the washing machine, walked the dog and returned to make the packed lunches, she heard the shower begin above her. Ian was rising from his restful slumber.

At 7.15am, Abbie was barking at the children, wishing for time to slow down and for them to speed up. She was rushing to gather bags, shoes, and PE kits. She was shouting and moaning - and occasionally swearing. She was growing anger, frustration and anxiety, while her children were growing disappointment, upset and perhaps even a little hatred. But the madness of the morning was playing out in a different world to the one Ian was in.

Locked securely within the bathroom upstairs, Ian was engulfed by the steam of his gentle shower and the sound of Bob Dylan, plodding rhythmically through the speaker.

Abbie's morning car journey was fraught. The first three minutes were standard. Her retort to the children about how important it is that she leaves on time and the repercussions of her being late to her morning meeting, were always met with silence. *Were they listening or judging?* The rest of the journey found her driving erratically, swerving the other fools on the road and beeping her horn aggressively at their idiocy.

By the time she reached her parents' house to drop the children off, they were feeling miserable and she was feeling guilty.

Ian, however, enjoyed his morning commute to the sounds of Alan and Ally on the radio, serving up their witty sporting anecdotes and opinions, as he chuckled along with them.

Abbie's day had started in a rush and it had not

stopped. She ran into the building at 8.01am, sliding into the only remaining seat in the room, where the meeting had already begun. On leaving the room at 8.14am, she now had five new tasks to complete.

She had ten minutes to check the ever growing Inbox of Doom, before tutor time began at 8.30am. The assigned tasks:

- a uniform check
- a homework check
- a behaviour and attendance check.

James and Leah failed each one, so Abbie informed them that she would be forced to put their names forward to Mr Jones. This was met with a series of threats:

'How dare you?!'

'Wait til my mum hears about this!'

'It's fucking stupid. How exactly does my skirt length affect my education?'

The joy of today's youths!

Abbie had a full day of teaching - five lessons. All had been planned to perfection. She'd stayed up until midnight the night before, just in case that woman from The Trust was walking around - again. The threat of inspection was always present, despite the recent Ofsted. The Leadership had started calling them 'Climate Checks' or 'Walkthroughs' but Abbie was experienced enough to know the drill by now. They were constantly being watched and judged - Big Brother style.

The lessons that Abbie planned these days were not the same as the lessons she planned when she had trained to teach. They were no longer just about imparting knowledge in an enjoyable and interesting way. Instead, they were an 'opportunity' to 'inspire' young people. She was expected to scaffold her teaching for differing abilities; to model excellent examples of writing and behaviour to the students; to show them how build on their prior learning; to offer opportunities for retrieval; to ask questions that deepened understanding; to captivate the students and insist on constant engagement; to live mark and give verbal feedback. All of this was to be achieved in every lesson, while also being supportive, firm, fair and understanding. She was to build relationships with the young people in front of her.

'Take the time to get to know your students,' they'd been told on Inset Day. The irony was not lost on her.

At break time, she was on duty in the canteen - successfully breaking up two fights. At lunch time, she was instructed to give up the opportunity to actually eat, in order to run an intervention session - supporting all those adorable little rugrats who failed to listen during their actual lesson, so were rewarded with a second shot at it in a smaller group setting.

After school, there was a meeting to scrutinise results and decide upon the actions needed in the Department Improvement Plan. A plan, of course, that would require hours more work to be input by these teachers, who were clearly not working hard enough.

Once the meeting finished, 4.45pm arrived and Abbie could trawl through her emails again... one hundred and twenty four today. She had ten minutes to work through them, before she needed to leave and collect her children. The rest would need to be answered once the kids had gone to bed. A time that, over the past few years, had crept later and later. Thank God for 'schedule send'. She'd hate anyone to know she was working at night time.

Once home, it was 5.45pm and the children needed feeding, the washing needed to be put on and the dishwasher needed emptying. The hoover was to be run round and the dog would be walked again. She had no choice but to ignore her children during these tasks. *How else would she get it all done?* So George sat in the lounge, watching TV, while Lucy slinked away to her bedroom, her face firmly planted in her phone.

At 6.30pm, Ian sauntered back through the door. He threw his bag on the floor and collapsed onto the sofa.

'Couldn't grab us a drink, could you babe?' Was his opening comment.

The memory hit her like a slap in the face.

Abbie could feel the warmth building inside her once more. It was rising from the pit of her stomach and into her chest.

She glanced back towards her husband and the snoring swirled around the room as he breathed in and out. He looked so peaceful. How could he sleep at a time like this? Why wasn't he awake with her, holding her tightly and telling her that everything was going to be okay, because they were a team - a partnership - and he would protect her, protect them all?

Abbie worked so God-damn hard for this family, yet it was all taken for granted. She kept all the plates spinning at all times. Yet, she had become the bad guy. She was the failure. She was the wife who wasn't quite loving enough, the mother who wasn't quite attentive enough, the teacher who wasn't quite committed enough. If Ian tried to walk a day in her shoes, he would make it no further than the end of the driveway. Yet she was the one who was not good enough.

Abbie pulled her phone towards her once more and opened up the familiar app. The words faced her sharply - bold and clear.

Period - two days late.

Abbie's stomach lurched. *Could it be?*

She tracked back through the calendar and saw the hearts that signified the days when her and Ian had had sex. A drunken Saturday, two weeks ago and a Wednesday before that. Wednesday was odd, she thought, before recognising the date and remembering his birthday.

They didn't have a lot of sex anymore, but she still tracked it. At thirty seven, she needed to know what her body was doing and, as her fertility tracker app liked to remind her, perimenopause was probably on the way.

Abbie knew that Ian wanted no more children. He had made that clear on more than one occasion, but Abbie couldn't shake the thought of it. A baby might bring them closer; it might give her something joyful to focus on. A baby might be just what they needed: the answer to all of their problems.

She glanced back at the app and clicked on the option: *Could you be pregnant?*

Abbie read the options:

Why might your period be late?
- *Pregnancy*
- *Stress*
- *Travel*
- *Underlying health condition*
- *Natural cycle changes*
- *Perimenopause*

Abbie clicked on number one and started

reading:

A late or missed period is one of the most common signs of pregnancy. However a late or missed period can also be due to several other factors. If you have also been experiencing other symptoms, it may be time to take a pregnancy test.

Abbie read through the symptoms and considered the possibility.

Sad or anxious mood - check.

Difficulty sleeping or bad dreams - check.

Unusual appetite, cravings or feelings of nausea - check.

She climbed carefully out of bed and headed for her underwear drawer, her eyes still adjusting to the darkness as she stepped, tentatively, forward. She found the pregnancy test that had been stashed there since the last time. *How long ago was that? Six months?*

She was usually so regular, so two days really did seem unusual.

Abbie collected the test and slowly pushed the drawer shut. She spun on her heels and headed for the bathroom. As she carefully pulled open the door to the en suite, she heard a shift in Ian's breathing.

She froze, staring straight at him, one hand on the door, the other, clutching the test. Silence filled the room. Had he woken up? She imagined him opening his eyes to see her, caught red handed, like a burglar trying to escape. Thankfully, his snore reverberated around the room again, allowing her to slink into the toilet, and close the door behind her.

Abbie performed the routine steps that she had done so many times before:
- *Collect cup*
- *Open test*

- *Pee in cup*
- *Dip test*
- *Lid back on, pants back up and place the test on the other side of the room.*

She sat back down on the toilet seat. Three minutes always seemed like such a long time when waiting for the test to decide its verdict. She allowed her mind to wander as she gently placed her hands against her stomach.

Abbie imagined the little baby growing inside of her and calmness engulfed her body.

She pictured the twenty week scan and the joy at finding out the baby's gender. She imagined the birth - a home birth this time - a pool of warm water in the living room while soothing music played and Ian sat beside her, clutching her hand and wiping her brow. He'd be so proud of her for staying so calm and having the strength to guide this human being out of her. She could see the expression on his face - pure love and admiration.

A baby would definitely reinstate some kind of lost spark between them. They always appreciated each other the most after the children were born. She heard that the first six months after having a baby was the worst time for most couples as the stress and the sleep deprivation generally caused them to argue more and disagree on parenting decisions. Abbie, however, was filled with a deeper connection to Ian after Lucy was born, and again after George. She remembered the nights when Lucy would cry and cry, refusing to sleep. They'd check that she was fed, changed, burped, the right temperature etc. and would find no solution to the problem. Just when she was at her wits end, fearing that she could not succeed in this parenting malarkey, Ian embraced her with his giant bear arms and held her so tightly, she thought she might melt right into him.

'We are in this together.' He had said. And they sat together, crying and holding each other all evening, breaking only to head upstairs together and attempt another soothe before returning Lucy back down to her cot. Abbie had never felt more connected to another human being than she did during those nights.

Abbie thought about her teenager. She imagined Lucy taking so well to big-sisterhood again. Lucy would embrace trying to settle the baby down to sleep at night. She would take so much joy from dressing up her little sibling in the latest designer outfits and ridiculous little booties. Lucy would soften and calm. She'd find a new appreciation for her mother for going through this ordeal. She'd realise what Abbie went through to bring Lucy into this world and would instantly show appreciation and thanks, having never considered the sacrifice before. Lucy would take great pride in showing off the baby at the school gates.

The school gates.

Yes. Abbie would be able to drop her children off at school; something she had never really been able to do.

'Teach!' They'd told her in her early twenties. *'If you want to have it all, teach! The job works so well around motherhood. Just think of the summer holidays!'*

In reality, Abbie had spent the last thirteen years missing every sports day and every nativity play; she'd not done a school drop off for five years and the last pick up was six months ago when the heating broke at school so they all got to leave early. For thirteen years, Abbie had spent most of her half term breaks sick (the curse of a teacher) and had worked at least four of the six weeks every summer.

Maternity leave - would she take the whole year? A whole year off from work. And then she could never go back full time. At age thirty eight, she'd really need to spend some time at home with the baby to make sure they reached all their developmental milestones properly. The chances of disabilities or learning difficulties would likely be higher now, given her age, so she would need to invest proper time and effort into raising the little darling.

Abbie checked her watch. Two minutes and forty five seconds. *It was time.*

Suddenly, Abbie felt fearful. For those few minutes she'd allowed herself to imagine a new world, a utopia where their lives could start again, they could have a second chance at happiness, but what if it wasn't to be?

Abbie recognised, perhaps for the first time, just how miserable she was. She was so caught up in the humdrum of life that she had stopped actually living. When was the last time she felt joy? When was the last time she involuntarily laughed? When was the last time she felt contentment?

A baby was what they all needed. The embrace of new life would reinvigorate all of theirs. A baby would bring joy, hope and laughter back to them all. It would allow time to share and enjoy and make the most of each moment.

She reached out and carefully collected the stick, guiding it towards her like a precious jewel, suddenly so aware of the power and significance held inside this piece of plastic. She cupped it in both hands so as to obscure the result.

Was she ready for this? As soon as she released her hands, this would be the start of a huge adventure for them all.

She could feel her heart pounding inside her chest and the sweat from her hands made holding on tight a challenge. She slowed her breathing and allowed herself to smile. *This was a good thing. This is just what they all needed.*

Abbie slowly turned the pregnancy test over in her hands. Her right hand gently cradled it, while her left stroked the top of it soothingly.

'Here we go,' she whispered to herself, as she glided her left hand away.

Her eyes darted down at the test but the writing on the stick was a blur. She composed herself and allowed the black smudges to slowly fade into focus - the words that would alter their lives forever.

She blinked and suddenly the words were clear. Staring back at her, bold and expectantly.

Not Pregnant

Abbie stared at the test for another few seconds before dropping it hard on the floor. Slowly, she clutched her knees into her chest, one by one, and locked her arms around them. She placed her head down onto her knees and allowed the darkness to envelope her.

For forty five minutes, the house was still. No movement occurred. No lights were flicked on or off. No children tiptoed from their beds to fetch a glass of water. No adults woke from their slumber for a middle-of-the-night wee.

From the outside, this house was filled with

sleepers - a family resting peacefully in the darkness until the new day's dawn would welcome them to tomorrow.

If anyone had ventured into the house, first impressions would have been the same, until the noises became audible. Only two were present in that house that night:

Abbie's weeping sobs, creeping out from under the bathroom door.

And just ten feet away, on the other side of the door, Ian's restful snoring.

BEFORE

CHAPTER 9

As she itched her cheek, she felt the dampness. She looked down at her palms, hunting for the source of the moisture before realising that it was being produced by her own hands. She suddenly felt self-conscious. *Was her face sweating too?* The temperature in the room was rising with every minute and she made a mental note to google: *effects of climate change on April weather* when she got home.

The white-washed walls made the room feel too clinical and the harsh smell of cleaning products left a bitter residue in her nose.

She shuffled uncomfortably in her chair and stared down at her feet - fixing her eyes on the faux leather shoes that had held her up all day. The buckle on her left foot was beginning to fray - she'd need to buy a new pair.

All the eyes inside this room were working hard to avert their gaze in order to avoid meeting another. They focused instead on one of two things: one's phone or one's shoes. There was to be no shared eye contact with any other woman within this space. No acknowledgement of the reason why they might be there, no consolidatory sharing of a glance. *Who had first agreed upon this rule and how did everyone know it?* It was unwritten but well known, unlike the other notices, plastered around the building:

No Smoking.

Rude or aggressive behaviour towards our staff will not be tolerated.

Waiting times may be longer than usual. Please be

patient with us.

The final sign made her chuckle silently to herself as she attempted to remember a time when she had been seen promptly inside an NHS building.

Her eyes rose naturally and it was a second too long before she recognised that she was observing the women sitting across from her. The woman was in her early twenties, wearing a dark brown duffle coat, buttoned up to the neck, leaving just enough space for her thick auburn hair to escape out of the sides, flowing gently and exposing an airpod tucked neatly in one ear. The coat spanned down to her mid calf, where the base of her leggings could be seen, tucked into her white Nike socks and her gleaming trainers. *How was she not boiling?* The woman seemed calm and composed. She did not seem in a hurry to be seen and certainly did not appear anxious. *Why was she here? Was this woman not filled with the same dread and worry as her?*

She began creating this woman's story: she was fresh out of uni and had been in a relationship for three years with her reliable, banker boyfriend. No ring confirmed that an engagement was not on the cards. *Maybe marriage is old fashioned nowadays?* She was sailing through the first few weeks of pregnancy and all was well. She was simply here for an extra check up because her mother had a history of miscarriage and during a routine check up when she was a teen, a junior doctor had suggested that she may also carry the same susceptibility.

She looked too calm though. Surely any pregnancy in your early twenties provoked some sort of reaction. If not fear, then excitement, or anticipation. She studied her face closer, watching the corners of her mouth wrinkle slightly at the video she was watching on her phone, her eyes lighting up with different tints of colour as the pictures on her phone changed. Suddenly, the girl's eyes darted up and straight across at the woman who dared to look directly at her.

It was too late. She'd broken rule number one and had been caught.

Her eyes shot straight back down to the floor, focusing once again on her broken shoe.

Time within this room was frozen.

As the statued figures sat idle and uncommunicative, the lack of appearance from a medical professional made her begin to wonder if this was no hospital at all, but a prank TV show, filming its contestants to see how long they would mindlessly wait before considering that something odd might be afoot.

A ripple of pain glided across her lower abdomen again, but she shrugged it off.

The wooden frame smashed itself open as a nurse appeared in the haunting opening, threatening to capture one of these sitting ducks and lead them into a new realm, where their lives might be changed forever.

She was already halfway to standing, desperate to escape this airless pod of time that trapped her, when her name was called.

As she stepped out of the waiting room, she felt the eyes of all four women firmly fixed on her back. *This was the only time to look.* She let the door smash shut behind her, removing their voyeurism from the rest of her journey.

As she walked down the corridor, she noticed

her steps sync in unison with the nurse: left foot, right foot. She was two paces behind, and as she listened to the clicking of her heels on the harsh linoleum floor she enjoyed their synchronicity and began attempting to match the rhythm with every step. *Control what you can, while you can.*

'Through this way,' guided the nurse, holding open a door and ushering her in.

The room was darker and smaller than she expected and the doctor did not turn to greet them. Instead, he remained seated on the stool, his back to them, staring at the ultrasound screen before him, moving his mouse and making some final adjustments.

'Take a seat just there, my love,' the nurse beckoned, pointing at the hard brown chair squished on the right of the bed.

She took a seat on the edge of the chair and glanced up at the nurse, waiting for the next instruction. The nurse nodded her head and smiled, comfortingly, but said nothing. She realised they were waiting for the doctor.

After too long, the doctor announced he was ready to begin. 'Righteo,' he said, clapping his hands together and turning his chair to face his patient. 'What do we have here then?'

She was startled by his cheery tone and spun her head again to the nurse, perhaps for reassurance. She nodded and smiled from behind his back.

'Well,' she started, hesitantly. 'I think I am about nine weeks pregnant,' she began, before hesitating and then adding, 'According to my dates and the test I have taken.'

She waited for a response, but the doctor

continued to stare at her, wordless and expressionless. She tried to read his signal but it would not compute.

'But,' she continued, 'I began bleeding a few days ago.'

His face remained unchanged. *Should she say more? Surely it was his turn to speak?*

Eventually, he began shaking his head from side to side, tutting as he moved. *Had she said something wrong? Was she incorrect? Was she in trouble?*

'Hmmm,' the doctor muttered, a wrinkle appearing between his eyebrows.

'It was light,' she attempted to assure him. Why did she feel like she was having to defend herself? 'Not bright red,' she said, perhaps with a little too much force, 'but pinkish. And it only lasted a day or so.'

'I see,' hummed the doctor, clearly not convinced by her show. 'Any pain?' He asked, shifting his focus back to the screen, as if he was about to check off his reel of usual questions, that presumably other people answered 'no' to.

'A little,' she lied as the stab hit her stomach again. 'It comes and goes.'

The doctor's face continued to stare forward but his eyes shifted right to meet hers. He seemed curious.

She avoided his gaze and moved her eyes back down to the ground - safety - but on the way, she noticed her leg. It crossed tightly and neatly over its partner, but it was trembling furiously. She had not noticed until now. She reached out and grabbed it firmly, trying to quieten its obvious fear. Too late, the doctor had seen it too.

'Now, don't fear, Miss. Let's see how the little one is growing shall we? Pop off your lower half and then jump up onto the bed. Nurse Goodacre will cover you over and we will do a quick examination.'

His words sounded comforting. *Had she misread him? He had probably done this hundreds of times. If he didn't seem worried, why should she be?*

The doctor slipped behind the plastic sheet of a screen, and barked instructions at her.

She obliged as quickly as she could, for fear that he would peek back from the sheet before she was fully ready for him. She stripped her lower half in record time and climbed onto the bed. The mute nurse covered her over with a sheet and offered her another comforting smile.

'Bum to the edge of the bed, ankles and knees together,' the doctor hollered from behind the sheet.

The volume made her jump, she was clearly on edge. She laid back on the bed and placed her ankles together. She could not tell if she was cold or terrified but she could see her knees knocking together beneath the cover as the shivering began to spread up to her arms.

The nurse rested a gentle hand on her knee. No words, but the look in her eye told her that she was a mother too and she understood. *A little comfort.*

'Ready doctor!' the nurse announced and he swished back the screen without a pause, shuffling himself back onto his stool.

'Okay, then. Nine weeks is early so the scan will need to be internal. It may feel a little uncomfortable, so the more you relax, the easier it will be.'

She breathed in deeply, willing her pelvic muscles to relax enough to allow the examination to be as painless as possible. Smear tests of the past had taught her that relaxing the muscles was definitely the best option.

'Okay, then, ankles stay together and knees part ways, please.' He guided her knees down. 'I will begin to insert the camera and we will see where this baby is.'

The instrument was cold and intrusive, but not painful. She took a deep breath and he began.

She stared up at the ceiling. *Was it better to look at their expressions or remain neutral?* The ceiling was white artex, little bumps and cracks all across it. She traced her eyes from left to right, wondering if she could count them. There were stains too - some light, some darker. *What were the stains?* She had a flashing image of a birth she'd witnessed on TV - *the blood spatter.* She shook the thought away and focused back on the ceiling.

A wince as the doctor pushed the camera to the right.

'Sorry, dear. We need to check both sides as well as the womb in the middle.'

He continued to push harder. She couldn't wince again so she held her breath and counted.

It was fourteen seconds before he released and readjusted his camera. A few seconds of relief, perhaps.

She had no idea how long she would be on the bed for, or how long it would take to find the baby and assure her with the news that all was well. She had assumed a few seconds would reveal the sights he needed to see, but he had not yet confirmed anything.

She took the gamble and turned to see his face.

He was concentrating hard, squinting and turning his head from side to side, like a confused labrador. At first his age made her feel like he was experienced, but now she was thinking twice. Maybe he retrained when he was middle aged. Perhaps he had previously been a science teacher or a pharmacist. Maybe he was always a doctor but previously specialised in oncology or neuroscience, choosing to move to gynaecology in his later years. *Why would any man want to work in gynaecology? What a way to put you off sex for life!*

His face continued to squint as he started clicking the mouse. He was taking pictures. *Surely that was a good sign?* He moved the rod to a new direction and clicked again.

She studied his face. He had thick, dark hair which he had combed over to one side and fixed there with some kind of wax. His eyebrows were dark and overgrown, with stray hairs flicking out from several different angles. His eyes were dark brown. So dark that the pupils became lost within them. His nose was too big for his face, giving him a rather amusing caricature look, and her vantage point allowed her to see several grey hairs poking out from each nostril. His mouth was small, with thin lips concealing his teeth, teeth which she had yet to see as when he spoke, his mouth only opened the slightest fraction.

His eyes shot her a glance and she shifted her focus quickly, back towards the ceiling. *Why was it so embarrassing to be caught looking at someone?*

She would avoid him now, keeping her gaze focused on the ceiling instead. The bumpy, browning ceiling, with its cracks and stains, showed clues of the stories that had filled this room over the years. She allowed herself to get lost within their pages, hers being another story to add to the book.

The doctor stopped his clicking and leaned back into his chair, tilting it to face his patient. When he spoke, she heard only fragments of his sentences. She did not look at him. Instead, her eyes remained fixed on the bumps of the ceiling. As his words filled the room, she tried to concentrate by writing any words she'd heard in a fake ink across the ceiling with her eyes. She knew she needed to retain the facts, but it was no use.

'Sac incomplete…no yolk…no embryo.'

She could feel their eyes on her as she recoiled with embarrassment, but they kept digging deeper into her skin.

Please don't look at me.

'No heartbeat…likely miscarriage.'

She could not respond in words. She had to get through this moment and then she could compose herself before returning back to the real world that lay beyond this room.

'No one's fault…able to try again in a few months.'

She took a breath and began to count. She would give herself ten more seconds. Ten more seconds, then she could thank the doctor politely and climb off from this bed. She could shrug this off as an unfortunate experience and get back to her life. *There was so much to do this afternoon!*

Her eyes continued to stare, unblinking, at the ceiling. And then, the tears began to fall.

She could not stop them and she could not escape them.

She laid on the bed, still and silent, hoping that the salty streams which collected in pools around her ear lobes were unseeable to the others within the room.

No one spoke.

Her eyes remained focused on the ceiling, yet she knew that theirs were burning into her. She could feel them scorching her skin. The shame and embarrassment and humiliation at her failure. *Why were they allowed to stare?*

She allowed herself not ten, but thirty seconds before she moved.

Thirty seconds of grieving. Thirty seconds of pain. Thirty seconds of human honestly.

When thirty seconds were over, she shrugged off the misery and sat up on the bed. She began dressing quickly and in silence, while the doctor shuffled out of the way uncomfortably and rushed back behind the screen. *You've already seen my vagina, mate! There's nothing more to avoid!*

She collected her things and thanked them for their time, faking an important meeting that she 'must rush to'. She left the room and did not look back as they called to her that she'd forgotten her medical notes.

She looked straight ahead and marched towards the exit door. She had a day to continue on with.

CHAPTER 10

The night had been unexpectedly enjoyable.

She very nearly didn't go.

Earlier in the day, it felt like the dreaded January cold was coming for her and she was considering cancelling. But by 8pm, the sneezing had subsided and the headache had been controlled with two paracetamol, so she got herself dressed up and headed out, despite him encouraging her to stay in and allow him to 'nurse her back to health'.

Now, as she stumbled over the threshold and back into her haven, she recognised that perhaps she had enjoyed herself a little too much.

She stumbled into the kitchen and retrieved a glass from the cupboard, moving almost in slow motion, dedicating extra care and attention to her movements. She poured herself a glass of water and downed it in one go. A flashback of the evening hit her - *how many shots had she downed?* An instant wave of nausea swept over her. She hated alcohol. *Why had she got so swept up in their drinking? Never again!*

She filled the glass back up again and exited the kitchen, stalking the motion of her feet carefully, willing their every tiptoe to be as silent as possible. She negotiated her next move, but deciding that the sickness was only a passing wave, she turned left to the living room, rather than straight on to the loo.

Collapsing down onto the sofa, she felt welcomed by its soft embrace which wrapped her neatly into the safety and security of home.

The silence of the house was calming.

She considered how much energy it might take to walk up the thirteen steps needed to reach the bedroom, imagining hauling herself from her current position and climbing each step of the mountainous trek. Then there would be the effort of undressing when she reached the top. And she would probably need to brush her teeth too! *No, she would resign herself to the sofa for tonight.*

She tugged at the blanket and it released its grip from the edge of the sofa. She enveloped herself in its fluffy embrace and swiftly withdrew into the solitude of sleep.

In her dream, she was swimming.

At first she was in the ocean, with the sunlight beaming down on her. Then a dolphin swam past and welcomed her onto his back, carrying her gently towards the shore, but just as the glistening sand was beginning to come into view, he swiftly changed direction and started swimming back into the depths of the ocean.

He was moving faster now, creating confusion.

'Wrong way,' she tried to call out, but he would not listen.

She hung on tight to his fin, in an attempt to stay afloat, but as the ocean waves turned into river rapids, sloshing aggressively in every direction, she was flung off his back.

The dolphin vanished and a crocodile appeared in the distance. She thrashed her feet around, trying to escape the water that was now beginning to engulf her. She gulped for breath but inhaled a mouthful of cold, gushing water instead. She began to panic. She was underneath the waves and she could not find her way back to the surface. She tried to breathe again but another mouthful of icy water filled her lungs and she coughed out fiercely.

She startled awake, falling onto the floor and coughing out the water that was suffocating her. Her hands against her mouth felt wet and she realised that her hair was dripping down onto the carpet.

She tried to regain her thoughts, attempting to make sense of things. *How had her dream managed to become reality?*

Suddenly, she felt a hand clutch hold of the hair on the back of her head, pulling her up with force. She let out a feeble scream and hoisted herself to a standing position, meeting his gaze.

At eye level, she snapped back to consciousness quickly and tried to think logically about what her next steps needed to be.

With one hand, he placed the now empty glass down on the coffee table gently and with the other hand he released the grip on her hair.

'Where the fuck were you?' he spat at her.

She blinked hard and remembered her evening. 'I was at The Kings Arms,' she protested, 'I told you where I was going.'

'I messaged you,' he said.

She tried to recall the evening. *Her battery had died. Fuck. But that was just before 11pm.* She remembered it distinctly because that was when she decided to leave. People were finishing up their drinks by then anyway and she knew it wasn't safe to be a woman out late at night without a phone. She must have been home by 11.20pm. She glanced at the clock. The room was dark but she could just about make out its face: 11.49pm.

'I came home as soon as it died,' she willed to

him, reaching out a gentle arm. She knew it was futile. His eyes were dark and angry, staring into hers and she could see there was no connection to be made right now. He had clearly been drinking too. The best thing to do was avoid any more conflict until tomorrow. He'd be sorry then.

He stepped back from her so as to see her fully. His eyes traipsed up and down her body and she realised how she must have looked: half naked, smudged mascara and dripping wet.

'I don't know why you insist on treating me like this,' he whimpered. 'You deliberately ignore my messages, you screen my calls and you treat me like shit. You're a fucking bitch and you don't deserve me.'

He picked up her phone and held it out, in front of her face. 'You can have this back when you learn to act like a fucking adult,' he said as he marched his way out of the room.

His feet climbed their way back upstairs and the door to their bedroom clicked shut.

She fell backwards onto the sofa and dropped her head in her hands.

This was not okay.

SATURDAY

CHAPTER 11
SARAH

Sarah could hear the sound of the lawnmower in her dream. The vibrating whine echoed into her subconscious and slowly melted its way into her thoughts, so that before she opened her eyes, she knew what was happening.

She pivoted her head to the left and peeled open an eye. 7.49am. *Who mows the fucking grass at this time?*

She heaved herself up from the satin sheets and rested down to a sitting position on the edge of her bed, clocking herself in the mirror, a side angle that was less than flattering. Her mangled hair needed to find a comb and she had neglected to remove all of last night's makeup, so clumps of black mascara rested under her eyes, still attempting to cling on to the lower lashes. She sat up straight and ran her fingers through her hair, before sliding her hands down to her belly.

She was sure she looked fatter. *Had she put on weight?*

I've barely eaten for a week! Came the thought, before the remembrance smacked her hard.

Pregnant.

Fuck.

She shrugged off the memory and leaned herself up into a tall stretch, before standing. She pulled the covers straight behind her and tucked them in at the edges. *A made bed was an important first step each morning.*

The window was slightly ajar and she could smell the freshly cut grass wafting in through the curtains. She pulled them open and gazed out at their garden - her garden; it had been hers first - and sure as anything, there he was, pushing the motorised mower up and down the lawn in synchronised, parallel lines. *At least the storm didn't last long.*

Sarah watched him for a moment, tracing her eyes back and forth as he stumbled up and down the garden. Simon wasn't made for manual labour, that much was for sure. He kept tripping over his own feet, which was mildly comical, but also slightly pathetic. *What kind of idiot wears crocs when mowing the lawn?*

She tried to remember what it was that made her feel drawn to him when they'd met.

Katie had dragged Sarah to Mulligan's that night in an attempt to 'raise her spirits'. Sarah was still moping about Tom, but had buried herself in work as a distraction.

'Nonsense,' Katie shrugged, as she brushed aside Sarah's excuse that she needed to work tonight. 'No man loves a woman who is addicted to her work, Sarah. Let's go out and find you a husband.'

Sarah had never considered 'finding a husband' before and the thought intrigued her. *Where could these men be found? Were they lined up in rows in disused car parks like Tesla cars, waiting for collection? Were they hiding behind trees in the woods like clues for a scavenger hunt, waiting to be captured? Was there an option to choose the one you wanted or did you have to marry the first one you found?*

Sarah was successful in her own right and she knew that she did not need a man to support her or to define her. She figured that out pretty early on in life, perhaps even before the Jason incident. But that didn't mean she didn't hope to one day be sought after. *Who doesn't want someone to love them? Who doesn't yearn for that person to desire them, to see them as number one above all else? Everyone wants a partner to greet them as they arrive home in the evening; to discuss their amusing work anecdote with; to analyse the latest TV drama series with.*

But Sarah needed more. She needed fireworks, she needed passion, she needed infatuation - a man who doted on her and adored her more than anyone else in the world. Someone who would whisper sweet nothings in her ear, compliment her in front of her friends and cancel his plans to play golf in order to take her out shopping instead.

Tom had not been that man.

Then she met Simon.

Simon was unlike any man she had ever encountered. He oozed confidence, but not in an arrogant way; simply in the way of a man who knew what he wanted and was not afraid to go after it, publicly, openly, and without a care for what others may think.

Sarah was at the bar when their eyes met across the room. Sarah turned away first, embarrassed at having been caught clocking eyes with a stranger, but when she turned back a few seconds later, he was still staring straight at her. When recounting the moment afterwards, she described it like a scene from a romantic film.

He was sitting with a group of male friends, all in their early thirties, lounging around a table and drinking their pints. They were laughing and throwing banter around, but as Sarah continued to observe Simon, the other men faded into a peripheral blur. The chatter in the room melted to a dull murmur and the rhythm of *Wonderwall* raised its volume from the jukebox. Oasis were having a comeback.

Her gaze zoomed in slowly on Simon, and his features became sharper, as if the spotlight had been adjusted to show the audience that they should now be focusing only on Simon; all the other characters were insignificant. His dark eyes continued to pull her in and she was absorbed by his sensual stare.

As Simon rose to standing, his eyes still fixed on Sarah's, she adjusted her gaze to notice his attire: pressed chinos and his Vivienne Westwood shirt, tucked in. Smart but stylish. He made his way towards her, one hand in his pocket, the other swaying gently by his side, refusing to look away. His confidence was mesmerising.

Simon reached Sarah, placed one arm on the bar beside her and leaned in.

'Good evening, my name is Simon. You are absolutely beautiful; may I buy you a drink?'

Sarah glanced back at the mirror. *Beautiful right now, she was not. There was work she'd need to do before the party this evening.*

She had her outfit planned: a long, black, strappy dress with a low neckline and a slight ruching over the midriff. *That will hide any bulge.* It hung loosely against the wardrobe, lying in wait for its showcase this evening. Her shoes stood proudly beneath it. They were black, with a gold trim, and her earrings and necklace were placed on the dressing table, gifts from Simon last Christmas, gold and extravagant.

Sarah had mixed feelings about this evening.

She was excited for her father. Seventy was an impressive achievement and she was thrilled to be able to celebrate with him. Greg didn't often make a fuss, so a party was an unusual luxury to afford. He deserved to be the centre of attention amongst his many, many friends. There would be friends from the village; tennis associates; men he'd worked with over the years and their respective partners; family friends and their plus ones. Sarah paused at the thought of seeing Tom again and her stomach lurched. It was not unusual to see Tom, the man showed up everywhere, but there was something about him being at this party that made her feel uneasy, uncomfortable even. The intimacy of the event - her father's significant birthday, to celebrate and honour the life he had made and the important people who had influenced him and his journey. *Was Tom one of those people? Was Simon?*

Her thought was interrupted by the slamming of the back door. Sarah had not noticed the mower finish, but now the silence was palpable.

She wrapped herself in a slinky silk dressing gown and plodded her way down the stairs, where the smell of strong coffee wafted its way towards her.

'Bella!' Simon called to her upon seeing her arrival, arms outstretched for a hug. 'Good morning my darling, can I get you some coffee?'

Bella was a nickname that Simon had adopted for her since their first date. She had joked at the amount of times he'd called her 'beautiful' so it just stuck. Nowadays, the word sounded patronising and perhaps even mocking. He had once mentioned that he was a quarter Italian (to impress her?) but the word sounded foreign and arrogant on his tongue.

She shuffled past his outstretched arms and plopped a tea bag into the nearest mug. Coffee was too strong for this morning and she feared the taste may provoke some sickness within her. She assumed that morning sickness mainly happened within the first few hours of waking, so she'd take no chances.

'How did you sleep?' asked Simon, clearly trying to shrug off the shunned opportunity for embrace.

Sarah sighed. 'Well, being woken by that racket kind of ruined it, if I am honest.' She spoke without glancing in his direction, walking straight past and retrieving the milk from the fridge.

'Ah, the mowing!' Simon realised, before adding, ' Sorry, my darling, I just wanted to make things perfect for this weekend. I know there will be a lot to get done today, so I thought I'd make a start.'

'Okay,' Sarah replied, stirring the milk into the mug. 'That's all well and good, but I am not sure our neighbours will have appreciated the early wake up call either.' She shot him a disapproving side eye and walked the milk back to the fridge. 'And you realise the party isn't at *our* house, yes? No one will know if *our* back lawn has been perfectly mowed.'

Simon ignored the dig. 'People should be up at this time on a Saturday. The sunrise is beautiful, the day should be embraced and enjoyed. Only lazy people sleep in.'

Sarah considered arguing with the insult, but thought better of it. She changed the subject instead.

'Have you chosen what you're wearing this evening?'

'Not sure yet,' he brushed off the chat, grabbing the kitchen spray and beginning to wipe down the surfaces. 'Probably my blue suit trousers and the white shirt I bought last month.

'No Simon!' Sarah barked, turning now to face him. 'You cannot wear that!'

Simon recoiled in shock, as if he had missed some important information that had been shared about the dress code. Had he misunderstood the assignment? He was sure Sarah had said to dress smart.

'I'm wearing *black*!' she protested, staring him straight in the face, assuming the sentence was clear enough for him to comprehend her meaning.

Simon stared back blankly.

'*Black*, Simon. So you can't wear *blue*!' Her voice was shrill and overreacting. She knew she was pushing his buttons, and she knew it was unfair, but something within her couldn't stop. 'Jesus,' she continued. 'It feels like having to dress a child at times!'

There were a few moments of still silence before she stole a glance towards him. It took a moment to analyse his face. *Had she stoked something within him?* She locked eyes with him and she continued to hold her stare. She would not be the first to look away. She would continue to hold her ground, no matter how irrational or unreasonable she was being. She was strong, she was powerful, she was in control. His eyes hardened and his stare grew fiercer, the black centre of his eyes growing with every second. They became a void into him and, as she continued to stare, she found herself sinking down deep within it.

Suddenly, he blinked and the darkness was gone, replaced with a soft blue tinge of warmth. He looked away and spun back to face the countertop, rubbing it back and forth with the cloth, polishing it neatly.

'Not a problem,' he chirped with his back to her. 'We can find something else for me to wear. I'm sure it won't be too hard.'

Sarah could feel herself getting frustrated. Why was she getting so annoyed? It was the pressure of the day, the bloody parasite growing inside her and the anxiety over seeing Tom. She reached out and stroked Simon's shoulder.

'Yes,' she spoke softly to his back. 'We will find something else together.'

He did not respond to the stroking, but continued to wipe the cloth back and forth, back and forth. Sarah wondered if he might end up wiping straight through the granite.

#

Sarah kept re-reading the same sentence. She knew it needed tweaking but she could not work out how. This was what she was good at, it was her bread and butter, but every time she read the words they became jumbled and confused. Was this the pregnancy brain she'd read of? *Surely not yet.*

This manuscript needed returning by Monday morning and she had neglected to get it finished. She kept putting it off - *bigger things to deal with* - but now the deadline was approaching fast, and she had to focus. She'd set herself two hours this morning to knuckle down, but she was already over an hour in and she could feel the futility.

She pushed the keyboard away from her and leaned back into the chair. She needed to get today over with and then she could refocus. She had read the instruction leaflet three times. If she took the pills tomorrow morning, their effects would start to kick in by lunch time. Some mild pain and discomfort first, the bleeding would follow. The instructions weren't clear on the levels of 'discomfort'. They ranged from 'mild' to 'severe' depending on the person. *What the fuck did that mean?*

Of course, she'd consulted Google to do her own independent research, but she had to stop after a few reviews. Some reported extreme pain - 'worse than childbirth' - while others felt 'minor period cramps'. Essentially, she had no idea what to expect, so she would need to plan for the worst.

Simon would be gone by midday tomorrow. His tennis retreat was a four day affair, so that would give her until Wednesday night to get herself back in shape. When he returned from the Devonshire castle, having spent four days being trained by an ex-pro, eating luxurious meals and drinking champagne, she would be over the worst of it and would be ready to play pretend again.

But what if I'm not okay? She considered, before immediately shrugging the idea away. *She would need to be okay. She was Sarah Abbingdon and she was an independent woman. She would be fine, just like the many women before her who had found themselves in this position and been fine. She did not need the support or the comfort of anyone else.*

Katie had offered some condolences, but she seemed more consumed with the drama of the incident than the realities of how Sarah would cope with it. Her questions were oppressive.

'But how did this happen?'
'Were you not using protection?'
'Does Simon even know?'

She hadn't the guts to answer her bluntly, but

imagined the conversation confidently.

'*Well, Katie, it happened because sperm managed to penetrate its way through the hole in the condom and into my - apparently very fertile - womb and so yes, I was using protection, and no, of course Simon does not bloody know.*'

Sarah had thought a lot about her decision. She had not taken it lightly. There had even been a moment where she allowed herself time to think about the alternative: the idea of having a child with Simon; raising a baby together and teaching it how to adapt to their environments and live within their habitats. That just felt wrong. Even the language she used when thinking about it sounded cold, animalistic. She told herself what she had always known: she was not the maternal type. She had no desire for it and she knew, deep down, that she didn't want to risk being a bad parent. There were too many children in the world as it was; the last thing the world needed was another child being brought into it, without parents who are fully willing and able to raise them well.

Sarah knew it was a divisive topic, which is why she had chosen to stay so quiet. She didn't even know how Simon felt about it. She had no clue if he agreed with abortion or not. Perhaps he felt it was only appropriate in the most extreme cases. *Was this extreme? This was not what she had ordered, it was not what she had planned!*

Sarah felt her face flush with a mixture of shame and despair. She needed to walk.

Without a second thought, she grabbed her denim jacket off the hook; slipped into her converse; picked up her keys and phone; and walked out of the front door.

The air hit her hard. *Where had this wind picked back up from?* The clouds overhead had bundled together, forming a group of angry looking bullies, waiting to launch their attack on the unsuspecting victims.

Poor dad, he would be the unsuspecting victim!

Rain was in the air but it had not yet started to fall, so she figured she had at least ten minutes to get a quick power walk around the block. That might clear her head. Then, she'd go straight back to editing - an hour on that, before gathering her things and heading to mum's. There was a whole list of pre-party jobs to be dished out, before they would all get ready together. A 6pm event in the lounge was scheduled for 'an intimate family celebration', before the doors opened for everyone at 7pm.

There was so much to do. But now was time for quiet.

'Meditative thoughts,' she willed herself, stepping briskly onto the pavement and strutting her way down the road towards the hills. At least this weather meant a quieter walk. No one would be out in this, with the impending rain due to make an appearance at any moment.

Her steps grew quicker as her mind slowed down.

She planned her route: up the hill to observe the view, over the hill and breathe in the fresh air, down the hill and pay attention to each step you take. Feel the ground beneath your feet.

Her mind was still; she was calm and in control.

'Sarah!'

Sarah's attention shifted.

'Sarah, love!' she heard the cry again, rousing her from her tranquillity.

Sarah spun her head to the left, but she already knew the voice, it was unmistakable.

'Sarah, dear, have you got a sec?'

Sarah sighed. 'Coming, Jenny.'

CHAPTER 12
ABBIE

'Lonely?' questioned Ian, raising an eyebrow and staring over at his wife, objectively.

They'd risen at the same time that morning, but managed to make it through showering, dressing and making their morning coffees - hers black and strong, his sweet and milky - without having to acknowledge one another. Now that they sat, face to face across the same table, there was no escaping it. Ian had served first with, 'How are you feeling?' and she returned within a beat, not even having to think about her reply.

The word had struck her last night as she crawled back into bed and scrunched herself meekly into the silky sheets. She adopted a protective foetal position, pulled the covers up above her head, with room for only her nose to poke out. She made herself as compact as possible, in an attempt at self preservation, and it was only then, as she attempted to soothe herself, while her husband of fifteen years lay within touching distance in the bed they both shared, that the word came to her.

Loneliness.

Not alone, of course. Abbie was always surrounded by people, but she felt disconnected from them all. It was a feeling she hadn't previously been able to identify, and she certainly hadn't been able to articulate it. But this morning, while slumped over her steaming coffee, feeling the weight of her world crushing down on her back, he asked her how she felt and the word tumbled out.

She had surprised herself with her response. Lonely sounded sad, pathetic, maybe even rather obscure, given the seriousness of her situation, but there it was. It had been released into the air like a poisonous gas and, as it swirled in the air around them, it continued to spread further, like a fog of honesty, and she realised there was no way to recall or contain it again.

'What do you mean 'lonely'?'

Ian cocked his head to the side and she was instantly reminded of Barney. His eyes said, 'I think I am intrigued by what you're saying but I have no idea what you mean.'

Abbie stared dead ahead at her husband, the man she had chosen to spend her life with, and she recognised the pity within his warm brown eyes. She couldn't help but hear the disappointment in his voice, fused with the business-like tone.

He had never been one for talking about feelings. He found it uncomfortable, awkward, and unnecessary. When his mother died of cancer, a few years back, Abbie had read several books on how to help someone through the grieving process. The diagnosis was unexpected but her decline and then her final passing spanned several months. Abbie followed the steps carefully: she'd given him space, comforted him gently, probed him encouragingly to discuss his feelings, but he had other plans. He switched immediately into action mode, ensuring their wills were correct, planning for the funeral and making arrangements for his dad's care after she passed. He did not take time to process or grieve, at least not with his words or the support of his loved ones, his way to get through things was to work towards solutions.

Abbie did not want to work towards a solution right now. There *was* no solution, and that was the problem. She had reached a dead-end and there was no space to make a three point turn. She could not control what happened next and she did not need Ian to attempt to guide her towards it. She needed space to grieve, time to heal, connection to work through her issues.

'Abbie?' he asked again, with either tenderness or annoyance. Abbie could no longer tell the difference.

'I mean … I am feeling … well … sad, I suppose, Ian.'

'Sad. Okay.' he nodded and she could see the cogs turning. He could cope with *sad*. That was more normal. That was a feeling that could be squashed with a hug or a chocolate biscuit.

'Well,' he began, lifting his coffee to his mouth to buy himself some thinking time. He took a sip and replaced the steaming mug on the table.

'You should make the most of a few days off! What you did isn't ideal. I mean, there will be some tidying up to be done, but Joe will be working on that now. I reckon by Tuesday or Wednesday, it will all have blown over and you'll be able to go back to work like normal. So, until then, just try to forget about it and focus your attention on something else, maybe you could repaint the patchy bits in the bathroom like we've been discussing for months.'

Ian smiled, surveying his work like a builder might, leaning back and admiring his brick wall - *Yep, good job!* He adjusted himself on the chair and turned his attention to the back page of the newspaper which was spread next to him across the table.

Abbie's instincts had been correct. He was trying to fix things, plaster over the cracks (or in this case, paint over the patches) rather than dig in and find the root cause. She was disappointed, but not surprised.

'I am not sure it's quite that simple.' Abbie tucked a wisp of hair behind her ear. She wasn't going to let this go, no matter how uncomfortable it made her. He needed to hear how she felt and she needed him to engage, no matter how difficult that might be for him. They were a couple, a team, and she *needed* him now. Needed him to listen to her with the intent of *hearing*. Needed him to empathise with what she was dealing with, to consider how she was feeling. She didn't need solutions.

'I'm not sure there is any 'going back to normal'.' Abbie admitted, hoping that he would hear the desperation in her voice and cling on to the thread.

Ian's attention was drawn away from the newspaper and he looked up at her again. His face was blank and she detected a wisp of disappointment in his eye, before it switched back to thinking mode. She hadn't allowed him to fix things; he'd need to work harder.

'Hmm…' Ian scratched his chin and his eyebrows wrinkled slightly.

After his mother died, Abbie had been open about the ways in which she felt he should try to open up. She even shared the strategies she'd been trying to use on him in an attempt to coax out some emotion. At the time, he'd been dismissive, but she'd left the books scattered around the house, in the hope that he might even glance at the back cover of one, in an attempt to figure out how to be more in touch with his emotions. She wondered if he was scanning back through those notes now.

He shuffled on his chair again and brushed the newspaper to one side, just out of reading space.

'Okay, Abbie,' he began. 'Perhaps things won't go back to exactly how they were. In which case, what would you like to happen next?'

Abbie was caught off guard. She was hopeful that he meant to use tip number one: *ask open questions*, but his tone sounded slightly passive aggressive. Perhaps he was getting frustrated with her instead.

'What do I want next?' She repeated the question back at him to buy her a little more time. It felt like a school test that she hadn't revised for. *How the hell did she know what she wanted? To feel less sad? To feel less lonely? To feel more human? She wanted some time to be able to feel those things, before having to decide what she wanted next.*

'Yes.' He reached for his mug again - 'Best Dad' printed below Lucy's baby face - and sat back in his chair. 'If the world was in your hands and you could choose your next move, what would it be?' He folded his arms and sat back in his chair.

Abbie let out a mocking laugh at his question. She could feel her face redden as her frustration began to rise. *Was this a trick? Was he trying to catch her out?*

She considered the number she'd seen on their most recent bank statement. Their savings pot had stagnated over the past two years and they were just about managing to get by with what came into their current account. *Why was he asking her about 'what ifs'? They did not live in some alternate universe where they could write their own destiny! They had responsibilities that required a certain amount of adulting! As if there wasn't a mortgage to pay! Why would she spend her time thinking about what ifs, when the realities of life were here and now?*

He was still glaring expectantly, straight at her, his stance unchanged, waiting for her response. His glare and his folded arms felt intimidating and she broke away first, pushing her chair back with force and rising from her seat.

'I don't know, Ian.' She collected her coffee mug and dragged her feet towards the dishwasher, pulling the door open and placing her mug inside. As the mug tipped, brown liquid spilled its way down the front of the cupboard door and plopped onto the floor. 'For fuck's sake,' she muttered, kicking the door of the dishwasher closed and reaching for a sponge.

She heard Ian's chair scrape across the tiles behind her. She wiped the cupboard door and scooped the liquid from the floor, before tossing the sponge back into the sink. As she rose to standing, Ian's hand touched her waist and she startled. She'd assumed he had left the room, not followed her over to the sink. Her body tensed.

Ian spun her around and pulled her into him, squeezing her tightly and holding her in an awkward embrace.

She shrugged him off and shuffled her way across the room, to where the dishes from yesterday's dinner were still scattered around the place. She was not in the mood for a soft embrace. *There was a time for that and it wasn't now.*

'Why can no one clear up after themselves?' she

screeched into the room.

'Abbie, leave the dishes.'

Ian motioned towards her again and reached for her arm.

Once again, she brushed him off, carrying the plates back to the dishwasher and loading them in with too much force.

'I can't leave the dishes, because no one else will do them. And I can't leave the laundry because no one else will do that. And I can't leave the bathroom dirty because no one else will think to clean it!' Her voice was getting louder and she was aware that she was being dramatic, but the burning in her stomach was egging her on.

Control. She needed to control the mess in the room, then the mess in the house and then, if she controlled enough things, the things that she couldn't control wouldn't matter so much and her world wouldn't threaten to spin completely out of control.

'I thought you wanted to talk.' Ian huffed, collecting the pans from last night's dinner and placing them into the machine.

Abbie stood beside him, watching as he attempted to squeeze the saucepan into the wrong place. It was too big for the gap on the lower shelf, and as he tried to manoeuvre it, she shifted in frustration, huffing and waiting for him to give up so that she could intervene and place them in properly.

'Just leave it, Ian. You're making things worse,' she snapped and he stepped back out of her way.

'I'm trying to help you.' His voice had lost its calm edge and was becoming sharper.

'I don't need you to do the job that I am currently doing, Ian.' A plate slipped from her grasp and dropped into the machine with a loud clang. She saw a small chip fly off of its edge. 'Help would have been doing the dishes last night while I was putting George to bed. Help is not getting in the way while I am doing them now.' She continued to collect the dishes and rush back and forth across both sides of the room. Each drop of cutlery or crockery fell onto the dishwasher with more force.

'I cannot win.' Ian muttered under his breath as he began to retreat.

'So I guess that conversation is finished then. Great effort Ian,' she snapped, still busying herself and refusing to look at him.

Ian stopped in his tracks and spun on his heels to face his wife. 'Abbie, I just tried to talk to you!'

'Barely!'

'I try to talk, and you don't answer me, I try to help, and you tell me I am in the way. What do you want from me?'

Abbie kicked the door of the dishwasher closed and grabbed the kitchen spray and wipe. She paused, momentarily, before issuing him her retort.

'Ian, you don't actually try to talk to me. You don't actually care about how I feel or what is going on with me. You think communication means trying to fix every problem and then moving on. I want to actually talk to you and share how I'm feeling.' She turned and started spraying the countertops. 'But I don't feel like I can talk to you at all any more.'

'Don't tell me I don't care, Abbie.' His voice was rising now and she could tell she'd touched a nerve.

Finally, a little emotion, she thought.

'I just don't know what has gotten into you lately. You're like a different person. You're always so angry with me and the kids, so angry with the world.'

She threw the cloth onto the counter and turned to face him. 'I'm not fucking angry, Ian,' she shouted. 'I am sad!'

She could feel the liquid beginning to prick in the corners of her eyes and the blood came rushing into her cheeks. 'I am sad and I am lonely.' she continued, shouting her words at him. 'And I am scared, and I am anxious, and I am finding it all too much.' Her words were becoming weepy and she was aware that she was sounding rather irrational, but she could not stop herself. 'I am not happy Ian and I don't know what to do. Everyone hates me.' The tears were now streaming down her face and she felt them start to drip onto her t-shirt. 'Everyone at work hates me. Everyone at home hates me. Even *you* think I'm pathetic!'

She saw the nervousness in her husband's eyes and the guilt crept into her again. She drew her eyes away from him and sulked down at the floor. The tears became sobs and the sobs became silent whimpers.

She stood still, staring at the grey tiled floor, before noticing his shadow silhouette begin to move.

The shadow paused, just inches from her own.

Abbie felt a pang of pain. She was completely broken.

Try again, she willed. *Come closer. Hold me now. I need you now*.

If he had attempted to embrace her, she would have stood rigid for a while. She would have stood firm for a moment or two, before slowly softening and eventually melting into him. Her pride was too strong. Her willingness to relent was too firm. She knew all that. But eventually, if he had held her for long enough, she would have begun to feel safe; she would have trusted him; she would have allowed herself to relax into his body and she would have breathed with his breaths until they began to breathe as one and become a single entity, a team, a unit.

But Ian did not try to embrace her.

'It's going to be okay,' he whispered, placing a cold hand on her shoulder.

She wanted to fall into him, to allow his muscular body to hold her weight, but she resisted the urge to succumb to the togetherness. She was weak, an embarrassment, a mess. She stayed rooted to the floor, her arms down by her sides and her head drooped to the tiles.

For a moment, despite the lack of embrace, Abbie felt calmer. For a moment, she wondered if she'd broken through a wall. For a moment, she allowed herself to believe that maybe he understood and things could change. She wanted him to tell her that he was there for her, that things could get better, that there was nothing that life could throw their way that they couldn't tackle together. She wanted him to know that she needed him, without having to actually tell him.

When Ian spoke, the words came out softly. 'Mistakes are a natural part of life, Abbie. You have to shrug them off and just keep on moving.'

She closed her eyes, but the drops continued to fall. Her heart sank and the feeling of loneliness swarmed her once again.

I just have to shrug them off and keep moving. She repeated his words in her mind. *On my own. I just have to deal with things. Be strong. Be mature. Be resilient. Be everything.*

Abbie ducked down slightly to remove his pressure on her shoulder and slowly tiptoed away from him, her eyes still fixed firmly on the floor.

'I'm going to have a shower.'

CHAPTER 13
SARAH

'The problem with this village,' Sarah moaned, 'is that everybody knows everybody else!'

She revved the car into gear and the tyres screeched as she accelerated away from the traffic lights.

'Isn't that a nice thing?' Simon offered, feigning an interest in the conversation, while staring down at the phone in his lap.

Sarah glanced to her side, hoping to catch his eye, but his eyes did not rise from the screen.

She was becoming inpatient.

'It's fucking annoying, is what it is.'

She turned back to face the road, but caught sight of her hands that gripped the wheel instead. Her knuckles had begun to whiten as she clung tightly to the steering wheel. She relinquished her grip and watched her knuckles slowly begin to melt back to their regular pinkish hue. Her knuckles wore a crackled coat of wrinkles that criss crossed across the back of her hand. The smoothness that she had once known was no longer present, replaced instead by a series of fine and delicate markings. The taut flesh that once surrounded her fingers had relented its hold and her skin now hung loose, attempting to cling on to the muscles and bone below. Her hands were no longer the hands she remembered. These hands were not her own. These were the hands of her mother.

When had they changed?

She had distinct memories of sitting in the

backseat of her mother's Ford Cavalier (Abbie always got the front seat) and observing the hands that groped the steering wheel. Her nails were always immaculately painted - usually red - but the signs of ageing could not be hidden in the wrinkles on her knuckles and the thinning of the skin that stretched over her hands. While they glided gently over the wheel, Sarah would sit, transfixed by the way the skin confessed to the truth of age. Back then, she would look down at her own plump fingers and tell herself to always make the most of being young. *Had she been doing that?*

The honk of a horn jolted her from her daydream and she shot her eyes back on the road, just in time to swerve away from the oncoming truck. She straightened herself onto her side of the road and slowed the car down, a subconscious act that she assumed was customary after a near miss.

The truck driver did not slow down. Instead he continued to bully his way past her. As he shot by her window, one hand still firmly pressing the horn, she observed the plump skin that encompassed his knuckles as he gave her an aggressive middle finger. *No wrinkles in sight.*

'Jesus, Sarah!' Simon snapped. 'Watch the bloody road won't you?'

She considered slamming her foot on the brakes, before turning to him and announcing that he should *learn to drive his-fucking-self*, but she thought better of it.

'I'm distracted.' She half apologised as she shook her head and began to gain speed once more.

'I can see that. But I'd rather not arrive at your parents house in a body bag.'

It had never bothered her that Simon couldn't drive. She liked to drive, and it seemed to suit their dynamic quite well. Sarah enjoyed the control that came with driving. Plus, she barely drank, so she didn't resent being the designated driver on nights out.

She was a good driver too. When not distracted! But today, she had too much on her mind: the Abbie issue, the pregnancy dilemma, the Jenny conversation. She needed to enable her *issues* to float from her mind. *Focus on the road*, she thought to herself.

She calmed her breathing and pretended she was on her driving test, the way she sometimes liked to do, while impressing upon her riders that she passed her test with only one minor. She still remembered all the details of how to drive *properly*.

- Hands at ten and two.
- Thread the steering wheel through her hands.
- Check the rear and wing mirrors before indicating.
- Watch out for hazards everywhere.

Mid concentration, her focus was stolen by Simon reaching out to the stereo. He cranked up the volume to thirteen and began to sing along to the tune.

She leaned over and corrected the dial. *Twelve*. Even numbers only.

He didn't notice.

'When it all breaks down, I'll be there!' Simon bellowed, louder than was necessary and an octave away from correct.

Sarah rolled her eyes. *Say nothing.*

'When it all breaks down, I'll be there!' He continued mimicking the vocals, now adding an

Irish accent, while tapping his fingers on his thigh, mindlessly and simultaneously scrolling through his social media app.

Say nothing.

The singing continued, and she wondered why she'd never noticed the number of refrains in this song before.

'It's 'melts down',' she muttered quietly, continuing to stare straight ahead at the road.

'Hmmm?' he questioned.

He continued humming.

She reached for the volume knob and spun it down several notches.

'It's: 'melts down',' she snapped, glancing sideways at his blank face. 'The words are: When it all melts down, not 'breaks down'.'.

Simon shrugged his shoulders and spun the volume back up again. *Thirteen.*

'Tomato, Tomarto.'

Sarah kept her eyes fixed firmly on the road, forcing herself not to turn her head back to Simon - or the number on the stereo.

Leave it alone. Focus on the road.

The irritation inside her was growing. While she knew it was completely illogical - irrational even - she could not contain the feeling swelling within her.

She fixed her eyes on the peak of the horizon and breathed in deeply. She tried to block out any external noises: the roar of the engine, the rush of the wind, Simon's incessant humming. She focused instead on the singer's voice that danced out of the stereo, and just kept on driving.

♩ *Hard to tell the real from the dreams you imagine … Just know this too shall pass* ♩

As soon as she pulled onto the driveway, Sarah spotted her mother through the kitchen window, illuminated in artificial light. Despite the mid-afternoon hour, lights were necessary as, outside, the clouds had gathered, forming a darkening rage above them. Her mother rushed back and forth furiously; her face haggard and her white-blonde hair dishevelled around her shoulders. Sarah could not see what her mother was carrying, but every few seconds, her movements paused, she stood still, shook her head at what she was carrying, and moved on again.

Hoisting the bags from the car, Sarah spotted a shadow behind the front door. Juggling three bags, she fumbled into her pocket, reaching for the key that would close her boot. Simon was checking his reflection in the visor mirror and straightening out his hair. She wouldn't wait for him.

She readjusted the bags to even out the weight and turned to face the house. Strands of her hair whipped her cheek, thanks to the rising wind, and she flung her head to one side in an attempt to clear her view. Squinting through the mess of hair, she approached the door just as it flung open.

'Sarah!' her father called, arms outstretched, leaning in for a kiss on the cheek and releasing a bag from her grip.

'Hi Dad,' she replied, pecking him back. 'Sorry we're late.'

'That's not a problem, sweetheart,' Greg replied, 'Come on in quick. The storm's on its way.'

Sarah stepped through the threshold and onto the welcome mat.

'It's been all systems go over here.'

Greg gave a quick head nod and wide mouth towards the kitchen. The silent language was clear: mother was stressed!

'GREG, old chap!' Simon called, reaching forward and hugging him firmly.

Greg tapped Simon on the back and he released his grip.

'How are you sweetheart?' Greg asked, turning back to his daughter and attempting to relieve her of the remaining bags.

'Shame about the weather, hey?' Simon interjected, before pushing his way past them both and into the kitchen.

'I'm good thanks, Dad,' she smiled at him, releasing the bags onto the floor and standing up tall. She tossed her hair from side to side and glanced over her dad's shoulder to the hallway mirror.

'Gosh, what a state,' she exclaimed. 'The wind has shot me to pieces in seconds.'

'You're always beautiful,' Greg said confidently while clicking the front door shut. He held his arm outstretched, gesturing for Sarah to walk through to the kitchen.

'It's been a busy morning.' He sighed as he entered the kitchen behind his daughter. 'Mum is just trying to reassemble the cake, which unfortunately got a little messed up in delivery.'

'A little?' scoffed Judy without looking up from her work. 'That bloody bakery has ruined everything! How hard is it to deliver a three-tiered cake without destroying it in transit?'

As Judy glanced up, her eyes shifted from a scowl to a widened joy.

'Oh Simon,' she sighed, 'Thank goodness you're

here. I need your culinary expertise.'

Simon ushered his way immediately towards his future mother-in-law, ready to play *hero*. Sarah side-eyed her father, who was doing the same back at her, but her attention was immediately stolen by the sight of Lucy and George. Through the glass-fronted doors, her niece and nephew were just visible, both hunched in their seats, engrossed in their devices - Lucy on her phone and George on a tablet - their headphones firmly covering their ears.

Why were the kids here already?

'I didn't know the kids were here,' Sarah said with mock calmness. 'Where's Abbie?'

Sarah knew she was stoking a fire that did not need stoking. She knew that Abbie wasn't there; that she'd probably dropped the kids round this morning to give themselves more time to get ready in peace.

'Abbie dropped them round at about midday,' her father replied. 'She said she'd aim to be here at five.'

Five? Thought Sarah. *It was 2pm now. So they'd have to do all the leg work, while her sister had some time to get ready in peace? Standard Abbie behaviour.*

'Ha,' the noise escaped her, before she added, 'So you have to babysit her kids? While also getting your house ready? For your party? That you are hosting?'

No response.

She carried on.

'While she affords herself the time to get herself ready, in peace?'

No one looked up to answer her, but her mother brushed her off.

'She's a busy girl, Sarah. It's not a problem.'

Sarah would not relent.

'It just seems kind of selfish, that's all. They're

her children and you guys have to look after them all the time.' The rage was building again. 'The one time you guys actually ask for a bit of help and not only does she not come round, she makes *you* look after *her* children.'

Judy stopped fiddling with the cake and turned to face her daughter, one palm raised out in front of her. Her voice was not raised but it emanated a firmness, 'Stop it Sarah!'

Sarah was taken aback. 'I am trying to stick up for you, Mum,' she snapped back, filled with hurt and disappointment. 'It's not fair that you have to do so much for her!'

She turned in search of the support of her father, but she was unable to catch his eye as his attention had been snatched by his watch strap, which he was now fiddling with furiously. She turned back to her mother, who had spun herself back around and was frantically spreading icing along a narrow ridge of cake, staring with pinpoint precision, while Simon helped to steady her hand.

'Dad, do you understand what I'm saying?' she attempted, but before her father could answer, the door to the dining room swung open and George ran towards her.

'Aunty Sarah!' he called with the excitement and joy that only a young child can express.

She reached out and scooped him up in her arms, swinging him round in a bear hug and kissing his cheek and neck until he squealed with laughter.

'Hello young man,' Sarah said, taking his hand and leading him back to the room he had come from. 'Come and show me what you've been doing on that tablet of yours.'

Sarah followed George into the dining room, his hair flopping merrily as he skipped back to his seat. He plopped himself down and carried on with his game, turning the screen every few seconds to show his aunty, his face filling with glee as he did so, waiting for her response. Sarah nodded back with raised eyebrows, feigning interest in his artwork. She marvelled at how his eyes lit up above the screen, his rosy cheeks bulging as his smile broadened. She peered down at his chubby fingers gliding across the screen and wondered how these game designers managed to create games to hook children in, while simultaneously repelling adults. *Why would anyone want to play paint by numbers on a screen?*

Sarah spun her head to find Lucy, who was slumped over her phone on the snuggle chair that positioned itself in the corner of the room, her headphones lodged firmly over her ears. She tiptoed towards her and squidged herself into the remaining gap on the edge of the seat, pushing herself tightly against her niece's warmth and placing an arm around her. Lucy's body reacted immediately, snuggling her head down into Sarah's chest and embracing the contact.

Sarah loved the relationship she had with her niece. She had always dreamed of being 'Cool Aunt Sarah' and the dream had actually come true. Sarah knew that the next few years would be the time where she would really come into her own. Puberty had already started, but there was still so much to come: boys, exams, alcohol, drugs! All her areas of expertise.

Lucy nestled her head further into Sarah and she clicked the lock button on the side of her phone, so she was now staring down at blankness. Sarah read the cue and gently removed Lucy's headphones, placing them on the side table next to them.

'How are you doing, gorgeous?' Sarah asked.

Lucy didn't move, speaking down into Sarah's jumper.

'Fine,' she replied, unconvincingly.

'Everything okay at home?' probed Sarah, hoping that Lucy would take the bait.

Lucy cocked her head up to scan Sarah, who raised her eyebrows and pursed her lips in a fake smile, indicating awareness of the unspoken elephant in the room.

Lucy straightened up and shuffled her bum so that she was facing Sarah, square on.

'So you heard what Mum did, then?'

Despite seeing Lucy every week, Sarah was always shocked at how much more grown up she seemed on each occasion. Today, Sarah was stunned by Lucy's complexion: pale and smooth, with a layer of moisturising concealer, topped with a glowing cheek and a tinted lip gloss. Her thick blonde hair fell in effortless wavy locks. She was stunning.

'Yes boo, I've heard.'

'It's everywhere, Sarah.' Lucy continued. 'You know there's a video doing the rounds online. It's absolutely mortifying!'

Sarah considered her niece's words. She hadn't known there was video evidence. *Jesus.*

'I bet that is upsetting, but remember that your mum is upset too.'

'Ha' scoffed Lucy. 'Well she doesn't seem upset to me. Or embarrassed. Or ashamed. Or any other emotion that you might expect from a normal person.' Lucy's voice was rising.

Sarah needed to choose her words carefully. She needed to make sure that Lucy felt listened to and heard.

'Well how does she seem?'

Lucy paused. She bowed her head down to her lap, considering the question.

'Angry,' she murmured.

The word hung in the air for several seconds, before Lucy's eyes rolled back up to meet Sarah's.

Sarah recognised real sadness in Lucy's eyes. The poor child was about to embark on the hardest phase of life. Being a teenage girl was no mean feat, and she needed a mother who could support and guide her through that with care and love. And Lucy was right, Abbie did seem angry lately.

'I think she's got a lot on,' Sarah spoke calmly. 'But that must be hard for you, Luce.' She needed to show Lucy that she cared about her and her feelings. She reached out a hand and placed it gently on Lucy's knee that sat folded into her body.

'She just snaps at me constantly. It's like I can't do anything right. I really feel like she just doesn't even like me, Sarah.'

The child's eyes began to prick with tears and she quickly spun her head away, wiping furiously at her face with the sleeve of her jumper.

'Oh Lucy,' Sarah soothed. 'Your mum loves you immensely! I guess she's just got a lot on her plate right now. Maybe she's struggling to manage it all.'

Sarah tried her hardest to empathise, but deep down she was struggling. *How dare her sister fail to remember the most important people in her life? How dare she treat this perfect little person in any way that made her feel unloved. How dare she not spend every single moment in this child's presence telling her how wonderful she truly is.*

Lucy's big, brown, watery eyes peered up at Sarah's. Her eyes were normally tawny pools of confidence - the eyes of her dad - but now they appeared sullen and desperate. When her words came out, they were slow and sharp.

'I'm not sure that a child should be seen as *another thing to have to manage.*'

The pause hung in the air for a moment too long, before it was punctuated by Simon's booming voice.

'Hey there, soldier!'

Immediately, George dropped his tablet on the wooden table with a thump and jumped up to greet Simon with their well rehearsed handshake.

Sarah turned to Lucy and gave her an eye roll, suggesting Simon's silliness.

Lucy stood up from her chair and threw a waving hand in the air to acknowledge Simon's arrival. She picked up her phone and turned back to face Sarah.

'I guess I just need to learn to live with the fact that my mother is a bitch.'

Lucy slinked out of the room, leaving a dumbfounded Sarah glued to the chair. She'd never heard Lucy swear before - and certainly not at her own mother. *This really was bad.*

'GREGORY!' came a yell from the dining room.

Simon pivoted quickly to find the source of the commotion and Sarah leapt up from her chair.

'THE GAZEBO!' came a second yelp, as Judy ran to the french-glazed doors, pointing and shrieking in despair.

Greg was hot on her heels and as Sarah reached them, she followed her mother's guiding fingers to see the violent gusts of wind flapping the fabric of the white sheeted structure.

A series of groans followed, as the pressure on the poles grew too intense. The entire frame rose from the ground, before settling back down again, breathing its weight in and out like a parachute.

'DO SOMETHING!' Judy called to no one in particular, but her command was futile.

A sudden gust of wind met a series of cracks, as the poles began to snap like twigs under the strain of the storm. The stakes in the ground flew from their fixings and the frame twisted itself free of its moorings. The fabric flung itself into the air, twisting, tumbling and soaring unpredictably through the grey sunken sky. It swirled around the skies, bashing trees and fences on its way, passing above the gardens of their neighbours, leaving a trail of debris in its wake.

Sarah threw her hands to her mouth and let out an audible squeak as she watched the ivory gazebo fly past the remaining houses and continue on its journey towards the rolling hills, like a ghost gliding its way towards an evening of spooking.

Judy dropped to her knees, like a grieving widow, and Simon stood behind her, rubbing her back with empathetic strokes.

She placed her hands against the glass, as if she were reaching out for a long lost lover. 'What the hell are we going to do now?'

CHAPTER 14
ABBIE

Abbie's gym membership had been active for years, but she rarely made the most of its cost. Occasionally, she attended Pilates or - if feeling particularly brave - a body combat class, but the gym was normally off limits. For starters, she was about twenty years older than most of the clientele, but she also had no idea how to use most of the equipment.

When she'd first joined, a helpful man called 'Chuck' had offered to assist her. The free introduction came as part of the membership package, but his muscular physique and intimidating youth put her off. She'd figure it out herself, thank you.

As she climbed into her lyra leggings, she wondered where she would start today. By now, she'd mastered the rowing machine and the treadmill - mainly due to their automatic start and stop buttons - but anything else was far too daunting.

She slipped on her trainers and stood up with confidence. She glanced in the mirror - full length and unflattering - and imagined the Abbie she could be in three months time. Full glow up and toned to perfection. She shrugged the idea away. As she observed her wobbling tummy and saw the way the sagging skin at the top of her arms jiggled as she swayed, she was under no illusions. In reality she just needed something else to focus on, something to distract her and occupy her mind. Toning up and strength training would just be a bonus.

Abbie surveyed at the wooden door of the

changing room that lay between her and the gym and drummed up the courage to exit, but as she went to stand, a gaggle of women bundled through it from the other side, squawking and laughing in unison.

The surprise disturbed her confidence, so she turned back to her sports bag instead, rummaging through it in a feign attempt to retrieve an imaginary item.

'Nick's taking us out somewhere special tonight,' one of the ladies smirked, waiting for a reaction.

'Ohhh,' came the chorus of replies.

'Tonight could be the night,' spoke another.

'Oh, I don't know,' she continued, head held high and soaking in the attention. 'But I'll make sure my nails are painted, just in case.'

The ladies shrieked at the thought of her proposal and hurried around her in delight.

Abbie glanced up from her bag and allowed herself to observe the women. From where she was sitting, in the corner of the changing room, she wondered if anyone would even notice her. Later, if the receptionist asked the gaggle about the middle aged woman on the wooden bench, waiting to enter the gym, would they be able to recall her presence?

Abbie was turning invisible, while these women, all in their twenties she guessed, were in the prime of life. She observed how, despite having come through the door that held the gym on the other side, none of them looked like they had broken a sweat. In fact, all appeared to be wearing makeup and at least two of them had either fake boobs or fake bums. Their faces were etched to precision and they all seemed as though their last proper meal was consumed over a decade ago.

One of the women slid past another and whipped her top off, with complete disregard for onlookers. She grabbed a towel and some expensive looking shampoo, and headed for the showers. As she stepped forward, she caught Abbie's gaze. Abbie spun away quickly, turning her attention back to the imaginary item in her bag.

Shit. Caught staring at a half naked woman - that's just what I need.

'Excuse me?' came the call, but Abbie continued to ignore it, desperately searching inside her bag in an attempt to appear busy.

'Excuse me?' it came again and this time Abbie saw her shadow move across the room, etching its way towards her. She glanced up guiltily and locked eyes with the beautiful stranger who was still strutting nonchalantly with her breasts perky and loose.

'Is this yours, madam?'

Abbie squinted at the object being held out in the woman's hand. It took her eyes a few moments to adjust. She had been expecting the woman to hurl an abusive comment at her, not offer her a lost item.

'You look as though you've lost something and I found this on the floor over there.'

Abbie scowled again at the object being held between the outstretched fingers of this woman. It was a white bottle, with an obscured label which was beginning to peel away from the edges. The bottle was all white, other than the bold black letters across the label that read: *Anti-dandruff Shampoo.*

Abbie stared for a moment too long, before slowly turning her gaze back towards the woman, a blank expression on her face.

Anti dandruff shampoo? Unbranded. Label peeling. Is that the kind of woman she looked like?

The stranger, clearly recognising the blankness in her face, placed the bottle down next to Abbie's feet.

'I'll just leave this here for you, dear,' she said, slowly and slightly too loud, the way one might speak to an elderly relative who is hard of hearing. The woman turned back to the showers and met the rest of her gaggle. Abbie heard her mumbled words over the hiss of the showers as they exited her view.

'Poor old dear...Probably doesn't speak English.'

As soon as the women were out of view, Abbie threw her bag into the locker and rushed through the doorway into the gym.

Did she really look that old? That poor? The foreign?

She tried to shrug the thoughts away as she headed towards the safety of the treadmills, but, to her dismay, they were all in use.

She turned and began heading towards the rowing machines instead, but as she walked in their direction she began to see the issue present itself. Three machines, two of them occupied and only the middle one free. She continued to move forward with hesitant steps, sussing out her options, while quickly scanning the rest of the room for an alternative. She clutched her water bottle tightly as her eyes flickered left and right.

At the last minute, Abbie rerouted left, adjusting her oversized sweater as she turned, hoping that she could shrink into it and become more invisible. She reached the dumbbells and picked one up with ease, before second-guessing herself and realigning her form, glancing at the other woman across the mats to check that she was doing it properly.

She heard laughter behind her and was certain that some of her fellow gym-goers had spotted the novice in the room and were talking about how ridiculous she looked.

Now, she was sure that if the receptionist were to survey the rest of these people later, they would all be able to recall the *uncomfortable looking, old lady who didn't even know how to use a dumbbell.*

She shrugged off the thought and switched arms.

Despite the anxiety that gnawed at her, she was determined to keep going. Maybe even, one day, she could feel like she belonged there.

#

After a forty five minute workout, Abbie was beginning to feel better. It was true what people said about exercise, it really did fill her with endorphins. *Maybe she should have tried this sooner?*

The gym session had not been a total disaster. She'd even made it onto the treadmill eventually and began to enjoy a few sprinting sessions as she hummed along to Ed Sheeran singing methodically through her airpods. But a glance at her watch made her realise the time, and she headed off to shower - with her L'oreal shampoo!

Ten minutes later, freshly washed and dressed again, she exited the changing rooms and made her way down the corridor to the building's exit. The tiled floor was clinical and she found herself oddly comforted by its cleanliness. The air in her lungs breathed in deeper and she sucked in the oxygen with a new lease of life.

As she approached the doorway, her attention was stolen by the coffee shop that housed itself to her right, tucked away gently just inside the foyer of the building. Finding herself drawn towards it, she adjusted her direction and walked up to the counter. She ordered a black americano and a banana (*no use undoing all that hard work*) and sat herself down to observe the passers by. *It was her turn to watch.*

The front of the coffee shop was also the front of the building, a translucent wall of glass that left no space for hiding. However, nestled on the correct side of the glass, warm and cosy in her deep armchair, Abbie didn't feel exposed. Instead, she watched the strangers on the outside of her serenity and considered their stories.

The first to park up and head towards the building were a young couple. They were in their early twenties, still primed with the gift of youth and hope for the future. They held hands continually, even as he reached to open the door. Abbie wondered if the determination to stay physically connected was a front for something more sinister happening in their relationship. *Did they want to appear united in public to make up for the arguments at home?*

Abbie considered the concept of arguments. *Could she remember the last time she'd properly argued with Ian?* Nowadays they opted for judging glares or a passive aggressive silent treatment to announce their disapproval or upset. Arguing was too exhausting - too much effort. There was no satisfaction to be gained from it either. The last time she'd shouted at him was when he went AWOL on his golfing day with Tom. They were due home at 5pm, but by 8.15pm, she'd not heard a thing from him. Neither he, nor Tom, were answering their phones and she was convinced that they'd both been killed in a car crash.

When he sauntered in at 8.45pm, she'd read him the riot act: 'How could he be so selfish? She was worried sick. Did he have no respect for her or the kids?'

He stood in the hallway, staring at her like she was a mad woman.

'Ran out of battery,' he announced, holding up his phone as proof, before kissing her gently on the cheek and walking off into the kitchen to make some food.

She remembered when arguments used to be explosive, exciting affairs. Both parties would shout, sometimes things would be thrown, and eventually they'd fall into bed and have raucous, angry make-up sex. *Those days were certainly over.*

Next, Abbie watched a young girl exit the passenger seat of a silver Golf and strut towards the doors. The girl was no older than Lucy, which surprised Abbie. *Why were girls heading to the gym at such a young age? Was there too much media hype? Too much focus on healthy bodies and natural ways to enlarge certain areas while shrinking others?* Abbie had caught Lucy watching bum workout clips on TikTok recently and wondered when the trend for larger behinds had arrived on the scene. When she was a teenager, it was all about getting smaller, not bigger.

It wasn't just that which had changed, fashion was different too. While flares appeared to be back in, the dressing up culture had died. Young people no longer donned a dress and heels for a night out, it was jeans and trainers instead. That was one thing that

Abbie could not seem to get her head around.

She thought back to the conversation in the car that afternoon. As she drove the children to her parents, she attempted to initiate a conversation with Lucy.

'What are you wearing this evening, then, Luce?'

Abbie knew full well what Lucy was planning - she'd seen her grab the clothes from the pile of clean laundry in the utility room and take them upstairs - but she wanted to offer an olive branch. The question received no reply. At least, not from Lucy. George noticed the uncomfortable silence and filled it himself.

'I'm wearing my new shirt, Mummy, the one you bought me this summer.'

Bless her sweet boy.

She wondered how long it might take before Lucy would talk to her again. There had been no words shared since the pinching incident last night. She needed to apologise properly, she knew that, but she needed an in, a conversation starter. It was too difficult to blurt out: 'I'm so sorry Lucy, I'm a terrible mother and I should never have done that to you.'

Abbie observed another car pull into a space. She vaguely recognised the vehicle, but could not place it. When the man stepped out of the car, Abbie was still none the wiser. He was a giant, too large for the delicate gym machines, surely?

He opened his boot and pulled out an umbrella. The rain was pelting down now, but the wind was whipping too. Abbie laughed to herself as she observed the galoot wrestle with the umbrella which refused to open calmly. With every attempt, the wind took hold of the object, threatening to tear it away.

Abbie averted her eyes, suddenly feeling guilty at her voyeuristic pleasure. She had become the people from the gym that were ogling her - she should pity this man rather than laugh at him. *Maybe she should actually help?*

She downed the last mouthful of her coffee and gathered her things, heading towards the door. By now, the wind-beaten man was only a few feet from the door and Abbie could foresee the dilemma that was about to approach him: he would have to fight one handed with the handle as the other attempted to lower the umbrella.

She was only a few steps from the door, so she knew she could help him. She'd hold the door open which would allow him both hands free to unfurl the umbrella. She'd make him aware of the basket where other discarded umbrellas had been left, so that he could place it to one side until it was time to leave again. *Good deeds are important.*

As she grabbed the handle and pulled the door open, feeling pleased with herself, she waited for the man to peer up and thank her. He shook his head like a wet dog, rain soaked hair flinging around him and straightened up to meet her eye.

The recognition hit them both immediately and they froze in unison, unsure of how to react. While the door remained open, whipping cold air into the foyer, both parties remained still, Abbie on one side, Mr Winterton on the other.

CHAPTER 15
SARAH

Sarah had been put in charge of music. At first, she was relieved - she knew music - but one glance at her parents' record collection, and a survey at the stereo system she would have to deal with, suddenly instilled the fear of God into her. She knew, immediately, that she needed reinforcements.

Lucy had sprung into action instantly, eager to be of assistance in the area she excelled in.

'You need to get the mood right,' she'd said, like a well rehearsed DJ. 'The party needs to warm up slowly and be at peak *dance mode* around 9pm. By that time, people will have had a few drinks and will be ready to start dancing. By 10pm, you can bang out the classics - eighties always goes down well, but these lot might prefer seventies, so we'll include a mix - and then we'll finish with something fun around midnight, just for our entertainment. None of the oldies will have any idea what's going on by then, so we could play Slipknot for all they'll care.'

Lucy was busy on her phone, arranging playlists on Spotify to suit the evening. She had one headphone in, playing the intro to a song and nodding or shaking her head, before switching to the next. Occasionally, she'd make a comment, but Sarah wasn't sure if they were directed at her or not.

'*I Wanna Dance with Somebody*... will that mix well into *Walking on Sunshine*?'

Sarah went to respond, 'Yeah, sure...' but Lucy had already changed her mind, shaking her head and muttering.

'No, let's try *Don't Stop Til You Get Enough*.'

Lucy was clearly in her element, but as a result, Sarah now felt rather redundant. She side-stepped her way out of the living room and wandered into the kitchen.

'I thought you were doing music?' Judy snapped, catching sight of Sarah entering the room. Immediately, she turned back to the tray of sandwiches and continued huffing as she moved them around, struggling to get the right layout.

'I was,' Sarah replied defensively, 'But Lucy is helping. I'll head back in a few minutes to see how she's getting on.'

Sarah observed her mother's hair swish back and forth - *was she shaking her head?*

'Is everything okay, Mum?'

Judy exhaled a huffing sound and her arms dropped down by her sides. 'I just need everyone to pitch in and help, Sarah.'

'Yeees,' she replied, feeling confused as she ambled closer towards her mother and resting at her side. 'I am trying to help, Mum. Lucy's doing the music. So I've come to see what else I can help with.'

As Sarah reached her side, Judy shuffled across the room to the mini quiches, taking them from their containers and emptying them out onto the next available platter.

'Right,' her mother replied objectively, 'Well the food isn't going particularly well. Somehow, I need to get all of this on platters and displayed on the table in the next twenty minutes, but I've no idea how it's all even going to fit.'

Sarah glanced around the room. Her mother

was exaggerating and catastrophising. The food was almost finished and there was plenty of space. She was just stressed about hosting. She grabbed a stack of colourful bowls and began opening bags of sharing crisps, decanting them into their new homes and placing them strategically around the table.

'God knows what time Abbie will arrive today,' Sarah began, glancing at the clock which already showed 4.45pm.

Her mother did not respond, choosing instead to continue busying herself by arranging and then rearranging the board of cheese and crackers. The grapes were strategically placed on the left hand side, before being moved to the right. Judy huffed and shook her head, before switching them back to their original home. The crackers were fanned out in a circular fashion, before being moved to a straight line down the middle of the ensemble.

'That platter looks really good, Mum.' Sarah spoke encouragingly, attempting to calm her mother's nerves.

'Hmmm,' she replied unconvincingly, refusing to accept the compliment, before turning to observe her daughter's handiwork. 'No, no, no,' she yelped. 'You cannot open the crisps yet, Sarah, they will go stale!' Her mother gave her a side eye of disappointment, and began hurling the crisps back into their packets, searching for clips to seal them back up tight again.

Sarah stood speechless, watching her mother scramble around the kitchen like a woman possessed. *She was trying her best. Why could her mother not just be grateful? Why did she always see the worst?*

'Sorry, Mum, I wasn't thinking,' she offered,

trying her hardest to shrug off her mother's stress. *This was not about her. Her mother was just anxious about the party.*

She scanned the room, wondering what else she could help with. Preferably something she couldn't get wrong this time.

On the slate tiled window sill sat two piles of papers. Her parents had a habit of opening post and sorting them into groups. Group one: reference paperwork to be filed away. Group two: paperwork that needed actioning. The habit had been passed down to Sarah and Abbie, both of whom had always been grateful for her mother's organisational skills that meant they'd never missed an energy bill payment in their lives.

She walked towards the windowsill, aware of the storm brewing wilder beyond the glass. Her mother was still huffing and puffing behind her, trying to undo Sarah's interference with the food. This was something she could help to tidy away. Surely she would not be able to get this wrong.

She knew where the paperwork was eventually filed - she'd identify the correct pile and slide the papers into their plastic wallets in the folder housed in the cupboard in the bedroom. The other pile, she'd leave on her mother's bedside table. No wayward guests would find it there, so they would not need to worry about nosey neighbours finding the details of Greg's next prostate exam or Judy's latest eye check.

She lifted the first pile and immediately recognised it as the one to file. The top letter was from the gas company and her mother had written, *PAID* and yesterday's date across the top of it. *Another habit passed down to the girls.* She slid the pile into her hand

and tucked the second pile gently beneath it.

As Sarah turned to leave the room, she could hear Lucy's arrangement and smiled to herself. The playlist was on double speed and being skipped through quickly, slowing down only at the transitions to the next song so she could check that they blended seamlessly. *That child really has an ear for music!*

'What the hell are you doing?'

The scream came from nowhere. Sarah jumped at the sound, dropping the pile of papers across the floor in her startled terror. The music cut to silence. Lucy had heard the commotion too and was at the doorway in an instant.

Sarah spun around in shock, unaware what had happened to provoke the scream from her mother. Her first thought was the gazebo, but that was long gone. *Could something else have come loose in the garden?* She spun back to the window, searching out into the inky sky, trying to discover what had caused her mother to scream so fearfully, but the view remained as it had at her previous glance, just moments earlier.

Sarah was instantly filled with a hot fuzz of confusion and concern. *What was the problem?*

Judy was suddenly at her feet, scrabbling madly across the floor, scooping up the pieces of paper that were now scattered across the room. Sarah stood still momentarily, trying to understand why her mother was now collecting papers when there had clearly been another event that had shocked her greatly just seconds ago. She shrugged off the confusion and lent down to the icy floor, reaching out for the papers.

'Leave it!' her mother shouted, knocking a letter out of her grasp. 'You've done enough Sarah. Just leave me to sort this out!'

Slowly, she rose back to her feet, watching the oddness of the scene before her - the frail old lady on her hands and knees, refusing help. The scene should have made her feel empathetic. Concerned, perhaps. But instead, Sarah felt the anger rising in her again. *She was a fuck up. She'd always been a fuck up. Nothing had ever been good enough and her mother had never hidden the fact, but as they'd grown older it had become less obvious.*

Her mother rarely chastised her anymore, she didn't mock her for her intelligence or make quips about her weight. Her mother was more patient with her frivolous ideas nowadays and more tolerant of her dreams. *So what had sparked her today? What had Sarah done to warrant this shortness, this ridicule, this feeling of worthlessness? She'd been trying to help, for God's sake. At least she was here, which was more than could be said for that fucking Abbie.*

'What the fuck, Mum?' The words came out of her mouth before she could even consider that they were coming. They slipped from her tongue and hung like a stillness in the air, wafting slowly through the room like a bad smell.

Her mother froze. She was still on her hands and knees and her face was obscured by the table leg, meaning that Sarah could not see her expression, but she could imagine. Her mother hated swearing. And even more than swearing, she hated disrespect. Sarah's outburst would not be tolerated.

Sarah had sudden flashes of the scene that would play out next. She saw her mother smacking her legs, like she did when she was a child. She pictured her mother shouting words about being grounded. She imagined her mother yelling for her father to, 'get himself in here now and deal with his daughter!'.

But Judy did not move. She did not speak. Sarah wondered if she'd actually turned to ice on the spot.

'I think you'd better leave, Sarah.'

The voice was unexpected and Sarah was shocked when she realised the source of the sound.

'Maybe just take a few minutes upstairs and leave Nana alone for a while,' Lucy suggested from nowhere.

Sarah swivelled her view from her niece to her mother and back again, unsure of the hidden secret in the room that she appeared privy to.

Lucy was standing assertively, her hands on her hips, unthreatening but assuredly.

Her mother was moving again, slowly reaching for the last few papers, but keeping her eyes firmly fixed on the floor. *Was she deliberately refusing to look up at her daughter?*

Sarah was hit with a sinking feeling of loneliness. The crushing weight of her isolating secret throbbed deep inside her abdomen, while another unspoken truth placed her firmly on the outside of the family kitchen. She lacked the knowledge - the connection - to the people she loved most in the world, which meant she had to leave.

For a split second, she considered trying to show empathy, to ask a question: *Was everyone okay? Was there a problem?* She considered trying to offer support, but the shameful embarrassment washing over her stopped her. Instead, she hung her head and walked slowly out of the room, leaving relationships crumbling in her wake.

CHAPTER 16
ABBIE

Abbie pulled onto the driveway, shoved the car into park and leaned back into the seat. She exhaled the breath that she felt like she'd been holding since she opened the door to the gym. Seeing Joe's face staring straight at her, just two feet from her own, was the last thing she had expected. The shock hit her like a punch in the gut. So much so that she let go of the door immediately, which then flung back with force, smacking Joe hard on the nose.

In the commotion, she'd attempted to leave, thinking she could slink out before he noticed, but as she reached out again for the door handle, she fumbled over her feet and dropped her gym bag hard on the floor, the contents spilling out and sliding across the white sheen tiles.

She'd quickly scooped up what she could, happily resigned to losing whatever had slid too far from reach, but the reception staff had different ideas.

'Madam,' called the handsome teenager, 'Here you go.'

He was walking briskly towards her, with her sweaty gym shorts in his hand. She focused on the ground and wished that, perhaps just this once, the floor could actually open up and swallow her whole.

Joe was tending to his nose, dabbing his face with his hand and then holding it out in front of him, checking for signs of blood. A gaggle of staff were huddled around him, offering first aid, tissues, a glass of water. *Surely this was her chance to escape?*

A final scout around convinced her that she had retrieved as many of her things as she was able to. She rushed the door again, reaching her hand out this time in a desperate plea to successfully reach the grasp of the handle. She felt its cold, metal security in her grip and she tugged firmly. Then she heard him.

'Abbie, wait!'

She froze, wondering if she could continue her exit and feign that she hadn't heard his husky call. But her frozen stance had surely given her away. She looked up eagerly at the doorway, deciding to continue her escape, desperate to run from this interaction, but suddenly, the doorway was wedged with a herd of teenage boys, trying to enter. She tried to squeeze past one of them, but the space was too small. Instead, she was now a doorwoman, holding the entrance open for them as they sauntered in, unaware and ungrateful.

She paced on the spot, her feet dancing from side to side, willing the boys to move quicker. She refused to turn around and face him, choosing to stare straight ahead instead, but as she clocked eyes with one of the boys, she recognised him immediately - a sixth former at Longleaf Secondary. She squirmed. *Could this get any worse?*

She heard the call again.

'Abbie!'

This time, the sound was met by a hand placed firmly on her shoulder. The boys had passed and the doorway was free, but she'd dithered too long and now her escape plan was foiled.

She breathed in deeply and tried to fill her lungs with the adrenaline boosting confidence she had just been dealt, as she turned to face him.

'Abbie,' he repeated again, this time softer and

more delicate. 'How are you?'

She paused at the question. *How was she? Was he having a fucking laugh?*

'You look great!'

Her face flushed as she was caught off guard. She knew that she *did not* look great. Her mind whirred furiously at the reasons why he might have spoken such an obvious lie. Guilt? Embarrassment? Fear?

Her face must have displayed the mixture of anger and confusion that she felt, so he changed tack.

'I mean, have you been working out? You look glowing.'

He shuffled uncomfortably, shifting his weight from foot to foot as she continued to stare back blankly.

'Trying to take your mind off things, I suppose?'

She exhaled a quiff of laughter at his comment. *How fucking dare he?*

'Do you want to grab a quick coffee?' he continued, nodding towards the coffee shop from which she had just left. 'We could talk. It was all a little rushed yesterday and I hope you understand, I had to follow the governors' orders and adhere to protocol.'

Abbie wondered how long he would talk for if she continued in silence. Would he fill the silence with chit chat until someone intervened? The thought amused her. His desperate need for communication was intriguing and while he continued to speak, digging himself into a deeper pit, she continued to feel more powerful.

A glance at the clock behind his head shook the thought away.

'I need to leave,' she said dismissively.

He seemed hurt, as his eyes dropped and his cheeks sunk into their hollows. She continued to observe his face; his sad, pathetic face that refused to give her clarity on anything. *What did he want from her?*

She turned to leave, but as she stepped away, she felt his hand on her wrist. It held her firmly but the touch was gentle, pulling her back around to face him.

'Abbie,' he begged in a hushed whisper.

She paused, then slowly turned to face him once more. His eyes were soft and desperate. There was a longing in his face that she could not understand. *What did he want from her?*

He didn't speak immediately, as if he were choosing his words carefully. He didn't release her wrist. Instead, he continued to hold it firmly in his grasp, as if refusing to relinquish control. When he finally spoke, his voice held a tremor.

'I'm really sorry. You know how I feel about you.'

A flash of light from the side of the room disturbed them, bringing them back into reality. Without a second thought, she shook herself free, turning to the door and pushing it open with force, desperate for the fresh air that hung on the other side, air would free her to breathe once more.

#

His words had rattled around her mind all the way home and she couldn't release the fury she felt. The audacity of the man who had promised her so much but had produced so little. *How could he continue to offer her moments of tenderness, of emotion, of connection, yet abandon her and leave her isolated and lonely in her moments of need?*

She finally switched off the engine and made

her way to the house. She was dreading the next three hours alone with Ian, but her mother had insisted she drop the kids round early and take a few hours to herself.

As she opened the front door, she heard the clanging of tools from the floor above her. She had no idea how the land lay between her and her husband. She'd not said goodbye when she left this morning and he hadn't messaged to see where she had got to. *Were they even talking right now?* She knew she needed to find out, so she headed for the stairs and made her assent. Before she had landed her foot on the top step, she heard him call.

'Abbie, is that you? Can you pass me the wrench?'

Abbie walked into their bedroom and saw the tool box splayed out in front of her, its contents spilling out like a body opened for surgery. She scanned the box, hoping the wrench would make itself known. She shoved a few objects out of her way. Hammer, screwdriver, a set of allen keys. She lifted an object in ignorant hope and held it in the air.

'This one?' She guessed, holding it out into the open doorway of their en suite, where Ian was laid sprawled out on the floor.

Ian craned his neck. 'That'll do,' he groaned as he threw an outstretched arm behind him.

The shower had been leaking for months. At first, they ignored it. A few specks of mould on the wall wouldn't hurt. But this morning, as Abbie flung the bathroom door open, Ian was waiting for her with his hands on his hips, announcing that the leak had now penetrated the kitchen ceiling below. Avoidance was no longer possible.

'How hard can it be?' he'd quipped after a call to the local plumber had been unsuccessful.

Ian had removed the baseboard in an attempt to find the crack in the pipe below. The exposed space below the shower was not large enough for a complete view, so he crouched down, bum high in the air and shoulders sliding along the linoleum. His head was turned sideways with his cheek resting against the cool floor, and his phone lay precariously as the torch lit his view.

'I'm tightening the waste pipe,' Ian mumbled, more to himself than to Abbie, 'but I'm not sure if that's where it's coming from.'

Abbie backed away into the bedroom and sighed. She removed the red dress from the wardrobe and held it up against herself, eyeing her reflection. She frowned as she shifted her weight from leg to leg, hoping that a different angle might make it look more appealing against her frame. Abbie never wore red, but in a moment of madness, she'd succumbed to her mother's suggestion.

'You look gorgeous,' Judy had ushered, while she stood in the changing room, twisting and judging herself in the mirror. 'Just get it!'

'I'm just not sure it's very *me*,' Abbie had replied, but her mother brushed her comment away swiftly.

'Nonsense, Abbie. You look lovely. Have some confidence and just go for it!'

So she had.

Looking at the dress now, observing the way the sequins sparkled garishly in the light, she felt a sense of dread at being overdressed. The last thing she wanted was to be the centre of attention tonight.

'Did you drop the kids off alright?' Ian asked,

suddenly next to her and staring at her reflection in the mirrored wardrobes.

Abbie was jolted back into the room.

'Yes, they're fine.' she replied, not yet sure whether she was ready for small talk.

'Is your mum all ready for this evening?'

Abbie considered the question. 'She seemed a little stressed actually.' she admitted. *More guilt.*

'Well she was insistent that we drop them round early. They'll be a help, if anything. They're not babies anymore, they don't need looking after. Your mum is probably looking forward to putting them to work like little minions. In fact, I bet she's got Lucy decorating the table and George icing the cake as we speak.'

Abbie knew he was right. Her babies were no longer babies and they didn't need much looking after. The thought panged at a heartstring. In fact, they were both a great help to her parents. This summer, when their guttering needed clearing out, Lucy had actually volunteered to climb the ladder and do it. Abbie was speechless. And George relished any opportunity to earn himself a chocolate coin from his grandpops, even if it meant weeding the front lawn - a job he would never have done at home!

Abbie envied the relationship her parents had with her children and wondered if she might get that one day too, should her children have little ones of their own. But Abbie's mind didn't allow the fantasy to evolve, instead jumping back to the car journey and the silent treatment she'd received from her daughter. Maybe their relationship was broken forever.

'I've had to leave it there,' Ian pointed back towards the shower as he entered the room. 'We'll test it again tomorrow, but if it's still leaking, we will need to get a plumber round on Monday.'

'Okay,' Abbie replied, still eyeing her reflection with a scowl.

Ian noticed her distraction. 'That's new!'

Abbie flung the dress onto the bed, discarding it along with his comment. She headed towards the dressing table, plonking herself down on the stool. She glanced back at it, checking that the price tag was not on display, but luckily it had slipped below the garment. *Please don't pick it up.* The last thing she needed was more guilt. It was more than she would normally spend on herself - much more. In fact, she couldn't remember the last time she'd shopped anywhere but the discount stores, but in a moment of weakness, she'd succumbed to her mother's egging.

Now she felt foolish. Who knew how much longer she'd even have a job. She really shouldn't have been so frivolous, so stupid.

'You don't often wear red.' Ian continued.

What was that supposed to mean? Red was a mistake. What had she been thinking? As if she could pull off red.

'What should I wear?' he questioned, laying down on the bed and folding his hands behind his head.

She breathed in deep and rolled her eyes, refusing to meet his gaze. She didn't have time to parent him, too. He could make his own decisions.

She shrugged her shoulders, 'I don't know.'

Lifting the lid on her makeup box, she began surveying the contents. She had no idea where to start.

She pulled out the eyeshadow set she'd received

last Christmas and gawped at it. *Which colours compliment a red dress?*

She pulled her phone from her tracksuit pocket and began typing.

What colour eyeshadow should I wear with a red dress?

The results came streaming in:
Nude colours. Pink, brown or mauve tones.
Plum, burgundy and black.
Pink eyeshadow, paired with a purple mascara.

Fucking hell. Abbie didn't own purple mascara. She scrambled through the drawer and found brown mascara. *Would that do?*

'I think I'll wear my green shirt,' Ian continued.

The wind outside was growling and she could hear the sides of the trampoline flapping vigorously back and forth. A shudder ran down Abbie's back.

She turned her head and was able to make out a partial view of next door's garden through the bedroom window, the branches of their tree bashing against the shed door. The leaves that had begun to fall were whipping up and spinning through the air in furious circles.

Abbie rubbed her hands against her thighs, drying off the moist sweat that was building on them. She had never been able to explain why the wind impacted her so much. The power it held to destroy life felt immeasurable. She spun her head back to the safety of the dressing table.

In the reflection of the mirror she could see Ian arching his back with a stretch. His grey jogging bottoms, contrasted the navy suit trousers of his weekday attire and his polo top welcomed a scruffiness about him. She scanned his six foot frame

- normally intimidating - and noticed how fragile he looked as he lay back against the headboard.

He caught her eye and she immediately spun her face away, embarrassed to be seen watching him. She continued ruffling through the bag, before glancing up again. He was still watching her and a soft, earnestness had arrived in his eye.

'Come sit with me,' he suggested. His tone was calm but not convincing. She paused for a moment, considering her options. She knew she had to make an effort.

She stood up tentatively and made her way over to her side of the bed. As she perched herself on the edge, she offered an olive branch.

'A green shirt will be nice.'

They locked eyes and an unspoken awareness was shared between them. The moment hung in the air as they both considered what was needed.

Ian lifted his arm and held it out wide, a welcoming invitation for her to fall into him.

Despite an awkwardness, urging her to stay put, she pushed through the fear and gently obliged, accepting the invitation as she rested against his side.

His arm below her wrapped around her back and, although she lay rigid with arms down by her sides, she allowed her head to rest snuggly into his chest. A moment of vulnerability.

They both lay still.

As his chest rose up and down, Abbie concentrated on her own breathing until it matched his. His body was warm and she could feel his breath grazing the tip of her forehead. She felt the muscles in his arm twitch under her and his hand began to stroke her back.

She tried to cast her mind back to the last time they lay together, but the attempt was futile. His touch felt alien to her, but she tried to embrace the connection.

A bang from the garden made her flinch and he pulled her in closer, his hand still rubbing back and forth. She mustered the courage to graze her foot along the side of his leg. The submission to intimacy was small, but she was pleased with her progress. She watched as her toes caressed the fabric of his joggers, repaying the touch.

Abbie was startled at how comforting it felt to be touched. She tried to consider why she often found it so hard to melt into her husband, why she resisted his hugs and offered up a cheek when he lent in for kisses. The protective shield she held up prevented her from being able to succumb to vulnerability. *Perhaps she needed to change. Perhaps if she let her walls down slightly, Ian could peek over the top and begin to see her worries, her concerns, her problems. Maybe then she could get some help and some support.*

She lent in further and lifted an arm slightly to lay it across his belly, her hand resting only centimeters from his.

He moved his hand slightly and began to rub his thumb slowly against her own.

Baby steps.

Abbie was relieved at how easy this felt. She hoped that a little physical contact could be the segway into them talking.

She considered all the things that she might be able to vocalise, if only she felt sure enough to let the truth escape:

'*I feel so overworked.*'

'I feel so overwhelmed.'

'I feel like I'm at breaking point.'

Those were big feelings. Maybe she should start smaller:

'I am not enjoying my job.'

'I would like us to do more as a family.'

That was better. Those were manageable things to say. Admitting those small thoughts would show progress. They'd allow Ian to come in and understand a little of what she was feeling. She wasn't ready to break the walls down completely, but she could show him a glimpse. Maybe he would have some suggestions. Maybe she didn't need to do life all on her own. Maybe they were a team.

Abbie considered what Ian was thinking about, lying there in the silence. *Surely he was attempting to build trust so that she would talk. Maybe he'd heard what she had said this morning and he was trying to show her that he was there for her when she needed him.*

The thought of him putting her first and understanding her needs filled her with a confidence that she had not previously held. She stayed close to him, considering where to start. *Work was the obvious place.*

She kept her arm around him, but slowly tilted her head upwards to meet his eye. They locked eyes again and Abbie saw a glint of recognition, connection, and understanding. He was ready to listen.

Here we go.

She took a deep breath, but before she could utter her first word, Ian thrust himself towards her. He shifted his weight to lean over her, wriggling his arm free in the process. His lips pressed themselves against hers and he shoved his hot tongue into her mouth. His hands were suddenly all over her, caressing her hips, her breasts, snaking themselves over her body as he continued to press his face against hers.

Abbie was caught off guard. She raised her hands to create a barrier between them and, in an instinctive motion, her knee shot up between his legs.

Ian cried out and flung himself back in shock, before doubling over and cupping his balls in his hands.

The release allowed Abbie to spin herself to the side and leap up from the bed. Her heart was pounding hard as she beheld her husband, writhing in pain.

'What the fuck, Abbie?' cried Ian, flashing daggers up at her in bewilderment.

She stood still, her feet frozen to the spot. She tried to speak, but the words wouldn't come out. The heat of guilt flooded her chest as she considered what she had just done.

Ian pushed his back against the headboard, cradling his balls in his grasp, and rocking back and forth, groaning and muttering swear words that Abbie couldn't quite make out.

'I didn't mean to...' Abbie offered.

'What the actual fuck Abbie. Why the hell would you do that?' Ian spewed the words out, glancing up at Abbie before focusing back on his painful crotch.

Abbie felt stiff with fear. *Why had she reacted like that?*

'I just wasn't expecting...'

'Wasn't expecting what?' Ian interjected.

Abbie flinched at the volume of his words. There was a nausea in her stomach that was rising as she remained fixed to the floor.

'For me to kiss you?' Ian hissed, rubbing furiously at his balls. 'Jesus, Abbie. We're a married couple. I was initiating some intimacy with my wife. Why the fuck would you react like that?'

Abbie could feel the tears begin to prick in the corners of her eyes as she shook her head. 'I don't...' She attempted to suck in some air. 'I don't know. I thought you wanted to talk, so I ... I was preparing to talk ... I just ... I didn't know you were going to do that.'

'So you attacked me?'

That word again.

'I didn't mean ... I'm sorry,' sobbed Abbie.

Her whole body was frozen as she continued to stare down at her husband writhing in pain. She tried to make sense of her reaction. She had been so shocked at his forceful initiation of sex, at a time when she was trying to show emotional intimacy, it instantly filled her with a mixture of surprise and anger.

Ian slid off the bed and hobbled his way towards the bathroom, hunched over and limping, while staring sullenly at the floor.

Abbie could see his blurred silhouette through the tears, as her eyes followed his movements. When he reached the door, he paused next to the tool box that still lay with its contents spilling out. With his eyes firmly fixed on the linoleum floor, he took a breath, considering what to say.

Abbie watched him closely as he seemed to loosen slightly, the pain clearly beginning to ease off. From his side profile, she thought she saw his expression soften. He was considering his next words carefully.

As Abbie tried to control her breathing and suppress the tears, she wondered what Ian was about to say. She hoped that he would reflect and try to understand why she had reacted the way she had. Perhaps he would see it from her point of view - she'd been preparing to talk, to let her walls down, to be honest with him; she wasn't expecting sex!

'You know what, Abbie,' he began. 'I have no fucking clue what is wrong with you lately.'

Without even looking up, Ian slammed the door behind him, ending the conversation with force.

CHAPTER 17
SARAH

Sarah stepped into her heels and observed the ways her legs extended, showing off her hourglass frame in the mirror. The sheer black dress brushed the tops of her shoes, allowing only the tips to peak out. The rest of the fabric clung sensitively to the curves of her body, creating a sensual, yet sophisticated elegance.

She clipped the bangle to her wrist and pinned the matching golden hoops into her ears.

Her makeup was contoured perfectly - her eyes shone and her cheeks glowed - but despite looking confident and impressive, she was still filled with an unsettled anxiety.

The front door clicked open downstairs. *Her sister's grand entrance - finally.*

A shot at the clock displayed the time - 5.45pm. Sarah rolled her eyes impulsively, before sitting down on the bed. She wasn't yet ready to face the evening. She'd need to put on her brave face, shake off the worries she felt and focus on her dad's big night. This was all about him, after all. She was desperate for him to enjoy himself - he deserved it.

The bedroom door clicked open and Simon's face peeked around the white gloss, grinning like a cheshire cat.

'Bella!' he announced, raising his hands in the air and ogling her up and down. 'You look absolutely gorgeous!'

Simon bent double and shuffled towards her,

feigning a drool as he continued to gawp over her. He leaned into her neck and began caressing it gently with his lips, his hands becoming loose and suggestive across her waist.

She shrugged him off and slid to the side, escaping his hold and sliding to freedom. She stood up straight beside the bed.

'Is everyone here?' she asked calmly as she grabbed her lip gloss and added a finishing touch.

'Indeed,' he replied. 'Queen Abigail and King Ian have finally arrived, so the party can begin.'

Sarah chuckled at his bitchy edge. He knew when she was cross with her sister and he always took her side. She did appreciate that about him.

'How does she look?' Sarah questioned, attempting to sound nonchalant as she stuffed the lipgloss into her handbag.

'Yeah, nice,' he replied. 'But she has nothing on you!' He rose from the bed and snaked over to her once more, grabbing her and pulling her tightly towards him.

'Simon!' she snapped, smacking his hand away and stepping back away from him.

'Woah!' he cried, rubbing his hand gently. He glared up at her, the hurt of a young child in his eyes. 'What was that for?'

Sarah was embarrassed, but didn't quite know the words to say. She hadn't meant to slap him so hard, but she was not in the mood for intimacy right now. He always picked the wrong time, the most inopportune time. *What did he expect? A hand job from her while her parents waited downstairs?*

Neither of them spoke.

Simon continued to stare at Sarah, waiting for

an explanation, an apology, some kind of admission of guilt, but it didn't come.

'Sarah?' came the call, reverberating up the stairs.

Thank God.

'Sarah, darling?' The voice was getting louder and was quickly replaced by a knock at the door.

'Come in.'

Judy flung the door wide and stood, blocking the light from the doorway.

'Oh my!' she gasped, catching sight of her daughter. 'Sarah, you look absolutely stunning!'

Judy's smart pantsuit hung stylishly over her frame, her hair was parted to the side and donned a gentle curl. Her face, usually plain and simply moisturised, held a bronzed glow and slightly more makeup than suited her face, but the look was not garish. She looked pretty, and Sarah was impressed with her trying something new.

Judy's face was lit brightly at the sight of her daughter, which made Sarah instinctively curious. The compliment was out of place (even despite being juxtaposed so fiercely to the last words she'd screamed in her direction). The words seemed unfamiliar and abstract. *Her mother never paid her compliments.*

'Don't pay her compliments, Judy, she's in attack mode,' Simon threw his mock humour towards his future mother-in-law, who seemed to ignore his remark.

'Absolutely radiating!' Her mother continued.

Sarah scanned for signs of alcohol - perhaps her mother was already drunk - but there was no sway in her step and her eyes were clear and alert.

'Now, sweetheart, it's time to come down. Your

father is ready.'

All eyes were now on Sarah, who felt suddenly unprepared. She opened her bag again, checking its contents, before nodding at her mother. Simon took hold of Judy's arm and led her out of the room, with Sarah following closely behind, tentative with every step

'You've got a wonderful woman there,' she heard her mother whisper into Simon's ear as they walked in tandem. 'Don't you ever forget it.'

Sarah frowned skeptically and pulled the guest bedroom door shut behind her. She could feel the beginnings of a headache brewing and she scrunched her eyebrows together. *What the hell was going on in this house today?*

CHAPTER 18
ABBIE

The car journey passed in silence. Abbie had driven quickly, attempting small talk over the weather on two occasions, but Ian's silence was deafening. *It was going to be a long evening.*

As she pulled onto the driveway, she put the car into *Park* and sat with her hands in her lap. Neither she nor her husband moved. The radio clicked off, leaving only the noise of their stifled breaths and the wind that whipped around them.

Abbie felt for her hair. She'd attempted a curl this evening (something she would never normally try) but she wanted to look different - needed to look different. Now she felt foolish, recognising how quickly the curls would drop, leaving a frizzy mess in its wake. The walk to the house alone would blow the ringlets into oblivion and by the time she entered the house she'd look tired and dishevelled once more.

From inside the house, life was visible. Behind the curtains, a dull light glowed and shadows swayed back and forth. The final arrangements would be being made - last minute food arranged on the table, the playlist teed up, the balloons hung tightly to the door frames.

Abbie could see her husband from the corner of her eye, his stance unchanged, his body still. She wondered what he was thinking about. Was he dreading spending an evening making small talk with her family and friends? Was he looking forward to the opportunity of having a few beers and trying to take his mind off of the mess that was their current situation? She felt a pang of guilt. She was supposed to make his life better - in sickness and in health, for better and for worse, till death do them part. The last part had always scared her. It felt too serious, too extreme, too finite.

She made the first move, angling her hips slightly to face her husband and regarding him square on. He was handsome. From side on, his profile was chiseled and firm. His square jaw, speckled with brown and grey, had begun to soften slightly at the edges - the overindulgence of summer. His cheekbones added to his well-defined structure and his slightly crooked nose added character - thank you teenage rugby days. His short, neatly styled hair framed his face and his eyes were deep and gentle. He wasn't a striking man - not someone to take your breath away in the street - but his face was kind and gentle. The more she observed him, the more attractive he became.

She spoke first.

'I'm sorry again. About earlier.'

He turned to face her immediately, as if waiting patiently for her to say more. His expression was calm and gentle, not judging or cruel. She knew already that she was forgiven, but he had not yet managed to forget. Ian didn't hold grudges; he wasn't that sort of a man. But forgetting her string of recent misgivings would surely take some time. Maybe forever.

He continued gazing straight at her, unspeaking but expectant.

She breathed deeply. 'I hope we can try to enjoy this evening. Tomorrow, we can sit down and talk things through. Let's just get through tonight, shall we?'

Ian continued to behold her, his eyes burning into her own, before turning away and facing the front windscreen again. His eyes were sad, hurt, dejected.

He nodded slowly and uttered a barely audible grunt of acceptance, before casting his eyes down to his lap.

When he spoke, his words were soft and bruised.

'If you want to leave me Abbie, I'd rather you did so now.'

She was shocked. *Leave him? Why would she leave him?*

He continued. 'I mean, if it's over and the love has gone, please just be honest. The cruelest thing would be to string this along, trying to pretend and thinking you're covering it up, when actually, the truth is out there for the whole world to see.'

He continued staring straight ahead.

She was confused. *Where had this come from? Why these words? Why now?*

Suddenly, she noticed his phone placed upon his lap. It appeared to be a symbol. Perhaps it was the missing piece of the puzzle, something to explain his words.

'Ian,' she tried to say more, but the words would not come. *What was she to say?*

'It's okay,' he offered kindly. 'Please Abbie, just tell me the truth.'

She could feel herself getting cross, like she was being forced into an admission that wasn't true. *How could she say she wanted to leave him, when in fact nothing could be further from the truth? It was him who she believed would be the one to stray - never her.*

'Ian,' she blurted out, 'I am not planning on leaving you. Why would you think such a thing?'

Ian turned back to face his wife. His eyes had begun to water; a clear sheen filmed over their surface. He stared at her, deep in the eye, almost begging for some truth, some admission, but she was unable to give any. She had no truth to admit.

When no more words followed, Ian took hold of his phone and swiped at its code, opening the lock screen and illuminating a photo. From where she sat, she could not make out the features, and wondered if she should be looking at his phone at all - she knew it was an invasion of privacy, something she would never want him to catch her doing. Not again!

He turned the screen to face his wife and her eyes slowly adjusted to the picture. The image was instantly familiar, yet it took a few moments to fade into clear focus. The white glass tiles across the floor, the clinical walls and the reception desk. Two figures standing in the foreground, caught in an act of troubled wrongdoing. The embrace was feigned to the truth - the picture angled to make them appear closer than they truly were - his hand reaching out and holding hers. It seemed like a moment of tenderness, their faces glued to each other's, their expressions seemingly saying: 'I know this is wrong.'

She glanced from the screen back up to her husband, confused by the photo, unsure where it had come from and why it had ended up on his own phone. The incident, only hours earlier, had been caught in a flash. It should have displayed raw truth, yet somehow it spun the truth and weaved a web of deceit in its place.

'That isn't what it looks like!'

The words came out too forcefully and immediately, she heard the way they sounded: guilt at protesting too much.

'Ian, really,' she begged, leaning into him slightly. 'We bumped into each other at the gym and he wanted to apologise.'

She had no more words and was aware of not wanting to say too much. Suddenly, she imagined how it might feel to be wrongly accused of a crime. If the defendant spoke too much, they looked guilty, but offering 'no comment' also suggested criminality.

'It isn't just this.' Ian's words swilled around the car as she tried to make sense of them.

What did he mean?

'There are comments online too. About favouritism at work, embracing at work parties, loose hands making inappropriate touches.'

Abbie couldn't believe her ears. *Where had this come from? For how long had people been talking about her in this way?*

'Ian, honestly,' she began, but he stopped her, placing his hand out, as if pausing her voice from travelling across the car and over to him.

'I can't do this now, Abbie. I just needed to make you aware...' He paused. 'Aware of what people are saying.'

People? She thought. *Who were these people?*

'Lucy sent this to me about thirty minutes ago.' He spoke coldly, clinically. 'Apparently it's on a few online forums and it's gaining traction fast. Some of Lucy's friends will be here this evening and they will all be aware. Perhaps some of the adults too.'

Abbie couldn't think straight. She glanced at her husband and then back at the house, where her loved ones stood waiting. *Had they all seen it too?*

'You just need to protect yourself tonight and we can deal with what's next tomorrow.'

He began shuffling around the seat, clutching at the bag that sat down in the footwell and collecting his wallet from the car door.

Protect myself? Deal with what's next? What did that mean? How was she in this position? She'd done nothing wrong.

'We need to go inside now,' Ian said pragmatically. 'The others will have seen us park up and they'll be waiting.'

He got out of the car quickly and shut the door purposefully. He stood on the other side of the tin box, getting blown apart by the storm, while he waited for her. She tried to regain her thoughts. *How had it come to this?* She turned to observe her husband and felt a pressure to get out of the car, despite it going against all of her natural instincts. She couldn't keep him waiting. The air was too cold, the gale was too strong.

She wasn't in control of her body as her hand reached for the door handle and she stepped out of the car. She did not notice how the wind whipped her hair or threw her dress around in a frenzied panic. She did not feel her feet as they stepped across the driveway and landed on the front doormat. She was numb from head to toe as she followed her husband over the threshold and into the lion's den.

CHAPTER 19
SARAH

The grandfather clock chimed six times, the sound reverberating down the hallway and through into the lounge. Everyone was positioned in their assigned seats. Sarah and Simon sat rigid on the kitchen chairs that had been brought through to create extra seating. The three seater was assigned to Abbie, Ian and the kids, while Greg and Judy stood in front of the fireplace, champagne flutes in hand.

There was an uncomfortable tension in the air, as they waited for either Judy or Greg to speak. The formality of the gathering seemed odd, but her parents had been adamant that a 6pm meeting was required before the rest of the guests began arriving. They needed a chance to be together - as a family.

Sarah glanced across at Lucy, catching her eye and giving her a comforting smile. Lucy faked a smile back and looked back at her grandparents, who nodded in unison at one another and turned to face their audience.

'Seventy years,' Judy began. 'It's more than some people get in a lifetime.'

Sarah instantly sat to attention. Her mother held an air of authority in her voice.

'Tonight is going to be a celebration - all in honour of this man right here. Now, I hope you don't mind getting up close and personal,' Judy turned to scowl out of the window. 'The weather has dampened our plans to spill out into the garden, so it's going to get cosy in here.'

Judy smiled to her audience, but Sarah could see the concern in her eyes.

'But, as I was saying, you don't get to this age without learning a thing or two,' she continued, 'And your father - grandfather,' she nodded at Lucy and George, 'has learned a few important lessons along his journey so far.'

She turned to Greg and smiled reassuringly.

'It's inevitable that at seventy years old, one will begin to reflect on the life they've lived. One may even start questioning the decisions that were made or the paths once followed. But none of those things really matter.'

Sarah was acutely aware of the vulnerability in her mother's voice. Judy was a confident woman, a commander of people, a voice of authority. She was not one to show emotion.

Judy took a breath and, immediately, the squeak in her voice was dispersed.

'You start to realise that it doesn't really matter what house you lived in, how much money you earned or how many holidays you went on. Your father - grandfather - and I have been talking recently about what we would like people to say about us in our eulogies.'

There was a visible movement in the room as people shuffled uncomfortably in their seats.

'Jeez, Mum!' Abbie called out, but Judy held out a finger to shush her, before continuing on.

'We want people to talk about us: our qualities, our personalities, the things we did for others and the good we have spread along the way. That's really all that matters, isn't it? The effect we have had on others. The imprint we leave on the hearts of the people we leave behind us.'

Judy peered out at her family. Sarah could see her glare sweep across the room, eyeing each member individually - Lucy squidged into the side of the sofa, her arm placed on the rest; Ian lounged back, his arm laid on the cushion behind his daughter's head; George perched on the front of the sofa, his legs swigging free, eager to hear more; Abbie sat bolt upright, uncomfortable and tense.

The gaze passed over Simon, before landing on Sarah. Her mother's eyes showed a softness and a kindness. For a moment, Sarah felt a connection to her mother, as if she were trying, telepathically, to share a feeling or a thought between them both. But the look fled and the sound in the room was replaced by her father's voice.

'Thank you,' he smiled at his wife and then continued. 'The day I met your mother - grandmother - was the day my life began.'

Sarah grinned. Her father was an old romantic, a wonderful man who adored his wife. He was everything she had ever looked for in a man, but had never found.

'And, of course, today doesn't just mark my seventy years on this earth; it also marks fifty years since that joyous day. Although, we can't class it as an official anniversary as she refused to date me until two weeks later.'

A murmur of amusement came from Simon and George. Everyone else had heard the story many times before.

'Since that day, I have lived a full life. I've made the most of each day and I have embraced everything that has come my way. I've grown a career and I've grown friendships. I've helped to raise two independent young women, and now I get to help raise two wonderful grandchildren as well.' Greg shot smiles at Lucy and George. Both were returned.

'My life has been wonderful and, when I look back on it, I know the reason why. There have been challenges. I've lost jobs. I've lost money. We even lost a child.' He held his hand out to take that of his wife's.

Judy and Greg never spoke much about their miscarriage before Sarah was born. She knew it was late - twenty weeks - and they had never hidden the loss, but they didn't discuss it either.

'The reason we wanted to get you together this evening is to share an important message that we think you all need to hear.' He and Judy shared a final glance before he spoke again.

'Life is short. You'll have heard many prophecies before. Things such as: 'It's about the journey, not the destination.' And I agree, life isn't about the destination, but it isn't about the journey either.'

The room was captivated now. It was unusual for Greg to speak at length, even more unusual for him to deliver an emotional speech.

Sarah felt both calmed by his soothing voice and alert to his every word. She had an intense feeling as though the next thing she learned might change her profoundly. She was transfixed.

'It is not the pursuit of happiness that we must long for. Instead, we must aim to find happiness in the pursuit. Don't get to the end and think, 'What now?' Get to the end and think, I enjoyed that. Remember that we exist in a shard of light between two vast plains of darkness. It is a miracle that we are here, and our time here is only ever fleeting. We owe it to ourselves to make the most of it. Whatever that looks like to you, just make the most of it. Say what you think. Quit the job. Jump out of the plane.'

Greg raised his champagne flute.

'So please raise a glass.'

Everyone lifted their flute into the air, ready to toast.

'Here is to celebrating life and making the most of every day. Judy and I will be there to support you all along the way. Cheers.'

'Cheers,' came the toast in unison, as people lifted cold bubbles to their lips.

Suddenly, the room was in motion again. George ran for his grandfather, bundling into him and hugging him tightly, closely followed by Lucy, who offered a softer embrace and a kiss on the cheek. Simon rose for Judy and held her for a moment too long, congratulating her on the wise words they'd both shared. Ian moved towards his father-in-law, prising his son's suffocating grip from Greg's midriff and replacing it with his own firm embrace.

Judy grabbed for the remote and hit play on the stereo, so that the sound of Bon Jovi blasted into the room, much to Lucy's annoyance.

'Right,' Judy hollered, 'Let's finish the last minute prep before people arrive.'

She began ushering people off in different directions, taking Simon's hand and leading him to the kitchen.

Sarah remained glued to her chair as she watched the room empty. She tried to make sense of how she was feeling. Her father's words had hit her hard and she was still processing them. Yet she had so many unanswered questions. She couldn't allow herself to blindly accept his advice when she was consumed with concerns. *What about money? What about responsibilities?*

She could hear laughter coming from other rooms as she remained frozen and alone. Suddenly, she saw a shift in motion off to her left. She turned her head and was startled to see her sister, who also remained glued to her seat.

How had Sarah missed her? She was sure everyone else had left.

Perhaps Abbie too was filled with questions and needed a few moments to try and make sense of her father's words. But as she looked closer, Sarah observed an unusual expression on her sister's face. Abbie's drained pallor was startling. Her eyes stared blankly ahead into an empty space in the room and she sat up, rigid and frozen, a full glass of champagne still stuck in her grasp.

'Abbie?' she questioned, tentatively.

Abbie didn't move.

'Abbie?' she tried again, slightly louder this time.

Slowly, Abbie turned her face to Sarah's and they locked eyes. Abbie was vacant, empty and elsewhere. It was a look that Sarah had never before witnessed in the eyes of her sister and she was filled with fear.

They held their gaze for several seconds before Abbie blinked. Upon opening her lids again, Abbie's vacant look had vanished. Instead, her eyes were filled with a vulnerable weakness. Tears began to pour, uncontrollably, from her sockets, silently begging for help.

'Oh Abbie!'

CHAPTER 20
ABBIE

As she riffled through the wall cabinet, she willed herself to find what she'd been searching for. She pushed the high gloss door shut and noticed the wall tiles to her left. They were grey slate - an extravagance that her mother had afforded from her lump sum pension payout last year - but the grouting between them was already beginning to discolour. She made a mental note to offer to help more with the housework; her mother's standards were no longer what they used to be. Perhaps age had allowed them to slip. Either that, or her eyesight now meant that she couldn't see the dirt that was beginning to encrust between the ridges.

When they were children, Judy spent hours on her hands and knees, scrubbing the floors. It was her biggest pride - a spotless home. She'd worked part time, as a secretary in a local bank, but her home was where she spent most of her hours, so she put them to good use.

Returning home from school, Abbie and Sarah would be greeted with a yell: 'Remove your shoes before entering the house.'

Two pairs of slippers were always waiting in the hallway, ready to make the switch. They'd be ushered straight upstairs to change out of their uniform, into the freshly washed and folded loungewear that had been laid out on their immaculately made beds.

A place for everything, and everything in its place, she recalled.

She'd not heard that phrase in twenty years!

More memories rushed to her.

Saturday mornings. Waking to the sound of bickering from the kitchen below her bedroom. Traversing the stairs with trepidation to find her mother upset and her father bemused.

'But I'm only trying to make myself a coffee.'

'Can you just wait though! I need to put the dried dishes back in the cupboards and wipe the sides down. When I'm done, you can make a coffee.'

'But why can't I make coffee *while* you put away the dishes and wipe down the sides?'

'Because that's not how it works. I can't have mess on top of mess.'

Her mother had been militant. Regimented. Obsessive?

She peered back at the moulding grout and wondered when it had changed. Perhaps the compulsive cleaning had only ever been about keeping up appearances. Or perhaps she was desperate to find order and routine in the home so that she could keep the other cogs turning, all in sync. Perhaps she craved some control in her otherwise submissive life. Whatever it was, at some point since she and Sarah moved out of their childhood home, her standards began to slip. Abbie felt a pang of sadness and pity.

A shame to let the plates stop spinning. She thought. *Once they stop, it's hard to get them going again.*

A knock at the door reminded Abbie that there were others needing to use the loo as well.

'One moment!' she called out as she made a last ditch attempt to search the drawers below the sink. Her mother hadn't had a period for years now, but hopefully she kept a stash somewhere - for guests.

A ha! A lonely tampon revealed itself at the back of the third drawer. Abbie scrunched her nose at its appearance: dust covered and ancient, but still tightly cased within its wrapper, so it would have to do.

'Abbie? Are you in there?' called a familiar voice from the other side of the door.

Leave me the fuck alone, her internal voice screamed as she sat down on the toilet.

'I'll be a minute,' she called back, perhaps more snappy than intended.

Her mind hurtled back to the years of torment: sharing a bathroom as teenagers. Sarah spent what felt like hours in the shower (*What the hell did she do in there?*) and then another age brushing her hair in the mirror, while Abbie wore the carpet threadbare, traipsing back and forth across the landing, banging on the door over and over again. It wasn't until after they both moved out that her parents finally decided on the extension - with a ground floor w/c. *Thanks a lot, guys!*

Abbie flushed the chain and washed her hands at the sink, taking her time to enjoy the rhubarb fragrance of the 'fancy' hand wash, clearly brought out to impress the guests.

Sarah can wait this time, thought her petulant teenage voice, but before she had reached for the towel, she heard the door creak behind her. She spun around to catch her sister's cheeky grin emerging around the crack of light created by the opening, bobby pin in hand.

'The trick still works,' Sarah smirked, shutting the eighties music out with a firm close of the door behind her.

'Sarah!' Abbie whined, 'You can't break into the

bathroom while I'm on the loo!' she shrieked, aghast at her sister's brashness.

'Sure I can. Besides, I knew you were done, I heard the taps running. Nice soap huh?' she nodded towards the sink, yanked up her dress and plonked herself down onto the toilet.

Abbie rolled her eyes and turned her back on her sister, facing the discoloured wall, once again. She didn't want to *chat* and she certainly didn't want to chat *now*.

'It's getting busy out there and it's still only 8pm! I knew I should grab the loo now, while it's still free.'

Abbie let out an audible chortle at her sister's words. She couldn't hold back.

'It wasn't *free*, Sarah, I was in here!'

'You know what I mean,' Sarah dismissed, pulling up her tights and adjusting her dress.

Abbie remained fixed on the wall, refusing to look at her sister. This evening had been embarrassing enough. She didn't need to go into depth about things, certainly not right now, with a house full of people beyond the door.

Abbie had clearly shocked her sister earlier - God, she'd shocked herself. Where did that even come from? But she'd successfully managed to dismiss it away - 'PMS and a lot going on right now.' She'd jumped up and headed for the bathroom then too, taking five or six minutes to compose herself, reapply her makeup and spritz a bit of perfume, before emerging again, as good as new. No one else had even noticed her absence.

'Tom's arrived.' Sarah murmured, as if throwing out an insignificant, passing comment. 'Got to try and keep him and Simon away from one another,' she jested, attempting to make light of the situation, but Abbie knew her sister. She would only have mentioned it if she was actually concerned, but Abbie had no idea why she would be. Tom had remained a part of their lives for all these years - what was different now?

'Have you said hello yet?' Abbie questioned, still facing the wall so as not to catch her sister's gaze, hoping to sound innocuous.

'Not yet. He's busy chatting with Ian. Acting like they've not seen each other for years! Didn't they play golf together last weekend?'

They had played golf together, but that was nearly a week ago now. There would be a lot to catch up on. Abbie envied the relationship Ian and Tom had together - a pure friendship that was never to be broken. They weren't gossipy like girls might be. They didn't need to chat on the phone, or even text often. But when they were together, they were like soul mates, so connected and at ease. Abbie wondered what it might be like to feel that way with a friend. With her husband even.

She shook the thought away, as she reached for the door handle.

'Ready?' she called back to her sister.

'I suppose so,' Sarah sighed back. 'Let's go do this thing.'

As the door slid open, the sound of laughter erupted up the stairs towards them. Abbie's parents had always had parties, even when the girls were young, and people always seemed to congregate in the hallway. *Why was that?*

Abbie descended the stairs, the music getting louder with every step. She wondered how these oldies even heard one another with the music blaring so loud. Perhaps she should head towards the stereo and turn it down a notch. The live band would have been so much better - more subtle and refined - the music swaying through from the garden and drifting calmly around the house, but the weather had ruined that too.

'The band will never fit in the house,' Judy had squawked at her earlier, panicking about the necessary rearrangements. 'I'm going to have to cancel them.' She'd been nervous to make the phone call, but thankfully they'd been very understanding and even offered to refund her half of the money - a gesture of goodwill.

As she reached the final steps, she surveyed her options. To her left, she could see into the lounge, where her mother was busy holding a crowd. Judy stood in the centre of the room, while four of her friends circled her and hung on her every word, throwing out an explosion of laughter every few seconds. Judy was a storyteller and she had always had the ability to captivate others. Normally this was on a one-to-one basis - she'd make up a fantastical bedtime story to hook Abbie in, or she'd recount a sensational event at work, over dinner, to her husband - but after a few glasses of wine, Judy could storytell to a crowd too. She must be on glass number three, by now.

Around the centrepiece that was her mother, the room was heaving with people - neighbours, friends, old work colleagues - all bobbing back and forth. Some danced like teenagers, holding their glasses in the air and shaking their backsides, while others two stepped more reservedly in time with the music.

At the far length of the room, Abbie spotted her parents' neighbours, Glynn and Nicola, sitting on the sofa, merrily engrossed in conversation, leaning into each other's ear to be heard over the noise of the music. *It's a wonder that people of their age still have things to discuss,* she thought.

To her right, Abbie could see the filled hallway, with a guffaw of laughter coming from the kitchen on the other side, where her father was clearly entertaining his friends in a slightly quieter environment.

Either way she turned, she'd have to encounter people - and that meant conversation.

She spun her head left and then right again before taking a deep breath and heading towards the hallway. At least, that way, she could be heading for a destination - needing a drink - and therefore, she wouldn't need to stop for too long in any conversation trap that she met along the way.

She slipped past Lisa and John, throwing a cursory., 'hey!' while pointing at her empty glass, in order to show her desire to reach the kitchen.

She squeezed behind some unknown partygoers, offering 'sorry's as she brushed too close to them - ex colleagues perhaps?

She stepped between her aunt and uncle. No need to stop and talk, she'd already chatted to them when they arrived.

Finally, she stepped through the threshold to the kitchen, headed to the double doors and out into the open plan dining area, where the table of drinks laid themselves out on the far side. The whole left wall of the dining room had been rearranged, a huge table positioned against the wall held the food and drink. At one end lay a spread of sandwiches, vol-au-vents, mini quiches and crudites, with the resurrected birthday cake in the centre. At the other end, there were trays of glasses, lined next to buckets of beers and champagne on ice.

Abbie searched the table for orange juice. One glass of champagne had been enough. Her mouth was dry and she needed to keep her faculties about her this evening, so orange juice it was. She scanned back and forth, hunting with her eyes, but there appeared to be nothing but alcohol. She lifted the table cloth to observe the staging area beneath. She scanned behind her, to be sure that no one was watching her ruin the facade, then snatched up the orange juice with a stealth move, laying the table cloth swiftly back over the hidden extras.

'It's the staging area, that is,' came a familiar voice behind her.

She turned to see Tom's outstretched arms, awaiting an embrace.

'Don't let your mother catch you!' he joked, mock glancing from side to side like a detective.

Abbie hugged him back, enjoying the familiar hold.

'Hey you.'

'Just been chatting with the little man,' Tom smiled, taking the carton and pouring her a glass. 'But he dumped me for a kid called Jonathan.'

Tom raised an eyebrow in a curious way, and Abbie instinctively laughed, knowing his next words before he spoke them.

'Who calls their kid 'Jonathan'?' he mocked.

'Now, now,' Abbie returned, brushing away her laughter. 'That's the neighbour's boy, he's a sweet kid.'

'I'm sure he is,' continued Tom, passing the glass to Abbie and placing the carton on the table. 'I'm just jealous.' Tom's face turned serious and sombre. 'I miss the little squirt. I barely get to see him these days.'

From George's birth, until the age of five, Tom had been 'Uncle Tom'. While he and Sarah had never married, the accolade was as official as they came, and well deserved too. Tom was at every family event; he was constantly round the house at the weekend; he even helped with the school run when her or Ian got caught up at work. And their relationship was special. Their cool uncle. Their only uncle.

After the split, things became different. While they still saw one another, the frequency lessened and the 'uncle' badge was forcefully removed.

'There are so many people here tonight,' Tom beamed, 'A true credit to how wonderful the old boy is.'

Abbie felt a flush of pride. Her dad had always been popular and she realised that she did feel proud of that fact.

'Many people I don't know though,' he continued. 'Like this Simon guy. I haven't even met him yet. You'll have to introduce us.'

The sentence felt pointed, deliberate, as though he were trying to find a way to segway Simon into the conversation. Abbie considered his motives, as Tom remained still and silent before her. Tom was not the confrontational type, and definitely not the jealous type. *What could his motives be?*

'Sure,' she chose the word with all its simplicity, as a way of neutralising the topic. Noncommittal and nonchalant.

'And where's Lucy Loo?' Tom questioned,

content to shift the conversation on. 'I've not seen her yet this evening.'

'Your guess is as good as mine,' Abbie replied. Tom caught the shooting sadness that escaped as the words left her mouth.

'Is everything okay with you two?' he questioned softly, touching her gently on her folded arms.

Abbie shrugged it off. 'Yep, all fine. It really is good of you to come tonight, Tom.'

'Oh I wouldn't miss it!' Tom responded, successfully distracted. 'Such a shame about the weather though. I heard about the plans for the garden party.' He turned to the window, where darkness was close to setting, but the remaining daylight still illuminated the lashing rain and whipping wind that threw the tree branches around with fury. The gazebo's remains were still evident from the holes in the lawn. 'Bloody gazebos are no good.'

'Well, you know, she was desperate to emulate one of your famous garden parties!' Abbie shot him the compliment.

'Oh gosh,' he blushed. 'She didn't say that, did she?'

'Not in so many words,' Abbie continued, 'But we all know that's what she aspires to. Those parties at your house are legendary - even the kids say so. Lucy talks about your summer house every time spring rolls around: 'But Tom has a summer house, why can't we get one?"Abbie mimicked.

Tom gave her a friendly prod to the arm. 'Stop it, you. That girl is welcome whenever she wants. You all are. You know that.'

'I know, Tom.' Abbie changed her tone. 'I'm only

kidding. We just miss you, that's all. You've not been around much recently.'

'Oh, I know, Abs. I am sorry. It's been busy, you know?'

Abbie raised her eyebrows. 'Oh, I see. A mystery woman on the scene, is there?'

Tom choked on his beer, spluttering out his reply, 'No, no, just work. Summer months are always crazy!'

Abbie looked into Tom's eyes, which appeared to have both softened and hardened at the same time - as if a deep routed pain was trying to escape, before being forced back inside. He dropped his gaze and lowered his head slightly, almost in embarrassment. His tilt suddenly allowed Abbie to see another head emerge into focus behind him, as it slowly made its way towards them.

Shit, she thought. She did a quick scan of the room, attempting to find Sarah, before remembering that she's taken a left at the bottom of the stairs. She'd be boogying it up with the neighbours by now.

She did a second scan, attempting to find someone else who might be able to help break up the interaction that was about to take place.

Ian. Where was Ian? She hadn't seen him for ages. The last she knew, he was chatting to Katie - stupid cow.

The head was now only a few feet away, clearly destined for them. There was no hope; she'd have to mediate this one alone.

Tom noticed the concern in Abbie's eye as he watched her gaze fall over his left shoulder. He followed it, turning his head just in time to come face to face with the man he'd only ever seen on social media posts.

He recognised him at once.

'You must be Tom,' the man spoke with a confident voice, perhaps a little louder than was necessary for the volume of the room, while motioning an arm out to shake his hand.

The man was tall, but not as tall as Tom; muscular, but not as toned as Tom; confident, but with more of an arrogant air than Tom; yet Tom felt intimidation flood his body, turning it rigid and still.

'Indeed,' Tom replied, reaching out a moist hand to meet his new acquaintance. 'And you must be Simon.'

CHAPTER 21
SARAH

'Terrible shame, really. The poor girl was having a moment of madness. All us women have them.'

Jenny's voice was high and shrill over the sound of the music. It was deceptive. To her ears, she was probably speaking at an acceptable volume, but the noise of the speakers beside her distorted her conception of reality. Her neighbour did not need to lean in to hear her story. In fact, others enjoying their own conversations turned round regularly, distracted by the loudness of her remarks. Jenny, oblivious to her own disturbance, continued to offer her opinions out to the unsoliciting room.

As Sarah entered the room, she heard Jenny before she saw her.

'Some women just aren't able to handle it all. And that's nothing to be ashamed of. Full time mothering and full time work do not go hand in hand.'

Jenny's acquaintance spotted Sarah's entrance and attempted to redirect the conversation, aware of Jenny's lack of subtlety.

'Have you tried the mini quiche?' she attempted, holding her plate out.

The attempt was futile. Jenny waved away the offer.

'Back in my day, you see, you had to make a choice: work or motherhood. But nowadays, feminism has gone mad. Why do women need to try to have it all at the expense of their own health and wellbeing? It's just bizarre. What are they trying to prove?'

Jenny's champagne swished over the top of her glass as she gestured along to her words. The spill was unobserved by Jenny herself, who continued to throw her arms back and forth, pointing at people around the room.

'Take my Michelle, for example,' Jenny continued, pointing at her daughter. 'She's raising three strapping young boys while Michael brings home the bacon. And it works perfectly. In fact, young Isaac has just been named captain of the under ten's football team!'

Jenny beamed with the pride that only a grandparent can possess.

'And that would not have been possible without Shelley taking him to all those training sessions. If she was out working, he'd be stuck in after school clubs until God knows what hour of the day.'

Sarah considered walking back out the way she had come, but thought better of it. Several listeners had clocked her entrance. How would it look if she ignored the talk and slunk away?

She walked around the back of the room, so as to approach Jenny head on. Better to give her a few seconds to consider how to redirect the conversation.

Jenny did not take the hint.

At spotting Sarah, she threw her arms out wide, again swishing champagne over the rim of the glass, which landed with a plod on the cream carpet.

'Oh and look at the lovely Sarah!' She kept her arms outstretched, waiting for Sarah to arrive into her counterfeit hug and European air kiss to each cheek. 'Sarah and I bumped into each other this afternoon, didn't we dear, and I'll tell you now what I told her then.'

Jenny readjusted her feet in an attempt to stand to attention, but her heel buckled below her, so she stumbled, before regaining balance with the help of Sarah's arm.

'Sarah made her choice and good on her.' She nodded towards Sarah with a blink that outstayed itself. 'It's brave to be childless when approaching your forties, but Sarah has made that choice and good on her.'

Jenny's voice rose louder, attracting the attention of onlookers from further across the room. Sarah placed a gentle hand on Jenny's arm, guiding her slowly away from the speakers, hoping this might also guide a conversation change.

'She's so focused on her career - and good on her,' Jenny's words were slurring in their repetitiveness. 'And yes, that might be intimidating for some men, but who bloody cares, right Sarah? You go out there and you earn your own money. You don't need children to be a woman nowadays. You can be anything you want. You can be a man. I read about it on Facebook last week, you know. Gender fluidity, I think they call it.'

Sarah ushered Jenny to the side of the room, away from immediate neighbours, and coaxed her down into an armchair. The woman she was speaking to had disappeared, thankfully. She'd clearly taken Sarah's arrival as her own opportunity to escape.

'Gender fluidity is something else entirely, Jenny.' Sarah began. 'And as I mentioned earlier, there is no need to comment on people's life choices. We are all just trying to muddle through as best as we can. Now, have some water.'

Jenny brushed the water away, still clinging on

to her champagne glass.

'My dear, I am fine,' she dismissed. 'We have to muddle through, my dear, yes, but some people make it harder than it needs to be. Why not just take the easy route?'

Sarah considered the question, as she slumped herself onto the arm of the chair.

'Because easy isn't always better, Jenny. Perhaps easy isn't as fulfilling or as rewarding.'

'Pah!' Jenny threw a dismissive arm in the air once more. She spotted a champagne bottle on the other side of the room, which called out to her. She attempted to stand, reaching an arm out at Sarah in order to gain her balance, before composing herself and staring down at her feet. Sarah watched her seemingly willing them to take a confident step forward. As she began to move, with the grace and composure of a child who had just learned to walk, she muttered to herself.

'These young women ... no idea about it ... suffragettes turning in their graves ... bloody woke ...'

With a glance to the left, Sarah spotted Lucy. She was standing, huddled around an ipad with two of the neighbour's kids. She watched, as the three of them giggled at the screen, clearly enjoying whatever mischief they were up to.

Lucy looked older this evening. Her thirteen years could have been mistaken for fifteen. She wore a black, bodycon dress that clung to her developing curves with precision. Her legs were bare, and her feet housed white Nike trainers. She was gifted long, thick, brown hair that hung around her shoulders with ease - a contrast to the wispy strands Sarah had naturally inherited. *Thank God for extensions.*

Feeling the eyes that were burning into her, Lucy glanced up and caught her auntie's gaze. She offered a smile that widened her cheeks and narrowed her eyes, simultaneously, before turning back to her friends.

Sarah grinned, continuing to watch her niece. The kitchen drama was surely over and she was back in favour with her niece once more. She fixed her gaze on her a moment longer, before her attention was stolen by a flicker of crimson out of the corner of her eye. Sarah turned and saw Katie, strutting down the hallway with her short red dress and black stilettos.

Sarah lifted her arm and tapped at her watch.

'I know we're late!' she called, shuffling her way through the crowd and approaching Sarah with her arms out wide. 'Blame the babysitter.'

'The babysitter had nothing to do with you taking two hours to choose an outfit Katie,' her mother joked, appearing from behind her daughter and leaning into Sarah for an embrace.

'Where's Rob?' Questioned Sarah, glancing behind them to check she hadn't missed his entrance too.

'Your guess is as good as mine,' Katie answered, brushing past her and heading towards the kitchen. 'Now, where's the wine?'

'I'll explain later,' Lisa whispered, stroking her arm with kindness and following her daughter's lead.

Sarah spun around and followed them into the room.

'You both look gorgeous,' Sarah offered to Lisa. A rare but genuine compliment that she reserved for when she really meant it.

For a woman in her mid sixties, Lisa was

impressive. She maintained a firm and healthy physique, playing tennis twice a week and attending a series of day time gym sessions. Pilates, most frequently, but spin class was her latest obsession.

'It's like cycling on speed!' she'd remarked, after her first session, 'But surrounded by sexy men and women in their twenties and thirties. What's not to love?'

Sarah wanted to question how Lisa knew about speed, but she thought better of it. What Lisa got up to in the seventies was her own business.

Tonight, Lisa looked ten years her junior - at least. She was styling a black pantsuit with a purple blouse tucked in at the waist, and a low neckline which revealed her plump and bolstered breasts. A black heel gave her five foot frame a boost and her ash blonde, highlighted hair was freshly styled from her afternoon appointment at Boutique Barnett.

'Thank you sweetie,' Lisa returned, 'As do you. Your dress is simply stunning!'

Sarah admired the fact that Lisa could take a compliment. It gave her a confidence that Sarah could only dream of. No silly, British brush away remarks - 'Oh gosh, this old thing?' or 'I got ready in such a rush.' - she owned her look. And she worked hard for it, so she should soak up the compliments.

'Thanks, Lisa. It's new,' replied Sarah, borrowing some of Lisa's attitude. She couldn't remember the last time her own mother had paid her a compliment, so she would take one from Lisa and enjoy every moment of it.

'Now, where's your mother? I need to say hello.' Lisa looked about the room, scanning for Judy. 'And apologise for being so late.'

'She's in the lounge,' Sarah said, handing a glass to Lisa and pointing in the direction of her mother.

'Thank you,' she said, taking the glass from Sarah and turning on her heels, before strutting away towards the lounge.

Sarah drew her eyes away from Lisa's mesmerising walk, and turned her attention towards Katie, who had almost already drained her first glass of wine.

'Everything okay?' Sarah questioned tentatively.

'He's a bloody arsehole!' Katie spat, lifting the bottle and pouring a top up. She offered the bottle to Sarah, who threw a dismissive hand wave in its direction.

'Oh shit, sorry Sarah, I forgot about the ...' Katie rubbed her hand across Sarah's stomach.

Sarah reached out and grabbed Katie's hand, placing it back down by her own side. She spun her head around the room to see if anyone had noticed. Thankfully, everyone appeared engrossed in their own conversations.

'Katie, what the fuck?'

'It's okay, it's okay. No one saw,' she replied, lifting her glass again and emptying the contents.

'You should slow down.' Sarah suggested, knowing full well that Katie would not listen to her advice. She never had, so she wouldn't start now.

Katie ignored her.

'So we're having lunch, right, and suddenly he gets up from the table and announces, 'I can't do this anymore.' Just like that.'

'Oh dear,' Sarah offered.

'So he goes upstairs and starts packing a bag,'

Katie continued. Obviously, I follow him upstairs and say, 'What are you doing?' but he gives me the silent treatment. Refuses to talk.'

'So what did you do?'

'Well, what could I do? I told him that he was being pathetic. Immature. That the kids were more grown up than he was.'

'Right,' Sarah grimaced. 'And how did that go down?'

'He just continued to ignore me! Acted like I wasn't even there, like he couldn't even hear me. He just finished packing his bag and then left.' She hunted around for another bottle of wine. 'Fucking prick.'

On reaching the lemonade, she grabbed at it and proceeded to top her glass back up. Katie had never been good at holding her drink, so she had probably recognised that the wine buzz would hit too quickly - dilution would be necessary to avoid another bathroom vomit incident.

'The whole time, Aimee was at the kitchen table, just sitting in her highchair, crying her bloody eyes out.' Katie continued. 'He didn't even check on her before he left. Just walked straight out of the door.'

This did surprise Sarah. Rob could be an arse. *Couldn't all men?* But he was a good father. He doted on Aimee and would do anything for her. She remembered his fortieth, when the lads had planned a huge knees up at the cricket club. But Aimee was poorly - stomach bug or something - so he cancelled his plans to stay home with her instead. Much to his friends' dismay and dissatisfaction.

'He doesn't give a shit. Not about me or about Aimee. So good riddance to him.' Katie continued, fooling no one as tears began to prick in her eyes.

'Come on, Kate,' Sarah coaxed, 'You know that's not true.'

'It is true,' she dismissed. 'And I don't give a shit anyway. He can fuck right off for all I care. I can find a better man, anyway.' She began searching the room hopefully, but her expression soon changed at the realisation that a seventieth birthday housed mainly pensioners - not the best place to find a partner.

'I just need a decent man, you know?' She turned to face Sarah now, more earnest in her speech. 'Someone who will treat me right.'

Sarah's face softened. Katie did deserve a good man, but she was still unconvinced that Rob wasn't it.

'Speaking of which...' Katie's eyes lit up, as she brushed Sarah aside and took a step forward. 'Simon!' she called.

Sarah turned to see Simon heading towards them, moving with a briskness that suggested business. His face was stern and cold, but he held his arms out to greet Katie.

'Hello Katie,' he said, wrapping his arms around her and releasing himself again quickly. 'Glad you could make it.'

What did that mean? thought Sarah. *'Glad you could make it?' He was not the host. This was not his house.*

'May I steal this good woman quickly?' he questioned.

Without waiting for a response, Simon took hold of Sarah's arm and began guiding her towards the back doors.

Katie nodded and turned back to the table, searching for another bottle.

'Simon,' Sarah winced, leering down at her arm.

His fingers were wrapped around her skin and the impression caused a pinkness to surround each one.

Simon stared straight ahead, his eyes fixed on the room's exit as he led her towards the garden.

'It's cold outside babe. Can I grab my coat?' Sarah called, but the question remained unanswered. For a moment, Sarah wondered if the music was still too loud. Perhaps Simon had not heard her.

As they reached the patio doors, Simon grabbed the chrome handle with his spare hand, opening it wide.

'After you,' he gestured, his sickly-sweet whisky breath smacking her in the face.

She instinctively recoiled with nausea, before regaining her composure and stepping out into the garden.

The cold night air hit her hard. A gust of wind whipped a pile of leaves around on the floor in front of them and a shudder ran through her as he slammed the doors closed again behind them.

Sarah startled as she peered back at the doors. The hum of music and chatter from inside sounded muffled now as she watched the smiling faces illuminated through the glass.

The pain in her arm caused her to glance back down at it. Despite having reached their destination, Simon still held it tightly.

'Is everything okay?' she questioned, choosing her words carefully.

Silence.

She glared straight into Simon's deep blue eyes. He returned the stare, but his eyes were cold and unblinking. The vast, vacant caverns of his eyes meant only one thing.

Surely not here.
A lump grew in Sarah's throat.
Surely not now.

CHAPTER 22
ABBIE

'That stretch of road is hazardous!' Judy exclaimed. 'Just last week, I was driving back from town, when I saw a lorry coming at me from the direction of the village.'

'A lorry?' questioned Roger, aghast at the idea.

'Yes, Roger, a lorry!'

The listeners joined together, collectively tutting and shaking their heads in dismay.

'So I'm driving along, with this ten tonne vehicle hurtling towards me, and I'm thinking, this is it. I'm a goner.'

'Oh gosh,' Helen gasped, throwing a dramatic hand to her mouth.

'But there are signs!' Roger demanded.

'I know there are signs, Roger, but they don't obey the signs, do they, these lorry drivers! They just do what they like, they think they own the road. So I am driving along and he is coming at me with some speed.'

'Well maybe the signs should be bigger,' Roger continued. 'We could petition for new signs with the council. My friend Joe is still over there, I could ask him what he thinks'

'Roger, please, let her finish her story. I want to know what happened,' Helen interrupted, elbowing her husband in the side.

'Right,' said Roger, 'Sorry Judy.'

'So I'm driving towards this lorry, hugging the hedge as closely as I can, the passenger wing mirror is practically scraping it. And he starts to beep!'

'*He's* beeping at *you*?' yells Roger, in disbelief.

'Roger, please!' Helen snaps.

'Yes, sorry, Judy.'

'So, he's beeping at me and I am thinking, what should I do? Should I stop? Should I mount the curb?'

'Oh my!' whispered Helen.

'But I can't just stop and I don't want to ruin the car's alloys do I?'

'So what did you do?' Helen questioned.

'Well Helen, I'll tell you what I did. I took a deep breath, I squeezed my shoulders together, I closed my eyes shut and I prayed.'

'Oh gosh,' Helen gasped. 'And did it work?'

'Well, Helen, I can tell you that, yes, it did.' Judy beamed.

Helen clapped her hands together quickly in sharp bursts of applause. 'Oh wonderful!' she exclaimed.

'Hold on, hold on,' Jason interjected. 'So a lorry is coming towards you and you closed your eyes?' The smirk on his face was evident.

'Oh Jason, please, you're missing the point!' Laura nudged him. 'She prayed and her prayers were answered.'

'Indeed, Laura,' smiled Judy. 'I had always been sceptical, but in that moment of life or death, he was there for me and he chose to save me.'

'Unbelievable!' wondered Helen, in complete awe of the miracle.

'And you're sure it was God who saved you?' Jason continued, raising an eyebrow.

Judy shrugged off his dismissal, remaining earnest. 'It was, Jason, yes. I could feel it.'

'Feel it?' questioned Laura, earnestly.

'Yes, I could feel it.' continued Judy. 'His presence, there with me in the car. All went calm and I knew he would save me.'

'Amazing,' Helen murmured. 'Just amazing.'

'Maybe signs aren't enough,' Roger interjected. 'Perhaps we need cameras! Can you get cameras to catch lorries driving on restricted roads?'

'Yes, I think you can, Roger,' Jason replied. 'ANPR I believe they're called. I saw it on a crime series.'

'Right, well I'll speak to Joe about those too,' he assured, making a mental note to himself.

'And it's not the only time it's happened, either.' smirked Judy, looking over at Abbie with an air of pleasure. 'Abbie's experienced it too.'

'Noooo,' breathed Laura and Helen in unison.

'Well, not exactly,' Abbie spoke softly in an attempt to dismiss any attention.

'It was just last week,' Judy continued, taking control of the story. 'The same stretch of road, just slightly further down, towards the Barn Road turning.'

'Oh it narrows down that way, doesn't it?' Laura interjected.

Both women moved in closer to hear more from the gripping story, while their husbands broke off to the side, now engrossed in their discussion of the newest crime dramas on ITV.

The circle tightened.

'She was on the way home from work, when her phone began to ring.'

'Was it connected to the bluemouth?' Helen asked.

'Bluetooth, Helen.' Judy corrected her sternly.

Helen's cheeks reddened in embarrassment.

'But no, it had disconnected itself somehow,' Judy continued. 'Because of the loss of signal, I suppose.'

'Well, no Mum,' Abbie attempted, in the hope of explaining how bluetooth works, but her mother raised a hand, which Abbie understood to mean that she needn't interject.

'So she's fumbling about, trying to find the phone, when, out of nowhere, she sees a truck come skidding round the bend.'

'Oh no!' shrieked Helen.

'He was definitely speeding,' Abbie interjected, starting to enjoy the reaction to her drama.

'So she drops the phone and clutches both hands back on the wheel, but to her surprise, she jolts it too hard and the car pulls off to the right - straight into the path of the oncoming truck.'

'Oh my goodness, oh my goodness,' Helen muttered.

'Everything just froze, didn't it Abs?' Judy continued. 'One of those moments where time stands still and you wonder what fate holds in store for you. No control and no idea how to respond.'

'It must have been so scary!' Laura offered, rubbing Abbie's arm with tenderness.

'Tell them what you said, Abbie. The words you muttered in your moment of panic.' Judy egged her on, loving the drama, but allowing her to finish the story.

'Well, it wasn't planned. I don't really know why I said it actually, it was very odd.'

'She said, 'Oh please God, no!"' Judy shouted, stealing the thunder back.

Both Laura and Helen recoiled in shock,

throwing their hands to the sky, while Judy stood back, arms crossed over her body, smirking at their reactions.

'And he saved her.' Judy continued, settling the narrative back down to its resolution. 'Somehow the truck swerved around her and she managed to avoid the collision. She sat in the driver's seat for a moment, trying to piece together what had just happened, before her body took over again and she continued on her journey. Truly miraculous.'

'Well I never!' Helen spoke.

'Only an act of God could have saved her, and that is exactly what happened. Same stretch of road as me. Can you believe it?'

Abbie felt a tugging at her side. She glanced down and saw George pulling at her dress.

'Mummy, please can I have some chocolate cake?'

Abbie peered back at her mother and her friends, but there was no need to excuse herself; they no longer needed her. Judy had control of the conversation while Helen and Laura were hooked in.

'Pleeeeease, Mummy! Jonathan's got some.' George begged.

She glanced across the room at where Jonathan was seated, cross legged on the floor, chocolate cake smudged across his face. She flashed a gaze down at her son and smiled lovingly at his innocence.

'Of course you can, sweetie.'

Abbie took George's hand - his plump, warm fingers nestled into her grip - and led him towards the buffet table, where the chocolate cake sat, half demolished.

Abbie couldn't recall the cake being cut. *Was*

there a ceremonious cake cutting at birthday parties? Surely it came after they sang happy birthday, but she could not recall singing happy birthday either.

She glanced at the clock. 9.46pm. It felt later.

The night had been a bit of a blur so far. She'd barely seen George and she hadn't seen Lucy at all. As for Ian, he was completely absent - obviously enjoying the company of others more than her - so she hadn't tried to seek him out. But now it was getting late and she wanted to discuss their exit strategy. She'd need to find him soon.

'Here you go George,' Abbie said as she handed her son a paper plate with care.

George took it obligingly, his face beaming. 'Thanks, Mummy!'

'Careful with that, now,' she warned, but George had already grabbed the plate and begun running off towards Jonathan, crumbs spilling over the edge of the plate as he went.

She stood alone again, and surveyed the room, considering where Ian might be.

The dining room was packed with people, but Ian was not among them. She walked back through the doors and into the kitchen. Some of her parents' friends were seated around the kitchen table, deeply engrossed in conversation, unaware of her entrance.

She stepped out into the hallway, feeling the ache in her feet as she stepped. Mum would never normally allow shoes on the carpet, but social etiquette at parties was different. Abbie wouldn't take off her shoes tonight; the outfit desired shoes on at all times. She felt a momentary pang of guilt for the carpets. *They'd need a deep clean tomorrow!*

Abbie pushed her way through the guests,

heading towards the lounge, when a movement from the side of her eye caught her attention, encouraging her to change direction.

Moving stealthily towards the snug, she noticed the door was ajar and could just about make out two figures, sitting inside. She edged closer, intrigued by the mystery guests. As she reached the doorway, she pressed herself gently against the wooden frame, eager not to disturb the conversation. She tilted her head around the opening and peered in.

The room was small and dimly lit, the only light emanating from a free standing lamp to the rear of the room.

The figures sat side by side on a small velvet sofa, angled into each other, deep in conversation. The woman's legs were crossed and she leaned into the chat, swaying slightly from side to side as she spoke. Her head was tilted down, obscuring her face, but her wavy brown hair swished around as she spoke. Abbie could only see the back of the man's head, but his stance was more relaxed, leaning back into the chair, resting himself with ease.

The conversation was inaudible; drowned out by the music which had been turned up again in the lounge - bloody deaf pensioners - but the woman continued to fling her body back and forth, laughing at the man's jokes.

Abbie leaned in closer, desperate to continue the voyeuristic pleasure, but she leaned a little too far forward and the door creaked itself open a few inches.

Katie's face lifted and she shot a gawp up at the door. For a second, she froze and her eyes widened, like a deer caught in headlights. Then her face softened and she called out to Abbie.

'Hey Abbie, come on in!'

Ian's head spun 180 degrees, catching Abbie's eye. He stood up and welcomed Abbie into the room, holding his arm out pointedly at the now vacant seat for her.

'Do you want to sit down?' he asked.

Suspicious of his chivalry, she lowered herself into the seat, keeping her eyes locked on her husband as she sat.

Inside the room, the noise from the music was dulled and the emptiness of their speech filled the space instead.

Ian stood awkwardly, his hands shoved deep into his pockets. He shifted his weight from foot to foot.

As Abbie waited for someone to speak, she felt a sinking sensation in the pit of her stomach. Her husband was barely speaking to her, but here he was, sitting in a private room with Katie, enjoying her chat, making her laugh.

The sinking nausea was replaced with the ache of her menstration - an ironic stab at her loneliness.

Why was Ian not speaking? Why was he not apologising or explaining himself? Why was he not riddled with guilt at being caught with Katie? Why did he make her sit, rather than standing with her and putting a comforting arm around her shoulder? And what had he been speaking to Katie about, that needed to be said in secret? Oh God, she thought. *Surely he hadn't told her about the bedroom incident? Would he confide in Katie like that? They barely knew each other. Well, if he was telling secrets, she had a few that she could tell too!*

Ian broke the silence. 'Have you seen George? I've not seen him for ages.'

Of course you haven't, Ian. Because you've been cosied up in the snug with this tramp.

'Yep, he's just been pumped with more sugar - chocolate cake.' she replied, cold and to the point. Now was not the time for small talk. She wanted answers. 'What were you two doing in here, anyway?'

The directness of her question surprised even her. She wouldn't normally have been so blunt, but her patience was wearing thin - not just with Ian, but with everyone, everything. She needed to start taking charge, no matter how hard that might be.

She glanced back and forth between her husband and his likely new mistress. Katie was staring at the floor, clearly avoiding Abbie's gaze, her cheeks reddening by the minute. Ian was staring straight at Abbie, a blankness in his face, not guilt as such, more dispassionate detachment. *Maybe he had given up on them, on her, so much that he didn't even feel the shame anymore.* Abbie's stomach lurched again. *Was this really how her life was going to turn out? The abandoned spinster; losing her job, her husband and her children? Is this really what she deserved?*

Ian's eyes darted right and caught Katie's eyeline. The look they shared was all too familiar. They were certainly hiding something.

'Well, you see, I'd had a bit too much to drink.' Katie's voice startled Abbie. 'And young Ian here spotted me making something of a prat of myself.' She smiled in his direction. A smile that seemed to say: *my hero*. 'So he brought me in here to sober up a little.' She pointed to the glass of water strategically placed beside her.

Abbie focused on her husband who refused to meet her gaze. His eyes were firmly fixed on Katie.

The humiliation smacked her hard. *How could he not even look at her? He was choosing Katie instead. Was that really what he wanted? Did he really think so little of her? Was it all completely lost?*

Abbie could feel the panic rising up in her again, the feeling she'd experience too many times this weekend already. The heat growing from her abdomen and encouraging her heart to alter its rhythm, from a settled beat to a pounding, trying to escape from her chest. The heat from her neck began to cause an itching sensation. She pulled at the collar on her dress, in an attempt to let some soothing air seep in. Beyond the fabric, her skin would be reddening, the sure signs of anxiety peeking out to show the world, to display her vulnerabilities to everyone. Thank God for the high neckline.

Abbie was unaware that the shaking had started until she caught a glimpse of the fabric moving around her thighs. She wouldn't be able to hide her anxiety for much longer. It would explode right here in this room and expose her in front of them. She had to keep it together, she had to get out of here and hide away.

She needed to compose her breathing enough to get the words out. Just a few words and then she could leave. She'd go back to the bathroom and get through the next few minutes alone, before gathering up the remnants of her family and getting the hell out of there.

'I think we should head off soon. George will be getting tired. I'll go and find Lucy.'

She tightened her stomach muscles in an attempt to prepare for standing, but her legs had turned to jelly.

How the fuck am I going to make it out of here? She thought, the panic rising further.

A hand touched her shoulder and she looked up.

'I'll go.' Ian said.

He was still not giving her eye contact. Now, he was facing the door, already heading towards his exit strategy.

'You sit here for a moment and I'll gather up the kids and our things. I won't be long.'

Before Abbie could muster up a response, Ian had left the room and there she remained, sitting awkwardly next to Katie. She suppressed her instinct to laugh at the discomfort of the situation. *Had he really just chosen to leave the two of them together in the room. To do what? To talk about who was more deserving at winning Ian's affections? Well he could fuck right off. Who the hell did he think he was? The brashness! The arrogance of the man.*

Her thoughts were interrupted by Katie's blasé tone. 'Oh God, Abbie, I really shouldn't have drunk so much. Bloody wine - it doesn't sit well with me, but I'll never learn.'

Abbie glared at her as she spoke. Katie's eyes were mildly bloodshot and her mascara was slightly smudged down onto her left cheek, but she still looked beautiful.

She and Sarah were always more concerned by cosmetics and aesthetics than Abbie was, spending their weekends in John Lewis, experimenting with free makeup trials. Their TikTok accounts were full of influencers sharing the latest beauty trends and makeup secrets. Abbie didn't even have a TikTok account. Maybe she should have tried harder not to succumb to aging. Men don't love middle aged, anxiety induced, haggard mothers. They fall for beautiful women who have their shit together and still manage to look young and beautiful while styling out life.

'I spilled half a glass of red over Tom earlier!' She giggled an embarrassed laugh, before sensing the lack of humour in the room. Her face softened as she began to let the curtain slip, revealing the truth behind her false persona. 'It's just been a rough day, you know?' Katie continued, reaching for her glass and glugging down two gulps of the previously untouched water. Drinking water wasn't sexy - she must have been waiting for Ian to leave before succumbing to its refreshment.

Katie suddenly lurched forward, as if she'd been scared by a ghost, tipping the glass away from her mouth and choking out a cough. 'Oh shit, Abs,' she spluttered, 'What am I saying?' She placed the glass back down and composed herself. Turning a sympathetic cheek to Abbie, she tilted her head and continued. 'There's me moaning about my day when you've just had the day from hell.'

Abbie recoiled in shock. So Ian had told her about the arguments and the bedroom incident!

'What on earth were you thinking?' Katie continued.

Abbie was taken aback by the judgement in her voice. *Was she really wanting to talk about her failings as a wife, as a lover?* She was frozen in silence, watching Katie's face turn to pure pity. In Katie's eyes, she could see her reflection - a tired teacher, a worn down mother, a crappy wife with zero sex appeal.

Abbie shook her head in despair. She'd hit rock bottom, there was nowhere else to go. She placed her palms on her knees, begging them to stop trembling, but the attempt was futile. 'I don't really know,' she replied honestly.

She could feel her eyes watering, so she lifted her gaze to the ceiling and blinked furiously to dispel the tears.

'And in front of all those people!' Katie continued. 'I assume you're aware that there's a video doing the rounds?' she questioned.

Abbie spun to face Katie once more, her eyebrows scrunched in confusion. It took a second longer than it should have done for Abbie to register what she was talking about, but the lightbulb went off eventually.

'Oh,' she started, shaking herself back into the present, attempting to bring her attention to the new topic they were now discussing. She didn't know what was worse: talking to Katie about her failings as a professional or her failings as a lover. 'Yes, I heard about a video. I haven't seen it though.'

'Hmm,' Katie continued. 'It's on TikTok. I don't suppose you have TikTok, though.'

This dismissiveness of the comment felt like a slap across the face, despite the truth behind it.

'You can't see your face in it, if that's any consolation?' Katie tried. 'But the memes are pretty funny!'

Abbie had clearly looked hurt by the last comment, as Katie's face softened at the realisation of what she'd said.

'Not funny!' She backtracked. 'Just creative.'

'Right.'

'And then there's the hand holding picture,' Katie continued, raising a wry eyebrow to suggest her promiscuity. 'That one's only a few hours old. I must say, it is a little dodgy, but I'm sure it looks worse than it is.' Katie hiccuped, and Abbie felt crushed with embarrassment. *How was this drunken mess of a woman able to make her feel so bad about herself?*

'So have you been sacked, or what?' Katie perked up at the concept of more gossip.

Surely she could have got this detail from Ian. Or maybe they hadn't even spoken about Abbie. *The lure of an affair is probably sexier if you don't talk about each other's spouses.*

'Suspended, for now.' Abbie spoke honestly. At this point, what did she have to lose?

'Oh,' Katie sighed.

Was she disappointed?

'Well aren't we all in a pickle, hey?' Katie's tone perked up as she prodded an elbow into Abbie's side.

'Indeed.' Abbie replied, sarcastically. 'A pickle.'

'And now the photo as well,' Katie continued, side-eying her victim. 'There are comments being made online about the two of you.'

Katie mistakenly took Abbie's silence as a suggestion for her to continue talking.

'That the two of you are...you know.' Katie nudged Abbie with her elbow again and raised an eyebrow.

Abbie continued to stare back blankly. *Was this woman kidding?*

'*Affair* is the word being thrown around, although that feels a little extreme if it was just a bit of fun.'

Katie continued to ogle Abbie, waiting patiently for a reaction or an explanation.

'You're not, are you?' Katie asked, this time with

a hint of desperation in her voice.

Abbie considered her words carefully. Her instinct was to scream, to stand up and throw something across the room, to open the door wide and yell to the whole house that she was not this person that they were all making her out to be and could they all just leave her the fuck alone, please?!

Instead, she replied with a soothing reassurance.

'No, Katie. I most certainly am not having an affair with Mr Winterton.'

Katie watched her eyes carefully for a moment, as if trying to gauge whether or not the truth was being spoken. Seemingly satisfied, she inhaled deeply and switched her focus to the drinks cabinet on the far side of the room.

She made her way over to it quickly, stumbling the four or five paces across the carpet, and flinging the cabinet door open with too much haste, smashing it against the wall.

'Oops,' she apologised, searching the clinking bottles for her desired win. 'Aha!' she announced, holding up a bottle of tequila. 'This is what we need.'

Katie placed the bottle on the floor beside her as she continued to search for shot glasses. Abbie considered telling her that the search was in vain - the glasses were not kept in this room - but all energy had seeped from her body and she no longer felt as though she could speak.

'You with your sacking,' Katie's voice became a mumble, her head now wedged firmly into the cabinet as she continued to rummage. 'Me with my disaster of a marr...'

What had she said? 'Disaster of a marriage?' The

bloody cheek of her. How dare she rub it in like that?

'...And now Sarah with the baby!'

Abbie was still reeling from her own injustice, so it took her a moment too long to register what Katie had said.

Katie pulled her head out of the cabinet and sat back on her heels, surveying the cabinet from the outside. 'Where are these bloody glasses?'

Abbie stared at the back of Katie's head. *Had she just said that?*

Her words, when she spoke them, were slow and serious.

'I'm sorry...Sarah's what?'

Katie spun around and stared straight on at Abbie, reacting to her surprise. Instantly her face softened and fear crept in. She had the manner of a child who had just been caught stealing chocolate from the cupboard.

There was no mistaking it: what she had said was real.

'Oh shit,' Katie mumbled.

CHAPTER 23
SARAH

Sarah sat on the back doorstep, underneath the pergola, her head tilted upwards, admiring the night sky. The cacophony of blackness amassed endlessly across her vision. The stars, that promised new worlds, were concealed by a thick blanket of doom, as the rain continued to hurtle down to the ground.

Sarah was protected from the downpour by the ledge that sat above the door, but scouting out into the garden, she observed the full force of the pelting that attacked the flowers and shrubbery surrounding the lawn.

She took a long, deep breath and considered how she had made it here. Her seventeen year old self would never have believed that she could be rich, beautiful and successful in her mid (late) thirties. That girl would admire her now, with awe and amazement. She'd take a glance at her life and see money, beauty and success. She'd be so proud of what she'd achieved by her mid (late) thirties.

Is that how others saw her too? Did people glance in on her world and see beauty, riches and happiness? Did old school friends scroll through her social media feed with envy at what she had achieved? Did the boys from her youth, now balding and overweight, gawp at her pictures and say: 'phwoar'?

The blur of chatter behind her brought her back to the present moment.

Did the people behind that door see her tonight and think, 'Gosh, Greg and Judy's girl is doing well for herself'?

Did her parents flaunt her success at the tennis club, lording it over their friends: their eldest who was a real business woman, who owned her own house outright, who didn't need a man to support her? Or was Abbie the pride of the family? The well grounded, married, mother of two, who had a sensible job and a pension plan. The reliable, dependable, infallible Abbie.

Sarah once overheard her mother talking to a friend on the phone. The friend's daughter was getting divorced, and Judy had said: 'It's not the end of the world. Modern women don't always need a man. It's not like it was in our day. Just look at my Sarah.'

Sarah's immediate reaction was pride, believing her mother was suggesting that Sarah was independent and confident in her own skin. But the feeling was closely replaced with dejection, as the conversation continued.

'I don't think Sarah even wants a partner - she can do it all by herself. She's already paid off her mortgage! Besides, I'm not sure anyone could put up with her. She's not really the relationship type. She'd only make a man feel insecure.'

The truth was that Sarah did want a partner. She wanted love! Of course she did. She didn't need someone to split the bills with, no, but she still wanted compatibility; she wanted emotional security from another person. She was just less willing to settle than some of the other women she knew. She needed to know that the man she chose wouldn't let her down, wouldn't lie to her, wouldn't leave her. She hadn't found a single one of these men in life so far, so she could only assume they did not exist, and therefore she'd have to settle for being alone.

'You'll catch your death out here,' Greg warned,

appearing beside her.

She jumped in shock.

'Dad,' she responded, 'Where did you come from?'

'I've managed to sneak out,' he whispered, sliding himself to a seated position next to her and pulling a cigar from his pocket. 'Don't tell your mother.' He winked at her and placed the object in his mouth, striking a match to light the end.

Sarah giggled. Her father had been sneaking cigar breaks at special occasions for years. She had a strong suspicion that her mother knew very well that this was happening, but the act was always unspoken, protecting the secret pretence.

The first time she'd caught him, Sarah had been seventeen. It was her cousin's twenty first, and she'd sneaked behind the back of the cricket club to light a cigarette. She had the lighter to her face, when she turned the corner and came face to face with her dad. She dropped the lighter to the ground and froze, wondering how they should each react to catching each other red handed.

'I won't tell if you don't,' he'd winked at her, striking a match and holding it out to her, cupping it from the wind with his spare hand.

From then on, it was their hidden secret. Their escape plan when they needed to take a break from big events and get-togethers. Their five minutes of peace.

'Are you having fun, Dad?' Sarah asked, smiling towards her father.

He had made a real effort tonight. He'd dressed up, in the chinos that Sarah bought him for Christmas (his first introduction to the trouser) and a white shirt, buttoned almost to the top. His face was clean shaven and all undesired hairs had been removed from nostrils and eyebrows - her mother's doing, no doubt. He had a lightweight brown jacket and a shiny pair of shoes to match.

Greg took a deep inhale and blew a cloud of smoke out into the air. The wind grabbed hold of it instantly and took it away with force. 'I am, sweetheart, yes,' he answered. 'Are you?'

'Well, yes of course Dad,' Sarah smiled, 'But it's your party. You're supposed to be enjoying it!'

Greg laughed a kind and gentle laugh. 'Yes, I know.' he nodded, understandingly. 'But it's all for show, isn't it?'

'What do you mean?' Sarah questioned. Her mother had gone to such trouble. She would be distraught if she thought he wasn't having fun.

Sarah turned to face her father. She noticed new lines above his eyelids that she hadn't noticed before. As he spoke, a wrinkle appeared at the crease of his mouth, teasing his lip as it moved.

'I am a sociable man, and it's lovely to see all these faces. Some of which I haven't seen in years.' he smiled, humbled by the love that he had received tonight. 'I feel so honoured to have so many people show up and celebrate with me.'

Sarah nodded, unsure where he was going with this.

'But hitting seventy forces you to take stock of what you've achieved. As crude as it sounds, you begin to wonder what people will say about you once you're gone.' He inhaled deeply again and released the smoke once more. 'People aren't going to talk about the hours I invested at the office or how clean we kept our home.'

His voice softened and he stared out into the

darkness of the sky, his head unflinching, as if he'd spotted a long lost star and he couldn't look away in fear of losing it again.

'They won't remember how lavish my parties were, or how many holidays we went on. They won't talk about the furniture we bought or the fancy artwork up in the hallway. People won't look back at my life and say, 'Oh Greg, yes, he was a damn good financial accountant.' or 'That Greg, he hit the top grossing figures in the company three years in a row.' People aren't going to say, 'You should have seen the Laura Ashley curtains they owned' or 'Six cruises he went on - six!'

Sarah couldn't take her eyes off of her father. His words were calm and slow, honest and serious.

'But people might remember the way I made them feel when I was with them.' He breathed slowly, this time without a puff of his cigar, his eyes still firmly fixed out to the heavens. 'They might remember the kindness I showed them, or my philanthropic stance. People might remember my laugh, and may even describe it as infectious.' The corner of his mouth rose slightly at the thought. 'They will certainly talk about my legacy: the children I helped raise, the views and beliefs I influenced on others, the change I made for good in this world. And I want people to remember those things. I want them to say, 'Oh Greg, yes he was a family man, he made a difference to our lives,' but most importantly, I want them to say, 'He lived a good, honest, and happy life.'.'

He turned his face to Sarah's and stared deep into her hazelnut eyes, which were glassy and wide.

'This party is lovely, Sarah. But it's all a show. It's the old school equivalent of today's social media reel.

It's for other people, sweetheart, not just for me.'

Sarah nodded as a tear escaped her eye and rolled its way down her cheek. She understood what he was saying. She knew the gravity of his words and she trusted in his voice.

Greg put his arm around his daughter and she nestled her head into the nape of his neck.

'I'm so proud of you, Sarah,' he gushed, rubbing his hand soothingly down her arm. 'You've achieved so much and you're a true inspiration. You touch the lives of so many people and you have so much good in your heart. But I want you to be happy. I need you to be happy,' he paused. 'And right now, sweetheart, I'm not sure you are.'

Sarah was caught off guard. Her first instinct was to jump up and brush away the claim. To feign ignorance and make a funny joke. To dismiss his concern and suggest too much alcohol had been consumed for such a deep chat.

But Sarah didn't do that. Instead, she did nothing. She sat and breathed in time with her father, watching the plumes of smoke rise into the sky from his cigar. She felt his chest rise and fall, and soaked in the warmth of his touch.

For perhaps the first time ever, Sarah was aware of the finite nature of her parent's lives. They'd both always seemed so young, so spritely. She'd never considered their eventual demise - neither of them had ever really even been unwell. No cancer scares, no heart problems - they were fit as fiddles. But now, sitting in her father's embrace, succumbing to his paternal security she felt conflicted emotions of both safety and fear. One day - maybe one day soon - he would no longer be here for her, and then what was she to do? Face adulting alone? Is that when one becomes a true adult, when they no longer have parents above them to look up to?

The door behind them flew open with force and Greg instinctively threw his cigar across the garden as both he and Sarah hurled themselves to attention and spun their heads. *Maybe his smoking was more secret than she'd thought.*

'Have either of you seen Lucy?' yelled Ian, his breathing laboured with concern.

'Lucy?' questioned Greg, in surprise.

'In the last thirty minutes or so?' Ian added.

'I don't think so,' Greg said, scratching his head. 'I think the last time I saw her was about an hour ago, standing with that Sean boy in the dining room.'

Ian's breathing was quickening and he raised his hands up to his head, shaking it from side to side, considering his next move. His face was a picture of worry, which made Sarah uneasy. Ian was not usually a man who could be panicked.

'Ian,' Sarah said in a steady voice. 'What has happened? Tell us what's wrong?'

Ian turned back to the kitchen and did a quick sweep with his eyes before returning his glance back to Sarah. He shook his head back and forth, muttering inaudible words.

Sarah raised to standing, leaving her father perched behind on the step. She put her hands on Ian's arms and lowered them back down to his sides. She tilted her head to catch his eye and tried again. 'Ian, what's happened to Lucy?'

'She's gone,' he said.

CHAPTER 24
ABBIE

'Lucy's gone.'

Abbie glowered up at Ian, unable to comprehend his words.

'Abbie,' he tried again, 'Lucy has gone. No one knows where she is.'

Abbie shook herself back to reality with the determination of maternal instinct that every mother possesses. 'What do you mean, she's gone?'

Ian was frantic. He stood in the doorway with his coat on and his phone unlocked in his outstretched hand. 'No one has seen her for at least thirty minutes.' His voice was wobbly and panicked. 'Sean said he thought she seemed upset and Erica reckons she saw her go out the front door, but she's definitely been sneaking a few beers this evening, so I don't know how reliable she is.'

Abbie snapped to attention. 'Okay, I am assuming you've tried calling her.'

'First thing I tried,' he replied. 'It keeps going to voicemail.'

'And her Snapchat location?' She interrogated.

'Sarah checked it. She's turned it off.'

Why the fuck does Sarah know about this before me? She shook away the petulant thought and snapped back to business.

'I'm going to drive around and see if I can find her,' Ian said, thrusting his phone back into his pocket. 'Where are the keys?'

'No way!' Abbie cried. 'You've had far too much

to drink. I'll go.'

Ian obliged willingly as she rose to her feet and headed for the understairs cupboard, where she'd stashed her handbag upon arrival.

'Shall we call the police?' Ian's voice was shaky and powerless.

Abbie shook her head, brushing past him with confidence. 'They won't do anything yet - it's too soon.'

Ian nodded an understanding and followed behind her like a lost puppy.

She opened the door with force and brushed coats aside swiftly, searching for her bag. Her maternal instincts had taken over. The thought of her child in trouble trumped all else. In that minute, only one thing mattered. Not her guilt and disappointment, or her failed career. Not her spiralling marriage or her daughter's contempt for her. Not her severe misery or sorrow with her failure to reproduce. She was a mother, and she needed to get her daughter home to safety.

Abbie grabbed her coat and slung it around her shoulders, placing her phone and keys in the pocket, leaving the rest of her bag behind, and headed to the front door.

'Stay here and keep an eye on George,' she commanded. 'Keep your phone on loud. Get a team of people asking around - someone must have an idea as to where she's gone or why. Call me if you have any leads.'

Ian nodded at her instructions, making a mental note of each one.

'Okay,' he replied, but Abbie did not hear him. The door was already slammed shut behind her and she was heading to the car.

#

The engine roared to life as the key turned in the ignition. She yanked the car into first gear and skidded off, without considering the need for an indicator.

She had no idea where she was heading, but she knew that she had to search. She had to try and find her daughter.

She tried to infiltrate the mind of a thirteen year old girl. Where would Lucy go? It was cold, it was dark, and she'd left a house full of friends and family behind her. Why would she leave?

She wouldn't head for home; that was over three miles away, and in these conditions, it would take her hours. There were several other houses known to her around the village. Sarah's house was only a few streets away, but why would she head there? She didn't have her keys, so she would not be able to get in, anyway.

Lucy knew the village well: the cricket club, the youth club, the pub even - where several Sunday roasts had been consumed. Jack and Penny were the landlords, but they were back at the party, so the pub would be closed tonight.

Abbie couldn't explain why, but she knew that Lucy wasn't in any of those places. An instinct within her kept her driving south, through the village and heading out the other side.

Abbie spun left at the end of the road, pulling out onto the high street and a car beeped a vicious warning at her.

Shit.

She clicked the headlights on and flashed them to full beam. No cars ahead.

She slowed her pace and tried to think. Rushing

wasn't what she needed right now, she needed time to think and search the streets, carefully looking for her child.

She slowed the car right down to a snail's pace.

'I'm Lucy,' she thought to herself. *'It's Saturday night, ten o'clock and I've left the safety of my grandparents' house. Where am I heading?'*

Glancing left she saw the local shop: shutters down, lights off. Then the butchers: closed up for the weekend. The church beyond was desolate.

Would she head to the graveyard? Oh, don't be so morbid! Abbie thought to herself. *She's a child.*

'A child,' she said, this time out loud.

It had been a while since she had thought of Lucy as a child. George? Yes. he was still a baby. Her baby. But Lucy was something else. Not yet an adult but no longer a child.

Lucy didn't need Abbie anymore. In fact, she didn't even think she liked Abbie anymore. Abbie's job was done. She had raised the child and the child no longer needed her protection, her support, or her love.

Abbie thought back over the last few days. There had been no mothering there. *When had everything changed? When was the last time that Lucy had truly needed her mother? When was the last time she had gone to her for advice or guidance?*

Lucy didn't even need her mother to provide basic, functional care these days. She'd quite often sleep through dinner time and wake later, settling herself with beans on toast or a pot noodle for her tea. Abbie was completely redundant.

'So, what am I doing?' she mumbled to herself.

Why was she out, searching for a child that didn't need or want her? If Abbie found her, how would Lucy react? Would she refuse to get in the car, intent on continuing with her journey alone?

The pang of emptiness hit her hard.

As she continued her way through the village, she came to the clearing on the other side; the expanse of fields, disturbed only by the single track road that ran between them, leading its way towards the bypass. She knew Lucy would not have made it this far. *So why was she still driving?*

The wipers crashed themselves back and forth across the windscreen, the rain pelting aggressive shots down from the sky, hitting the car with force and bouncing off the ground, illuminated ahead of her.

The sleepy village was deserted of cars. No one else was out in this.

What was Abbie doing? What was the point? Of any of this?

She was failing.

She had failed.

There was no going back. She'd failed Lucy and Lucy was making her voice heard. She'd left, she didn't need Abbie to search for her, She didn't need Abbie to rescue her.

Abbie had failed as a teacher: exploded, lost her composure and hit out. She'd lose her job, for sure. That was suddenly clear to her, now.

She had failed as a wife. Ian didn't love her. He didn't even lust after her these days. He wanted something more. Something fun. Someone younger. More beautiful.

So, what was her purpose?

The car jolted hard to the left, skidding on an unseen puddle in the road. She grabbed the steering wheel tightly, straightening the car back out.

The rush of adrenaline flooded her senses. The feeling was refreshing.

She clung tightly to the wheel and watched her knuckles whiten as she gripped the leather harder and harder.

Slowly, she released her grip, watching her hands float up from the wheel, levitating, almost of their own accord, away from the steering wheel and out in front of her vision. She no longer had control. But that wasn't new. She had control of nothing anymore.

The car stayed straight on its path, following the road obediently.

She felt a clarity wash over her. *If she was no longer in control, nothing could be her fault. No one could blame her.*

Her hands continued to float in the air, their focus mesmerising, as the background blur of the road faded into insignificance beyond them. The hands were steady, calm and peaceful. She turned them around, observing the lines that traced the palms. The lines of life, head, heart, fate. Maybe destiny had always been there, written on the lines of her palms. If only she'd noticed them.

Abbie pushed her foot down hard on the accelerator, and watched the speedometer climb.

32 mph.

35 mph.

39 mph.

Succumbing to inevitability felt peaceful.

She allowed her arms to float back down, resting peacefully on her lap. She took a deep breath. She closed her eyes. She did not pray.

#

Later, they would say that the driving conditions were treacherous, that the wind made the car uncontrollable; that the rain was pelting down too hard to see the bend in the road. People would blame the lorry driver, who should not have been on the road at all, coming too fast around the corner. They would blame the council for the signs being too small and unlit, making them invisible.

No one would blame Abbie.

No one but Abbie would know that it was all her own fault.

BEFORE

CHAPTER 25

The key scratched uncomfortably around the lock, marking the chrome fitting, refusing to slot into its place.

The keys slipped from her grasp as it fumbled and clanked onto the step below. She succumbed to acceptance and she slinked down after them, landing with a plod on her backside.

Please don't let mum and dad have heard me, she begged to herself.

The air was still warm from the afternoon sun, now long set, and her walk back from the green added another layer of perspiration to her forehead. Katie had offered to walk with her, but she needed to go alone. If Katie saw her like this, she'd ask questions, and questions would uncover truths that she could not afford to release.

How had she been so stupid?

She held her head in her hands, and the memories flashed before her closed eyelids.

Sitting cross legged on the park bench, the others were standing, watching her. Shot after shot of vodka. *Had the others drunk so much?* She said she'd had enough. They laughed. She drank more…

Vomit down the slide and his hand on her back. They were alone. She was tired. Had she closed her eyes?

'I'll take care of you.'

His words were soft and gentle.

Katie was no longer with her.

A flash of his face.

Cold mud on her lower back and the view of tree tops.

Pressure on her stomach and shaking her head.

'No thank you.'

Sharp pain between her legs and a squeal of agony.

Grunting and hot breath on her face.

Laughter in the distance. Shaking her head.

'No thank you.'

She lifted her head from her hands and saw a light flick on in the house across the street. She needed to get into the house. If the neighbours saw her, mum would be furious.

She glanced at her knees: a rip in her tights, her skirt stained with mud. Mud or blood? She couldn't tell. Perhaps it was both.

She grabbed at the keys and rose to her feet, fumbling for the front door key. It was brass and larger than the rest. It should be easy to find.

'Aha.'

As she pushed the key in the lock, the door handle jiggled and she felt a clunk from the inside. The door swung open, almost pulling her arm off with it.

She stumbled across the threshold as the door was quickly slammed shut behind them.

The feeling of safety was immediately overtaken by the feeling of fear, as she stared her mother dead in the face.

Her nightgown waved peacefully around her legs and her hair was fastened neatly. *Had she been sleeping or was she waiting up?*

Beyond her mother's silhouette, the hallway mirror scared a vision back at her and she realised, for the first time, just how awful she looked. Her previously, iron straight hair was now a dishevelled mess and her ivory face was streaked with black mascara.

'Where the hell have you been?' Came the aggressive whisper, as her mother towered over her ominously.

She cowered down and perched on the third step of the stairs, tucking her knees in tightly in an attempt to hide her appearance.

'Your tights are ripped, you've mud all over you and you look an absolute mess!' she continued. 'What the hell do you think you're doing?'

She lifted a hand, using the back of it to wipe at her face, in an attempt to remove the noir smudges. But as she touched her face, she noticed the salty tears that were streaming down her cheeks.

Her mother's eyes continued to burn down into her and she imagined how awful she must look: dirty, drunk, and crying on the stairs in the middle of the night.

'I don't really know what happened...' she started but her mother cut her off.

'I don't want to hear it,' she snapped in retaliation. 'What you choose to get up to in your own time is up to you, child. But I will tell you something for free.' She bent down low, her face too close, her eyes too wide. 'If any of the neighbours saw you this evening; if they start gossiping or asking questions, you're on your own.'

Her mother pushed past her and began to walk slowly up the stairs, before pausing, mid step. Her voice softened slightly.

'Now, get yourself cleaned up and get into bed. Before you wake the whole house.'

Her mother stood still, waiting. Perhaps for a response, perhaps for an admission, perhaps for an opportunity to console rather than chastise. But when no reply came, she continued her climb, entered her bedroom, and closed the door quietly behind her.

The silent sobs continued. She was unsure how long for. Finally, she stood, made her way up the stairs to the bathroom and attempted to clean herself, before climbing into bed.

She did not sleep that night. Every time she closed her eyes, a flash of his face flickered across her vision. His eyes scrunched shut, his jaw clenched, his thrusting stinging her.

How could I have been so stupid?

CHAPTER 26

The first time it happened, they'd been in the middle of a shopping trip. 'Girls' Day Out,' mum had called it. She'd obliged. *What teenager didn't want new clothes?* But in reality, they were not enjoying themselves. The crowds were too big, the shops were too warm and stuffy, and nothing they'd tried on seemed to fit quite right.

At age twelve, she was too old to hold her mother's hand, but too young to venture off on her own. The tweenage limbo - before the confidence of adolescence had sunk in, but after the desire for freedom had begun to claw at her.

The break for lunch had been needed. A quiet spot in a local cafe was a welcome relief from the bustle of the fast food outlets. Now, seated on a delicate stool, perched against a round high table, just big enough for two, she felt like she could breathe again.

The menu in her hands was written in French. Thankfully, English translations sat below the foreign words, meaning she could still pretend an air of superiority (no one would know whether or not she could translate the French, and that made her feel grown up and proper). She wondered whether all grown ups knew more than children, or if it was all just a grand ruse. Perhaps she was just as bright as her adult contemporaries. Maybe worldly wisdom was all that differentiated them.

'Do you know what you'd like to eat?' her mother asked. 'I'm contemplating the fish.'

She smiled at her mother's words. Only a few years prior, she would have needed to select from the kids' menu, which would have been shoved in her lap. Her mother would have told her what her options were: chicken or pizza. She never trusted the sausages in restaurants.

Now, she was being treated like an equal; allowed to peruse the menu and consider her own choices and her own fancies. She was old enough and mature enough to decide what meal would suit her best on a Saturday afternoon.

'Hmmm,' she replied. 'Fish sounds nice, but I'm considering the risotto.'

She never ate risotto. But something about the formality of the cafe and the adultness of the room made her act unusually. She wanted to be taken seriously, and for that, she needed a serious lunch.

'Risotto?' her mother asked, not glancing up from her own menu. 'That sounds lovely. I may join you in that, actually.'

She felt a surge of pride. Her mother was going to be swayed by her suggestion - now she really was a grown up!

'Judy, is that you?' The shrill voice came as an uninvited intrusion on their lunch date. She did not want anyone to interrupt them.

Could people not see that they were having a private lunch, a private conversation, connecting as mother and daughter?

'Rachel!' her mother replied, rising from her stool and giving a fake hug and an air kiss in her direction. 'How are you?'

She knew her mother and she knew when she was being insincere. She wondered why people insisted on pretending to like others, when in reality, their feelings were clear. She was sure that, on returning home, Rachel would report back to her husband about seeing Judy this afternoon and proceed to tell him about her widening hips and wrinkled brow. Judy, too, would be sure to tell her father about Rachel's poor dress sense and greying roots. Yet, when standing face to face, these two acted like long lost sisters.

She chose to ignore their falsehood, pretending to read the menu instead, despite having no desire to consider any more options. The French words were giving her a headache.

Her mother and Rachel kept chatting. She was amazed at how, if children pretended not to listen to the adults talk, the adults were quite content to pretend the children could not hear.

'What are you going for today?' Rachel asked, inquisitively. 'I hear the fish here is sublime!'

'How funny,' her mother replied. 'That's exactly what we were considering.'

'The little one too?' questioned Rachel, nodding towards her.

She continued to stare at the menu, her face obscured from sight, faking deafness at their conversation.

'Yes,' Judy whispered. 'Either that or the risotto.'

'Ooh' Rachel winced, scrunching up her face. 'Lots of cream in the risotto, you know. Think of the calories!'

Judy considered her words, before nodding. 'Yes, good point. I'm really trying to get her to watch her weight. It's a tricky age she's at.'

Her ears pricked up. *What had she just heard?*

'Oh I know!' Rachel replied. 'Hormones and puberty are a terrible combination at this age. Girls either shoot up tall and slim or plump out like a balloon. You gotta do what you can to help them.'

'Exactly.' Judy replied. 'God knows the last thing a teenage girl wants is to be overweight!'

'That's why I'm so glad I have boys!' the obtuse woman continued. 'So much easier. They can eat and eat but they burn it all off.'

'Oh gosh, so much easier!' Judy agreed.

Rachel's husband called her name from across the room and she made her excuses to leave.

'See you at the next gala dinner?' she asked, hopefully.

'I'll be there.'

'Good luck with the diet!' she called back, tilting her head towards Judy's distracted daughter.

And then Rachel was gone.

Frozen still, she kept her head firmly glued on the menu, fearing that if she moved even an inch, if she looked anywhere else or, God forbid, caught the eye of her mother, she might burst into tears right there and then.

She glanced down at her stomach and witnessed a small roll of puppy fat hanging idly below her t-shirt. She breathed in deep and sucked it back into place.

'Shall we order?' her mother questioned confidently. 'Fish or risotto?'

She considered her options, but suddenly the thought of both made her nauseous. She wasn't sure she could eat a thing.

She glanced back at the menu and the words illuminated themselves.

'Hello?' her mother questioned, impatient for a response.

'I think I'll have the side salad.'

'Great choice,' her mother said without skipping a beat. She placed both menus together, before raising her hand in the air and clicking. 'Waiter!'

SUNDAY

CHAPTER 27
SARAH

She wasn't shocked when the phone began to ring.

She'd been staring at its blank face for a few minutes, waiting for the blackness to illuminate. She didn't know if she had willed it to happen or if she had a sixth sense that it would.

The phone buzzed gently on the table top and she snatched at it, glancing over to the sofa to ensure that Simon hadn't been disturbed.

The ringing was no surprise but the unknown number was.

Who would be calling from an unknown number?

The party had ended promptly at the news that Lucy was missing. Abbie disappeared first, launching her own private search party - *typical Abbie.* Whereas others had devised a more strategic plan.

Judy would watch George, while Ian and Greg went out on foot, turning left at the end of the road. Tom would turn right, heading down the highstreet and back towards his own house. Roger and Helen would head to the park, Jason and Laura to the shops, and Jenny announced that she would start making posters, which everyone ignored - she was still far too tipsy!

Sarah and Simon were instructed to head home and wait in case Lucy arrived there. Everyone was on standby.

It was now 12.04am and she was sure this call

would be the stand down announcement. *But why wasn't the call coming from Abbie or Ian? Who would call from 'unknown'? The police? The morgue?*

She ran into the kitchen and shut the door behind her and she swiped the green button. The last thing she needed was Simon waking now.

'Sarah?' came the voice.

It was familiar, yet the unexpectedness of its sound caused Sarah to spend a second too long deciphering it.

'Tom? Is that you?'

'I'm sorry, I tried both Abbie and Ian but I couldn't get hold of either of them.'

'Okay...' Sarah spoke slowly, suddenly feeling her legs begin to tremble. She placed a hand on the table to steady herself and lowered herself down onto the kitchen chair.

'I've got Lucy,' he continued, his voice was calm and strong. 'She's absolutely fine - a little cold - but she's okay.'

'You've got Lucy?' she asked, trying to piece together the information she was receiving.

'It's a long story.'

He paused.

'Could you come over? I think there are a few things we need to discuss.'

She peeked through the glass door that separated her and Simon. *If she left, he could wake up. That would not look good. But she needed to go and collect Lucy, surely that was a good enough reason to head to her ex-boyfriend's house in the middle of the night.*

'Sarah?' Tom interrupted her thoughts.

'Of course,' she replied, grabbing at her keys and heading out the back door. 'I'm on my way, I'll be there in ten.'

#

It felt strange knocking on the door that she used to walk through freely. The blue painted wood felt alien against her knuckles. *Had the door always been blue?*

The door swung open almost instantly and Tom filled the doorway with his powerful stance. He had changed into joggers and a loose t-shirt, which fitted his athletic muscles well. His mousy hair looked soft and enticing (so different from Simon's oily gel). She remembered mornings where she'd run her fingers through it with ease.

Tom leaned forward and turned to glare down the street. Sarah followed his gaze, copying his moves like a mirror.

'Sirens in the field again,' he said, nodding out towards the village's exit. 'I'll be another burned out car, I bet,' he continued, not moving his gaze. 'Bloody kids!'

Sarah looked back at Tom, observing how his jaw jutted out confidently as he spoke.

'Speaking of which...' Tom moved aside, opening the doorway for her to enter.

She stepped over the door mat and into the lounge. The mat read: Welcome To Our Home. She remembered buying it at the garden centre when she'd first moved in. *Why had he not changed it in two years?*

The room was warm and dimly lit by the lamp in the far corner. The same blue velvet sofa lay against the back wall, but the cushions perched upon it had changed. Once pink and fluffy, they now held the same velvet sheen as the sofa, causing them to melt inconspicuously into it. The room had a different air to it. The sweet rhubarb scent was replaced by a fresh vanilla hum which hung, stagnant over the carpet.

It took a moment for her to notice her niece and, when she did, she was immediately surprised by how vulnerable and small she seemed.

Lucy was huddled in a blanket on an armchair in the far corner of the room. Beside her, a mug of hot chocolate sat steaming and Kitty nestled herself snuggly on her lap, protecting her from harm.

'Hi sweetie,' Sarah motioned towards her and sat herself down on the hardwood floor beside the chair. 'What happened to you?'

'I'm sorry Auntie Sarah,' she mumbled, 'I really hope I haven't caused too much trouble,' she continued, lifting a hand from below the covers and wiping her face. 'I just had to get out of there.'

Despite appearing small and scared, Sarah was surprised at how well she seemed. She had no scratches or bruises, no soiled clothes, no messy hair. Her eyes were watery and tired, but there were no bloodshot streaks - she had clearly not been drinking. But this made the mystery more confusing.

'Did something happen to you?' Sarah questioned comfortingly. Sarah knew how to interrogate this situation. Her own experiences had prepared her for this moment. If someone had harmed Lucy, she'd need a calm and comforting adult to support her, to make her feel safe and confident to recount the terrible events. 'You can tell me,' she whispered. 'I'm listening.'

Lucy shook her head hard, 'No, no,' she said. 'I'm fine.'

Tom lifted a futon and moved it to sit beside Lucy, so that she was sandwiched between both adults. He placed a gentle hand on the edge of her chair.

'It's okay, Lucy,' he said. 'Tell Sarah what you told me.

Oh great, Sarah thought. *So something has happened and now she doesn't even feel like she can talk to me about it.* This was her worst nightmare. She'd always wanted to be there for those children, always wanted to protect them from the dangers of the world - of the other sex. *What had happened to her? Was it a boy from school? Or a man alone in the park, lurking behind the trees. How could she have let this happen to her niece?*

'I know too many secrets,' Lucy whispered, peering down at her lap.

Sarah paused.

'Keep going, Lucy,' Tom prompted.

Lucy looked up at Tom expectantly and he nodded back to her.

She continued.

'Over the last few days, I've found things out.' She gulped. 'Too many things and I don't know what to do.'

Sarah glanced over at Tom, who did not meet her eye in return. Instead he kept his focus fixed on his former niece. Those kind, comforting eyes were watching, listening, supporting.

What was Lucy talking about?

'First mum...' Lucy choked on her words as tears gushed to her eyes. 'She doesn't want me anymore,' Lucy began to sob. 'She's had enough and she wants to replace me.'

Sarah shook her head and dismissed her immediately. 'That's not true Lucy.'

'It is!' she yelled, snapping her face up to scowl at her auntie, before softening again. 'She's been cross with me for months and it doesn't matter what I do.'

Sarah realised the mistake she had made; she needed to listen, not to dismiss her feelings. What Lucy was feeling was real, even if the facts were not. She sat back and rested her hands onto the floor, a move to show Lucy that she was relenting, listening.

'It doesn't matter what I do,' Lucy continued, twisting strands of her hair around her fingers, the same way her mother does when she's overwhelmed. 'I know I can be a bitch…'.

Sarah went to interject but she stopped herself. Lucy needed to speak her truth.

Lucy coughed before continuing.

'I can be a bitch, I'm not blind to that, but she just isn't ever there for me. It's like George is an angel and I'm the devil.' She paused, waiting for reassurance that she should continue.

'She actively avoids me, she ignores me, she never tries to listen or understand. And I just don't feel like that's okay. *I'm* the child!' Her voice began to rise, not in anger, but in disappointment and despair. '*She's* the parent, but she's given up trying to parent me. I know that I can be tricky at times, but doesn't she remember what it felt like to be a teenager? How fucking hard it is?' Lucy spluttered to a stop, her face streaming with tears.

The room fell to silence and Sarah considered what to say. *She sided with Lucy, she really did. She got it. But Abbie wasn't a bad person, and she wasn't a bad parent. Sarah knew how much Abbie loved that child. Somehow, a disconnect had emerged between them, causing a void to begin to grow.*

'Lucy,' Sarah started, and her niece nodded, ready to hear her words. 'I understand exactly how you feel,' she began, before pausing again.

Choose your words carefully.

'And there is no excuse for your mother making you feel that way. You feel how you feel and those feelings are real, no one can deny that.'

Lucy was nodding.

'Your mother has not been her best self recently, I have seen that too.' She reached out and held her hand. 'Perhaps she has neglected your feelings and forgotten how to put you first. That isn't okay.'

The love and protection that Sarah felt for her niece in that moment caused a physical ache in her chest.

'We've spoken about this before, Lucy - being a teenager is hard.' A flashback made her shiver. 'Really fucking hard.' She could feel Tom's eyes on her now. He was listening to her too. 'And those years are the times where you really need your parents - your mum - to support you, to understand you, to feel your woes and worries.'

'Exactly!' Lucy interjected. 'But mum does not want to even try. She just dismisses me as grumpy or rude or obnoxious. I am not trying to be those things!'

'I know you're not.' Sarah said calmly.

She couldn't lose her here.

'Of course you're not. You're going through so much and that's not to be underestimated. But Lucy, you have to remember that she is going through things too.'

Lucy shook her head dismissively. 'But those things are ruining my life! Do you know what people are saying? That she assaulted that girl Tia. That she's mentally unhinged. That she's going to get fired. And now they're saying she's having an affair with Mr Winterton!'

Sarah understood the weight of this all on her poor niece. She could not really imagine just how difficult this must be for a thirteen year old to comprehend and deal with. It was social suicide and utter despair. Yet, for perhaps the first time, she was not thinking about her niece. Instead she thought about Abbie, and began to really consider just how bad the situation was for her sister. *How had she gotten to this place, without her seeing?*

'She has her own struggles.' Sarah began. 'She has her own worries and I think she needs some help. She needs someone to lean on and to talk to. And sometimes when people are unable to control their own emotions or stress, it means that they do not have the capacity to help others - no matter how much they want to.'

Lucy was still silent.

'So that doesn't mean that she doesn't love or want you, sweetie.' Sarah said, feeling confident in her persuasive words.

'Sure,' Lucy said, standing up and brushing herself down, 'She just wants to replace me.'

Lucy grabbed her water and walked slowly into the next room. Sarah heard the door click shut.

'She would never want to replace you!' Sarah called after her, but it was in vain. Lucy could no longer hear her behind the closed door.

Sarah looked over at Tom and was suddenly aware of a secret she was not privy to. There was more to the story.

'So, what am I missing?' she asked.

Tom glanced back towards the closed door that Lucy had exited. For a moment, Sarah wondered if Tom was going to keep this from her - he'd always understood the importance of privacy - but this was different, Lucy was just a child.

He took a deep breath and turned back to face Sarah.

'She was searching for period products,' Tom began.

Sarah was surprised at his coolness. He'd never been comfortable talking about periods before. He used to avoid the bathroom if there were tampons around.

'But instead she found a stash of tests.'

'Tests?' Sarah questioned, beginning to feel impatient.

What the hell were they talking about?

'Pregnancy tests,' he explained.

Sarah's stomach somersaulted. *Surely not her too.*

'Loads of them apparently,' he continued. 'All negative.'

Sarah didn't understand. 'Well if they're negative, then what's the problem?' She was losing patience now. *At least her sister wasn't in the same bloody mess that she was.*

'Last night, she saw her go into the bathroom with a test in her hand,' Tom explained. 'Then she heard the sobbing.'

Sarah was confused. 'But they're negative!' she repeated, unable to piece the puzzle together.

Tom did not reply, he just looked at her blankly, waiting for the penny to drop.

'Oh,' Sarah said at last. 'Oh, I see.'

#

Sarah knocked gently on the bathroom door.

'Can I come in?' she pleaded.

The door lock clicked open.

Sarah didn't know what words she had, but that was okay. She couldn't make it better, but that was okay too. She just needed to show Lucy that she was there for her. That would be enough.

'I understand now,' she said, hugging her niece tight. 'I can understand how that might make you feel, and I'm so sorry.'

'It's not just that,' Lucy said, stepping away from her auntie and moving towards the mirror. She brushed out her hair and reached for a wipe. Carefully, she wiped her cheek, removing the light brush of blusher that had remained, despite the tears. Sarah would have to check which brand she was using.

'I understand what you said earlier, Sarah. I know that the world doesn't revolve around me. I'm not stupid.'

'I don't think you are!' Sarah jumped in, but Lucy brushed her off.

'I know, I know. I just mean, the stuff with Mum is tough, and I am sad that our relationship isn't great right now, but I know that it's not just her. I have a responsibility to try too.'

Sarah was in awe at her niece's maturity. *She'd not been quite so grown up, or emotionally intelligent at her age!*

'She's clearly got a lot going on and I want to be there for her.'

Lucy glanced down at her jumper and pulled at a loose string. 'Does Mum know about nan?'

'Nan?' Sarah asked. 'What about nan?'

'The lump,' Lucy said without hesitating. Immediately she realised her error.

Lucy saw Sarah's reflection, standing dumbfounded behind her in the mirror. She spun around to see her aunt in the flesh. 'You know about the lump right? You saw the letter!' Lucy willed.

Sarah shook her head, trying to remain calm and rational, while a thousand thoughts swam frantically around her brain.

'Oh God, Auntie Sarah, I'm sorry. I assumed all the adults knew. And when you were looking at the paperwork in the kitchen this afternoon, I just assumed there was another update, which is why nan had gotten cross with you.' Her face fell with guilt and sadness.

'Start at the beginning,' Sarah urged, calmly.

So Lucy did.

She explained about the letter she'd found in the drawer at her nan's house. It was addressed to Judy Abbingdon and it described the steps in the process now that she had found a lump. She explained having to scan the letter quickly as she could hear George coming in from the front room, but she saw the words: 'cancer ... treatment ... procedure.'

Lucy described noticing her nan's behaviour change over the next few days. She had caught her and Grandad hugging in the kitchen - alien behaviour - and she described noticing her nan's face softening, as if a secret had been released to the world. Grandad had been protective of her, bringing her cups of tea and making dinner while she rested. They kept sharing looks - secret glances that they thought no one else could see - but Lucy had seen.

Sarah's mind was rushing too fast. No thoughts

were complete before a new one arrived. She had to calm herself and slow her thinking, she had to try and make sense of the situation. She was suddenly very aware of the importance of her reaction; she could not risk panicking Lucy further. She would have to suppress her own emotions and try to focus on how to defuse the worry for her poor niece.

'That is a lot, Lucy.' Sarah began. 'You're dealing with a lot of stuff there. Grown up stuff that even adults would struggle with.'

Lucy nodded, looking straight ahead at Sarah, waiting for more.

'The first thing that I need to say is that you should never, ever, have to deal with anything like this alone. Secrets are evil; they eat you up from the inside out.' She almost choked on the irony of her own words. 'None of us should ever have to feel alone with the weight of a worry.'

Sarah was becoming stuck. What else was she supposed to say?

Lucy's attention was stolen as her eyes shifted over Sarah's shoulder.

'You did a good thing in sharing this with me tonight, Lucy.' Tom's voice was gentle and comforting. 'But you must listen to Auntie Sarah; she's right.' Sarah felt a tinge of pride in hearing Tom's words. 'No one should ever have to deal with the weight of worry alone. You are so loved. By so many people. We are all here for you. Forever.'

Sarah was startled by the 'we' in Tom's words. She'd tried to erase Tom from her life but in fact he was still so present in so many pockets of it - Lucy included.

Tom's hand brushed against Sarah's waist and

her heart fluttered.

'I'm going to pop the kettle on,' Tom said, beginning to walk back out of the bathroom. 'Lucy, you can sleep in the spare room tonight. Tomorrow, I think there are some honest conversations needed. For everyone's benefit.'

Tom's gaze switched with his final words, looking straight at Sarah instead. She watched him leave the room and wondered what he knew.

'Sarah,' came the meak voice, jolting her back into the room.

'Yes, sweetie.'

'There's something else.'

Oh for God's sake, she thought. *What more could there be?*

Lucy continued to observe Sarah, but her face had changed now. Sarah knew this face so well, but the expression she shared now was new - a mixture of embarrassment and, what else? Pity, perhaps.

'It's okay, Lucy, tell me what it is.'

Lucy gulped hard and began to wipe her hands down the sides of her legs, drying the perspiration.

'I was in the garden,' she whispered.

In the garden. What did that mean?

'Yes,' Sarah nodded, waiting for more clues.

'I was hiding down by the back gate, trying to take a moment to myself, to clear my thoughts.'

Suddenly, Sarah remembered the twitch in the darkness. She froze.

'I saw him,' she continued.

Sarah was grounded to the spot, the weight of the world pushing down through her body and cementing her feet to the floor. Inside, her instinct willed her to run away, but she was stuck still.

'I saw what he did to you.'

CHAPTER 28
ABBIE

She was alive.

There were sirens screaming too loudly, and muffled voices moving their way closer towards her. Her head throbbed.

A man's voice.

'We have to pop the door, love... don't panic... out of here before you know it.'

A drilling screech behind her ears. A wet, sticky liquid rolling down her cheek. Fading to blackness.

Eyes open.

A flicker of black hair brushing past her face.

The sirens quietening.

The drilling sound subsided.

A pull on her torso and a stabbing in her thigh.

Bright lights in the ambulance and the oxygen tanks and defibrillators positioned against the wall. A kind woman with blonde hair, tied back, sitting by her side, squeezing on her hand.

A putrid smell of disinfectant and a jolt as the van began to move.

She vomited over the edge of the gurney.

Embarrassment.

An attempt at an apology to the blonde woman who sprung into action.

Fading back to blackness.

CHAPTER 29
SARAH

She heard a groaning from the front room while she removed the oat milk from the fridge. The scent of the percolating coffee must have roused him.

Her return last night had not even caused him to stir. As she tiptoed through the back door, sliding it open softly in anticipation, she heard his thunderous roaring - punctuated every few seconds by a snort - and was comforted again. He would be out for the count and would rise, reproachfully once morning arrived.

The groan from the next room reverberated through to her. Instinctively, she grabbed another mug from the cupboard and began to pour into them both.

'Sore head?' she suggested, placing the steaming mug down beside him and taking a seat on the armchair.

'Just a bit,' he winced, sitting up and reaching out for the welcome drink. 'Thanks for this,' he gestured, tilting the coffee to her.

'That'll be the whisky,' she continued. 'You never learn.'

He rubbed at his stubble, the small pink smudge of his birth mark peeking out through the flecks of grey.

'I know, I know,' he moaned humbly, holding out an arm to welcome her over. 'Come and sit with me. I need a hug.'

She rose and moved towards him, placing

herself down gently beside him. As he leaned into her, his head rested against her breast, like a feeble child seeking comfort from a mother.

'Drink your coffee and you'll feel better,' she advised.

'I don't even remember getting home,' he admitted. 'No more alcohol for a month - I swear it,' he lied, attempting to fool himself. 'Just the gym and juices!'

She nodded along. He would certainly try, she knew that much was true. He'd do a week, maybe even two. But the drink would come back eventually, and so would the demons.

'Did you sleep well?' he asked her, 'I'm so sorry I didn't come up, I guess I didn't make it that far,' he declared with embarrassment.

'Not really,' she admitted. The truth would come out soon, so she should probably start by being honest straight away. He'd be calmer about it now. Now that he was sober again. His hungover mornings were always where he was at his most apologetic. He'd once bought her diamond earrings online, while simultaneously throwing up his hangover over the side of the basin.

'I got a call just after midnight to say that Lucy had been found.'

A spark of remembrance.

'Oh shit. Lucy!' he cried. 'Darling, I'm so sorry, I forgot. Lucy, of course. Is she okay?'

'She's fine, she's fine,' Sarah dismissed, waving a calming arm out. 'She was hiding in Tom's back garden.' She tossed the comment away like a piece of rubbish thrown casually into the bin, hoping it wouldn't draw too much attention. 'I went to fetch her, but she wanted to stay.'

She recounted the events with precision, calmly retelling the facts, looking ahead at the fireplace throughout. She only glanced away once to glance down at the mug that she held firmly between both hands. She could feel Simon's eyes burning through her cheek. The silence hung in the air like smoke.

Simon coughed. A delay tactic while he composed his thoughts.

'Well,' he started.

How would this go?

'I'm just thankful she's okay.'

Sarah turned to face him, but he had withdrawn his stare.

'Did Abbie and Ian not want to collect her?' he questioned calmly. He was beginning to try and unpick the story, trying to find holes in its fabric.

'We couldn't get through to either of them.'

'Hmmm,' he replied, sipping his coffee with a false composure.

'They were probably on the phone to the others,' she suggested. 'Whole bloody village was acting as a search party in the end.'

Simon seemed coy. *Was he embarrassed at the idea of everyone out searching for Lucy while he was at home like this?*

'We tried to call, then we sent a few texts. Eventually, I left her with Tom. One of them will have picked her up and taken her home by now,' she concluded.

As she spoke, she remembered that her first glance at her mobile this morning had not alerted her to any messages. She often had her notifications turned off, but she was sure she'd turned them back on last night. Perhaps she was mistaken and she'd forgotten to toggle them on during all the hysteria.

She reached for her phone, tucked securely in her dressing gown pocket and clicked the screen alight. Nothing.

'Weird that there's no new messages,' Simon interrupted, leaning over her shoulder.

She shifted away from him.

'My notifications are off,' she said. But as she spoke, a message pinged through. The banner identified the sender - Katie - and the first line was in capitals: 'JESUS, MY HEAD!'

'They seem rather on to me,' Simon lorded his catch over her.

She was bewildered. *Why had no one thought to update her? Not Abbie, not Ian, not even Tom.*

The messages continued to tumble through. Katie was awake and on a roll.

Is Lucy okay?

I swear I'm never touching tequila again! Rob is furious.

I think I might actually be sick.

And by the way, your sister is a lunatic, I swear she thought I was trying to shag her husband at one point!

Sarah ignored the pings and opened up the family group chat. No new messages.

She began typing: '

Just checking all is well and that Lucy made it home safely from Tom's. She seemed fine when I was with her xx

The message double ticked immediately. *All phones were on, then.*

She clicked out of the group and saw her dad typing just to her.

'Shall we go for a walk this morning?' Simon

questioned, begging to regain the focus.

'I'll need to check on Lucy and the others first,' she dismissed. *How could he not see what her priorities were today?*

'Of course, of course,' Simon agreed. 'Well I'm here until twelve, then Carl is picking me up.'

She nodded a dismissive agreement, still staring at the phone.

Typing

Why did it take old people so long to type?

Simon leaned in to her and kissed her cheek. She flinched instinctively and he recoiled backwards.

The humiliation on his face was glaring, his sunken eyes filled with remorse, as he held her gaze with sorrow.

'I'll miss you while I'm away,' he spoke softly.

She looked up and caught his eye.

'Huh?'

The tennis retreat! She'd forgotten all about it.

'I'll jump in the shower, shall I?' he asked, 'Then we can decide what our morning has in store for us before I have to go.' He began making his way across the room, his bare feet sticking to the wood with each step. 'I won't be long,' he called back, reaching the stairs and skipping his way up hurriedly.

Sarah did not reply. Her attention had been stolen by the message on her screen:

DAD

Abbie's in the hospital. Not sure of the details. Come round when you can. We are all here. x

As she heard the boiler click to life above her head, she switched her dressing gown for her coat, grabbed her keys from the side, slipped on a pair of shoes and marched straight for the door, slamming it

shut in her wake.
    Meanwhile, Simon sang idly along to the radio, as the steaming water poured down around him.
    'When it all breaks down, I'll be there.'

CHAPTER 30
ABBIE

There was a faint beeping of machines and hushed voices moving through the corridors. The bed she laid in felt too warm, too stiff and too unfamiliar, with crisp white sheets that scratched as she readjusted her position.

A pulsating pain in her thigh reminded her of the sirens and the drilling noise. *What had happened?*

A flash of images shook her to life - *sitting in the driver's seat, hands up in the air, the tree hurtling its way towards her.*

Where was she?

She opened her eyes and the bright white walls confirmed her suspicions.

Beside her stood a monitor, humming away mindlessly. An IV drip stretched its wires down into her arm, which she now noticed, laying patiently by her side. She was wearing a faded hospital gown, which hung loosely around her.

Where were her clothes?

Oh God, someone had seen her naked!

A thin chequered blanket lay across her legs, tucking her in neatly, refusing to let her escape the confines of the bed.

There was an ache in her neck, two pillows were too many, she'd have to adjust that. No other signs of damage - no visible cuts or bruises.

'Good morning,' came a familiar voice. She hadn't realised she had company. 'They told me you'd wake up soon. Gave us a bloody fright, you did!'

Ian leant in and pressed his lips against her cheek. His touch felt reassuring, comforting. She smiled an unconscious crease into her cheek as his kiss landed gently.

'How are you feeling?' he asked, his voice caressed with kindness, as he sat back down on the blue, foam chair by her side.

He looked tired. His hair was messy and his eyes were bloodshot red. His outfit was an odd choice, she thought. Why was he so dressed up and yet appearing so dishevelled at the same time?

'I'm not sure,' she answered, honestly. 'What happened?'

'The car lost control in the rain,' he said slowly. 'Probably startled by a lorry that was coming round the corner too fast. You must have spun out. The car hit a tree.' He reached forward and cupped her closest hand into his. 'You're extremely lucky to have come out of this with such minimal damage.'

She blinked slowly, attempting to piece together the puzzle. *Her father's party. Then she'd been driving in the rain. Why was she driving? A familiar feeling engulfed her: desperation, tinged with despair and fear.*

'Lucy!' she exhaled, before the memory had fully formed in her brain. 'Where is Lucy?' she shrieked, sitting up in bed, eyes wide and crazed.

Ian placed a hand on her shoulder and gently coaxed her back to a lying position. 'Calm down, Lucy's fine,' he shushed convincingly.

It made no sense. Lucy was lost. She was going to find her. She could be hurt or in some sort of danger.

Then the same intrusion appeared again – *Lucy doesn't want her, doesn't need her. No one needs her.*

She shook her head, erasing the words, trying to

create space in her brain for clarity.

'Where is she?' Abbie implored. 'Where *was* she?'

'It's a long story, but I promise you, she's absolutely fine. She was found safe and well. Before we even found you!' he added.

The irony hit her and she felt a wave of embarrassment.

As she scanned the room again, she noticed for the first time that they were not alone. The curtains that should have protected her privacy were wide open and she noticed five other cubicles that she shared her space with. Most had curtains closed, but directly in front of her lay an elderly woman. Until now, she'd been statuesque, not moving a single inch meaning that neither Abbie or Ian had cause to look over at her. But now, her finger placed itself against a button and her bed began to rise, slowly. When reaching its desired height, she removed her finger and continued to stare straight ahead at the soap opera that threatened to ignite itself in her field of vision.

'Do you think you could close the curtain?' Abbie whispered, nodding a sideways head towards their voyeur.

Ian obeyed the command and stood to slide the curtains shut, much to the annoyance of their new companion, who screwed her face in dismay and huffed in audible dissatisfaction.

'She wanted to come and see you this morning,' Ian continued, but Abbie had lost the trail of the conversation and needed to rejoin.

'Sorry?' she asked, shaking her head in confusion.

'Lucy,' he prompted. 'She wanted to come and see you this morning - George too.'

Abbie's heart dropped in her chest as the pieces began to connect. She'd felt utterly helpless last night. Everything was falling apart and she had no control over anything. Her job, her marriage, her children. And that wasn't all. She had a sinking feeling that there was more, but she couldn't remember what it was.

'I said it was too soon,' Ian continued.

Abbie interrupted him immediately. 'No!' she announced. 'I want to see them. Why can't I see them?' Her voice was becoming hysterical.

'Abbie, calm down,' Ian gestured for her to quieten her voice with his hands. 'You've just had a car crash. You've got a concussion and a broken leg for goodness sake, so I suggested that now was probably not the best time.'

'They are my children, Ian, and I can decide when I want to see...' she stopped mid sentence as her gaze slid down on the blanket. 'Broken leg?' she questioned.

Ian recognised her confusion and his face softened.

'Oh,' he whispered, lifting her blanket and exposing her left leg, suddenly alert to her lack of awareness.

Below the scratchy sheets, Abbie's leg was cocooned in a white plaster cast, stretching from her ankle to the top of her thigh. The leg was slightly raised on an extra cushion and it was double the width of her right. She wondered how she'd missed its size below the sheets.

Staring at her leg, the image seemed so silly, so

dramatic. She was horrified at the drama she'd caused, the fuss she'd created, the people that had been affected by her carelessness, her selfishness.

She glared back at Ian who was staring back at her. His look was unrecognisable. *What was he thinking? Was he judging her? Disgusted by her? Embarrassed by her?*

She continued to watch him, his warm brown eyes, his soft, undefined cheeks wrapping around his face. It was the same face she'd known for years, but his expression was different - she had never seen this stare before.

The howling noise startled her and she spun her focus around the room, shocked at the volume, but unaware of its source.

Ian's reaction was unflinching. He launched himself upon her, throwing his giant engulfing arms around her shoulders; protecting her with his firm grip and consoling her with his warm embrace as the noise grew louder.

It was only as he rocked her back and forth with a gentle shhing murmur in her ear, that she realised that the noise was coming from herself.

She felt the tension return to her chest, felt the rigidity clamber its way back to her upper body, felt the fear creep back into her brain.

'It's okay, Abbie.' he whispered, without releasing his grip. 'I am here and I have got you.' He continued to hold her.

She took a deep breath and allowed herself to melt into him.

The heap of boulders that towered, mountainous and colossal within her shifted slightly and she felt the release of one small stone.

#

The subdued, functional aroma of the antiseptic cleanliness was replaced with a scent of stewed vegetables and overcooked pasta. It wafted its way onto the ward, and her neighbours, who had obviously been there for too long, sat up to attention at the familiar recognition.

'Fancy some lunch?' Ian questioned. 'I hear the food has improved greatly since George was born.' His lie was obvious but sweet natured.

She'd always hated hospitals and Ian knew that. When George was born, they insisted on keeping her in for three days 'for observation'. George was fine but her blood pressure was 'slightly high' so they wouldn't let her leave.

'Of course it's slightly high, I've just pushed a nine pound baby out of my vagina!' she had screamed at the ward nurse. 'Of course I'm feeling a little more stressed than normal.'

The nurse had appeased her with a promise, 'You'll be home tomorrow, I'm sure.'

Tomorrow rolled around and the day glided by with the endless hope of escape. Abbie stalked the clock, willing the doctor to arrive on his rounds to finally discharge her. The hourly observations proved repetitive with the same promise: 'He shouldn't be much longer.' So at 5pm, she ripped the canular from her arm, packed up her bags, and announced to the reception staff that she would not spend one moment more in this establishment. She was off!

'No thank you,' Abbie replied to her husband. The thought of food made her nauseas.

'Okay,' he said, taking a seat beside her and scraping the chair across the hard flood so as to see her face-on. 'I think we need to talk.'

We need to talk. She heard the words repeat in her ears. *Had he finally had enough?*

She had constantly suspected that he would leave her, that there was someone else. The clues had been there, but she'd shoved them aside, hoping they were untrue.

She didn't have the strength to answer him. *We* need to talk meant *he* needed to talk. She'd let him speak. Let him admit to his affairs, how he no longer loved her and couldn't imagine spending any more time with such a worthless, middle aged wreck.

'It is pretty clear that things have been getting worse for some time now,' he began, his words echoing in slow motion around her, as if hearing them from an outer body place. 'It's time we made some changes.'

She had no words to reply. How could she reply? She had no control over this, she was merely a pawn in his game.

'Firstly, I think you need to take some time away from work.'

What was he on about? She was already suspended!

'I know they've already asked you to take some time off, but I think you should tell them that you're not willing to work for them at all any more. Not after the way they've treated you.'

She was confused. *What was this?*

'Or perhaps,' he continued. 'Maybe teaching isn't the right path for you anymore.'

She sat up straighter in the hospital bed and blinked hard, readjusting her position to see him more clearly, in an attempt to understand his words.

'Ian, what are you talking about?'

'That job!' He spoke surely and with confidence. 'You've been unhappy for ages, but I don't think it's just unhappiness anymore. I think you're overworked, overstressed, and underappreciated.'

She was dumbstruck by his words. *Where was this coming from?*

'And it's affecting you in ways that are starting to scare me.'

She blinked hard again. His eyes were soft and teary.

She shook herself and jolted back to reality. 'So how exactly will we pay the bills?' she spat at him, more aggressively than she meant to.

He pacified her concern. 'We've still got my earnings, and a fair bit saved in the bank. It will tide us over until you have taken some time to figure all this out.'

'Figure it all out?' she questioned.

'Yes,' he replied. 'Most people don't love their job, but most people don't hate it either. Most people don't get to a point where their job is infiltrating every other area of their lives with its poison.'

She was stunned.

'You've never spoken like that before,' she whispered, softening to his honesty.

'Well, I've never needed to.' he admitted. 'You used to love your job. And after that, you at least pretended that you loved it still. Only now is it clear - to all concerned - that you cannot continue like this. You cannot continue being this miserable. And I can no longer sit still and stay silent. No more mantras: *this too shall pass*. No. We need to make it pass.' He held onto her hand. 'You're my wife and I love you. We're a team.'

We're a team, she thought.

'Which brings me onto my second point,' he continued as the puzzlement continued to sway over her. 'We need to get you reconnecting with your children, and with me.'

Shame swept over her again. *Failure.*

'Abigail Hart, you are the most wonderful wife and the most kind, caring, maternal mother in this world.'

She gulped.

'But you haven't had the time or space to enjoy being a mother recently, and your sadness over that fact is palpable.'

Her face was still in shock, her eyes wide and staring hard.

'Slow things down, Abbie, and enjoy being who you are for a while. Everything else will fall into place.'

'But...' she went to speak but there were too many thoughts. She did not know where to start.

'I know there's a lot to sort out, the details are blurry, but I know one thing for sure, Abbie: it's better to slow down than to break down.'

Instinctively, she snorted a short, sharp laugh. 'But I am breaking down, Ian. I feel like that's exactly what I am doing.'

'Well maybe you have been breaking,' he admitted.

The truth hit her like a punch to the stomach.

'Maybe you have been breaking, Abbie,' he repeated, 'but you're not broken. We will mend the splintered pieces and build you back up. Together.'

'It's all been a lot,' she admitted.

She wasn't sure the words had ever escaped

her mouth before and she felt like she was setting something free, something that had been trapped inside her for far too long.

'It's like I woke up one day and suddenly, the person that I was was gone,' she began. Now the words were tumbling out, mixed between the ugly tears and the sobbing breaths. 'And for what? Certainly no one was grateful. Not the school children or their parents, not the headteacher or the CEO, not my family. No one even knows the woman I was - the woman I wanted to be - and I had no time to talk about it because I was drowning under the marking and the planning, the spreadsheets and the action plans, the laundry and the roast dinners.'

Ian understood. 'I know who you were, Abbie,' he smiled.

She remembered their first date, their honeymoon, the day they found out about Lucy.

'You were pretty fucking awesome! And I want you back again.'

'I've been desperate for a way out,' she admitted, and he nodded in acknowledgement.

'I wanted another baby,' she said. *No point holding the truth back now.*

He continued to nod.

She was unsure if what she was saying was news to him, or if he was just listening politely. She would keep talking either way, the words tumbling out before she even knew what they were.

'I'm not sure I even really wanted one though,' she continued. 'I think I wanted out of my job and I think I missed Lucy.'

She was crying hard again now.

'My sweet little girl who has been growing up

and growing away from me. I just wanted her back.'

'I understand,' he said.

She eyed him sceptically. *Did he really understand?*

'I miss her too,' he said. 'Mourn for her, even.'

Abbie was shocked. He'd never spoken this candidly before.

'It's so hard to stop one day and realise that your baby has grown up. And you feel like you missed it because you never got to appreciate the last times.' he whispered, tears pricking in his eyes. 'You don't realise the last times are the last times until they have already happened. The last time your baby wakes up from a bad dream, needing your comfort. The last time you watch them in a nativity play. The last time your child holds your hand in public.'

She saw him now, in a way she had never seen him before: raw, honest, true. *How had they missed knowing that they were sharing the same thoughts? The same feelings? The same mournings?*

They both wiped at their cheeks in unison.

'And I thought you were having an affair.' She said bluntly. 'While we're being honest.'

He laughed.

'You silly woman.' He leaned in and kissed her gently. 'Why would I ever want anyone other than you?'

#

She was aware of Lucy's presence before she opened her eyes.

In the nightmare she was having, the tree hurtling towards her gave way to a more peaceful scene. The tree spun off into the torrential wind and the air calmed to a still. Clouds faded from grey to white and the sun rose behind one, peeking out as if to check that it was safe to show its face. The air became warmer and a small fairy floated down from behind a cloud in the sky and rested itself on her lap. The car had disappeared and she was no longer sitting in its seat. Instead, she was aboard a flying carpet which bobbed around in the air, waiting for its journey to begin.

She was absorbed by a feeling of safety and contentment. In this dream, she was calm and secure. She had a deeper knowledge of what was to come and it was shielded from the anxiety that her previous nightmare had been engulfed with.

The fairy continued to watch Abbie, but she was silent. The look said all that was needed. I forgive you, I love you, we are going to be okay.

With her eyes still closed, Abbie reached her arm out and held her hand wide, expectantly. Within seconds, the hand met another and she knew that Lucy was there with her.

In that moment, she was desperate to keep her eyes closed; to stay in the space between her dream and her reality. The limbo felt tranquil and peaceful. She had the security from her warm dream, mixed with the reality of her daughter's hand. But she knew that she had to jump. She had to free herself from the illusion and trust in the fate of reality. She opened her eyes.

'Hi Mum,' smiled Lucy. 'What are you like? You'll do just about anything to steal the attention back won't you!'

Abbie laughed instinctively, causing her to pull a muscle in her stomach and wince with pain.

Lucy squeezed her mum's hand - two short

sharp bursts - and the memory flooded back: her first days of school when she'd been too anxious to leave her mother's side. They'd created a signal - two short squeezes to mean 'I love you'.

Abbie's heart lurched with fragility.

'I was worried about you,' Abbie admitted softly.

'I know, Mum,' Lucy spoke with shame in her voice. 'I'm so sorry. I didn't mean to worry you.'

'Why did you go to Uncle Tom's? She asked, genuinely bemused.

Lucy shrugged her shoulders. 'I just wanted to be somewhere comforting.'

Abbie was confused. 'Is that how you feel about Tom's house?'

Lucy considered the question, wondering how to verbally explain her feelings. *Why did she feel that way about Tom's house?*

'You remember his parties?' she started. 'In the summertime, in the garden.'

Abbie nodded.

'Well, when I think back to those days, there's a feeling that washes over me. I remember the laughter and the warmth, the fun and the comradery.'

Abbie was surprised by her daughter's eloquence. She didn't interrupt her, but let her continue to speak.

'It's a kind of nostalgia, I suppose. I mean, I was just a kid then and things always look better when you're younger, right?'

Her mother nodded. She was listening.

'There's blissful ignorance in childhood. Before you grow up and start to understand more about how the world really works.' Lucy paused. 'But it doesn't matter whether ignorance played a part, it doesn't really matter what the facts were or what was true, because the way those days made me feel was real - it was pure happiness.'

Abbie squinted at her daughter and noticed how her face had changed. Her chubby, dimpled cheeks had made way to high, naturally contoured cheekbones. 'I've never heard you speak like that, Luce,' she said, in a mixture of shock and admiration.

Lucy shrugged.

Abbie realised her moment and chose to take it. 'I suppose you're right, things get harder as you get older. More complicated too. And we all wish, at times, that we could slink back into the blissful ignorance of youth.'

Lucy was watching her mother and listening intently. No phone in sight. *What a welcome change.*

'I've been there myself.' Her words were calm and honest. 'I've found myself feeling scared that my life is changing too quickly, that my children are growing up too fast and that I am hurtling away from all those wonderful moments in my past. But there's beauty in growing up too,' she said, her words tumbling out honestly, before she was even aware of what they were. 'You get to grow into yourself and move ahead on to new pathways. Things don't always go to plan, but that's okay too. You can change direction or choose a different route if you want - it's exciting really.'

Lucy considered her mother's words. 'Sounds terrifying to me,' she said earnestly, 'Making decisions and being in charge of your own destiny, trying to face the world alone.'

'Ah,' Abbie interjected instinctively, 'but see that's where you're wrong.' She reached out a hand

and grabbed Lucy's once again. 'You can't do any of it alone, my dear. It's taken me a long time to learn that one. You have to lean on other people; work with other people; depend upon other people.'

Lucy considered her words carefully. She scrunched her eyebrows together, weighing up the pros and cons. 'But doesn't that open you up to the unknown? Doesn't it make you more vulnerable? More able to get hurt?'

'Perhaps,' she admitted, 'But what's the alternative? And the truth is that you can't ever really control things. We fool ourselves into thinking that we control our own path, but we can't really, no more than we can control our neighbour's path. So we have to find a way to open ourselves up to the fragility of life and enjoy being with others along the way.'

Lucy smiled. She could not remember the last time she spoke at length with her mother, or even had a conversation where they both looked and listened to one another.

Abbie smiled back. 'Everything in life that is worth a damn is people, Lucy. It's all about people.'

Lucy nodded in agreement and understanding. Their connection in that moment was palpable and beautiful.

Another stone crumbled free.

CHAPTER 31
SARAH

Stepping through the sliding glass doors, a thick, sterile air greeted her. Nurses moved briskly down across the gleaming white tiles, as she headed towards the welcome map on the far wall, to the left of the reception.

She was looking for Ward Three, and the map confirmed the directions that Ian had shared: Second floor. Turn right.

Sarah eyed the stairs, but settled in front of the lift instead, pressing the button and observing the bright illumination of the arrow.

She was alone as it began to rise, staring back at her reflection with concern. Her mother had lent her a pair of trousers and a jumper (she'd chosen black - unassuming and neutral) yet she still felt uncomfortably unfamiliar, awkward and itchy. She looked older than normal, more stressed, more haggard. The fake tan kept a luminescence in her cheek, but her eyes could not hide their exhaustion. She would never normally have left the house like this.

As the doors dinged open, she was greeted by a long corridor, lined with numbered rooms on each side. Her footsteps echoed down the hall as she passed bulletin boards of faded notices and health tips.

Top tips to improve your mental wellbeing
What happens when you quit smoking?
Are you ready for pregnancy?

She paused her step, composing herself for a moment. Of course, she had not forgotten about the pregnancy - the tablets were waiting patiently in her bedside drawer - but she had other things on her mind right now. That problem would have to wait.

As she turned into Ward Three, she spotted her sister immediately. Her lunch had just been placed before her and Abbie scrutinised it sceptically, debating whether or not to risk taking a bite.

'I wouldn't if I were you,' Sarah joked, heading towards her sister and leaning an obnoxious glare down at her lunch.

Abbie laughed. A genuine, honest laugh that reminded them both of childhood.

'Hey you,' Abbie said, as Sarah negotiated where the safest seat might be. She dismissed the plastic chair and perched herself onto the side of the bed instead, forcing Abbie to shuffle her good leg over.

'I suppose a private room wasn't available,' Sarah joked.

'Unfortunately not,' Abbie replied. 'They like to keep them free in case someone really worthy comes in. They don't just let any old riff raff have a private room, you know.'

Sarah let the smile fade naturally from her face, before attempting to cut through the mocking with anything serious. This had been a regular pattern throughout their entire relationship. Don't get in too deep. Don't discuss real feelings that might make the other party uncomfortable. Definitely don't cry!

'So, how are you?' Sarah began, softening her voice.

Abbie felt the shift and considered her reply. She prodded her lunch with a fork before speaking earnestly. 'Not great, really.'

'Ian said you've got a broken leg.'

'Yep,' Abbie replied, lifting the cover and displaying her cast.

'Are you in pain?'

'Not really. They're keeping me topped up.'

There was a moment of silence. It did not feel awkward. Instead, it spoke loudly of all the things that were still unsaid, reminding them of the connection they shared and the power they held to lessen each other's woes. Sarah felt the inevitability of the difficult conversation that would follow.

'Abbie,' she started. 'What happened?'

Abbie blinked hard and she spoke. The words, when they came, began to pour out.

'I think I've been miserable for some time,' she began. Sarah leant back slightly, listening intently. This time (for perhaps the first time) she really wanted to hear, to absorb and to understand what her sister was saying. *She needed to know the truth.*

'I've always been on the treadmill,' she continued. 'Cranking up the pace, little by little as the years went by. I was proud of my ambition, my achievements, my success.'

Sarah relaxed into the bed, understanding that Abbie's words were true and deep.

'But as time has moved on, I've found myself both unable to keep up and unable to jump off. I have always prided myself on my ability to juggle it all, so when it started to feel like too much, I didn't know where to turn or what to do. Work had become insufferable and I was reaching the end of every day with a to-do list longer than the one I had written at 7am that morning.

'Although it wasn't just the stress of the tasks that needed to be done, everything else that had made the job palatable was suddenly vanishing too. I could no longer enjoy the lightbulb moment for my year eight student when he finally understood the irony in Macbeth; or celebrate the success of my bottom set year ten student moving from a grade one to a grade three. None of that was good enough anymore. Instead, I had to churn out grade fives - over and over - for everyone! No time for personalised teaching along the way.'

Sarah nodded. She had never really considered Abbie's job like that before. Her world was self-governed. She wrote what she wanted and picked up freelance work as she pleased. No agenda that she needed to meet or deadline she needed to reach - only the ones she set for herself.

'Then the parents started to become disgruntled too: *My child needs more*, or *Where's the personalised support?* And I agreed! But there was just no time. It was an impossible job. I couldn't please them all. *'The Trust needs to see results,'* she continued to mimic. *'The data just doesn't look good enough.'*

Sarah continued watching her, in awe of her honesty and fragility.

'So by the time I was getting home at night, I was exhausted, overwhelmed and overstressed. The days were getting longer and the joy and pleasure I once got from teaching was lessening day by day.'

Sarah was dumbfounded. She had no idea that Abbie was feeling this way. Abbie had always taught, and had always been so passionate about it being her vocation. *When had things changed and why hadn't she noticed?*

'You've never said any of this before,' Sarah noted.

Abbie shook her head. 'I didn't want to admit to feeling like a failure,' she admitted. 'I just kept thinking that if I sacrificed something else or if I worked harder at my time management then I could find the secret to getting back on track.'

'But there was no secret,' Sarah said as her sister nodded in agreement. 'There is no magic fix. It wasn't what you were or weren't doing, it's a systemic issue. So you were always doomed to fail.'

'Exactly,' she admitted. 'Meanwhile, I had become so consumed by work, that I was forcing myself to neglect other areas of my life. Lucy became a teenager in the blink of an eye, and I didn't give it the attention it deserved. You know how much I love that child...' Abbie's voice broke as the words fell out.

'Of course I do,' Sarah replied.

Abbie had always been an amazing mum - naturally maternal and destined to produce the most miraculous little people that the world had ever seen. She read all the parenting books, educating her to the max, before cherry picking the sections she believed in most.

Abbie's children did not have explosive tantrums in the supermarket, they did not hit other children, they did not refuse their bedtimes. Because Abbie had raised them to understand rules, to have clear boundaries and to recognise how to manage conflict. She showered her children with praise and pride, while still keeping them humble.

Sarah's mind raced back to when Lucy had come home with her first reading age certificate. At age five, Lucy had a reading age of eight years and three months.

Sarah's instinct had been to wave the paper

around, announcing for all to hear that her niece was the smartest little girl that ever there was, but Abbie's approach had been different. She'd crouched down to Abbie and asked her how she felt about the result.

'I'm pleased with it,' Lucy had replied, 'because I tried really hard.'

'Then so am I,' Abbie spoke back to her daughter, 'because I will always be incredibly proud of you for trying your hardest, no matter what score you receive.'

Abbie squeezed her daughter tight and said no more on the subject.

At the time, Sarah was cross with her sister for not making more of a big deal of it, but in time she began to understand.

When Lucy was seven, Sarah began noticing the way Abbie handled conflict resolution. Instead of shouting at the children, she would listen to them and empathise with their upset (no matter how ridiculous it seemed) before offering a sympathetic cuddle and a kind word. Abbie did not lose her temper. She was the perfect mum and her children always knew just how loved they were.

'She knows that you love her,' Sarah interjected, as Abbie's bottom lip began to quiver.

Abbie shook her head. 'No,' she continued, 'I began to neglect her. The most precious thing in my life, and I did not have the time to try to understand her. She's going through the hardest time in her life and I need to be there for her; to let her slam doors and grunt and eye roll, without screaming back at her. Her hormones are flooding her body and she's dealing with so much, but instead of showing her warmth and compassion, I've been showing her hostility and a short temper.'

Sarah considered denying her sister's claims - she hated seeing her this upset - but the truth was, she was right. Recently, she had not been the supermum that she once was.

'I kept thinking of ways to buy myself time,' Abbie continued. 'Some time to be with the kids again and to stop them from pulling away from me. I was losing my grip and I needed to invent a way to pull them back.'

Sarah watched Abbie gulp and wandered where this was going.

'So I started trying to get pregnant,' she admitted. Her face flushed and she looked almost ashamed.

'I thought that a new baby would fix things, you know? I thought it would give Lucy an opportunity to connect with me - she'd be such a fab big sister again. But it would also, you know, buy me more years before they all grew up and abandoned me.'

'I understand that,' Sarah said, 'But did you really think that, in reality, that would work?'

Abbie shrugged her shoulders. 'I got pregnant once too.'

Sarah was shocked. *How had she not known this?*

'About eighteen months ago.'

Sarah felt a churning in her stomach. Saliva began to build in her mouth, bringing on the feeling that she might need to vomit. She suppressed it and continued listening.

'I didn't even tell Ian.' she admitted, shamefully. 'I kept it to myself for weeks. But then I started bleeding.'

Sarah did not speak, but placed a hand against

Abbie's thigh. She had never understood people's grief at losing a fetus that was never fully formed, but looking at Abbie now helped her to understand. It wasn't about losing a fetus, it was about losing the dream, the promise of something to come.

'I went for a scan, fearing the worst, and they confirmed it for me.' As she spoke, a single tear rolled down her cheek. 'So it was gone. It was over, just like that.'

'And you never told Ian?' Sarah's words sounded more confrontational than she meant for them to.

Abbie shook her head. 'Why would I? There was no need. What would have been gained?'

'The sharing of grief,' Sarah urged, 'The connection with someone else. The burden released from you!'

Abbie shrugged off her comments. 'It's fine, honestly. I was okay. I am okay. But it's just the hope, you know? The dream. I don't think that in reality I ever want another baby. A baby wouldn't fix things. A baby would disrupt what we have - and I love what we have!' She paused. 'It's just the fantasy of doing it again, going back to the start and having the expanse of time before us again, the security in knowing there's another eighteen years before they're gone. That's what I was scared to lose.'

Sarah understood.

All this time, she'd looked at her sister with mild irritation - the woman who had it all but didn't quite appreciate it. But now she saw it differently and realised that she could never really know what a person was going through unless she took the time to try and walk around in their shoes. Sarah had never taken the time.

'I'd just got myself to a bad place, thinking the worst. I was convinced that Ian was having an affair for a really long time.'

'Pah!' Sarah's laugh escaped before she could control it. 'Sorry,' she corrected herself. 'But you thought Ian was having an affair? *Ian?*'

'I did,' Abbie said earnestly.

'Oh Abbie, the man loves you more than any man has ever loved any woman alive. He would never cheat!'

'I think I know that now,' Abbie conceded. 'But I convinced myself that I wasn't enough for him. I made myself believe that no one could love me. I used to read his messages,' she admitted, embarrassed at the memory, 'and I'd jump to all sorts of crazy conclusions.'

Sarah felt a deep pit of empathy for her sister. How awful to live with that sort of pain.

'It all just became too much. I realise now that the thing I was feeling was crippling anxiety, but I didn't really know what that meant, or what that was. Anxiety isn't a concern over what's happening in the moment, it's a build up of fears, frets and thoughts about what is to come. Anxiety explodes from concern over things that are further along the treadmill, but are hurtling towards you at speed. It's a fear that when those things reach our feet, we will not have the strength or agility to kick them off the machine. That's what I've been suffering from. That's what I've been trying to figure out how to deal with.'

'I'm sorry I haven't been there for you,' Sarah admitted, honestly, her voice cracking slightly at the vulnerability.

'I'm sorry too,' Abbie replied, 'That I haven't

been there for you.' She nodded down at Sarah's stomach. 'You've got a thing or two going on in your own life, I hear.'

Sarah was caught off guard. *How on earth did Abbie know?* But before the thought had finished in her mind, the truth interrupted it. *Katie!*

'Are we all finished here, dear?' the nurse asked, arriving stealthily behind them and reaching for her plate. 'I bet you're feeling a bit better now, eh?'

Abbie smiled at her sister as the plate was cleared.

'Yes,' she said, staring straight at Sarah. 'Yes, I think I am.'

CHAPTER 32
ABBIE

'She'll be home by six,' he said, speaking into the receiver while smiling at his wife.

'Yes, yes, you can come straight round, I'm sure she'll be glad to see you.' Ian rolled his eyes in mild humour.

'Lasagne sounds lovely, but that really isn't necessary. We can pick up fish and chips en route,' he continued. 'Okay, lasagne it is. Thank you!'

Ian finished the conversation and walked back into the ward, where Abbie was waiting, perched hesitantly on the edge of the bed.

'She's jumped straight into overprotective mother mode,' Ian chuckled, shoving her trainers into the overnight bag he'd brought with him that morning. 'She's talking about coming round between nine and three every day to support you in the house, in between pickups and drop offs for the kids.'

Abbie smiled at the sincerity of her mother. She'd always dismissed the idea that she was a devoted maternal woman - 'I'm more than just your mother, you know!' she used to say in defence when they were younger - but, in fact, she always stepped up when they needed her. She remembered that now.

'Well, I suppose I will need to ask for some help, here and there, won't I?' she admitted, pointing down at her leg, which forked out awkwardly before her.

'There we are!' Ian cheered. 'You're learning already,' he smiled, leaning down to her. 'Sometimes we have to lean on each other.'

He kissed her on the forehead as she rolled her eyes and frowned at him, hiding a slight smile in the corner of her mouth.

'I'll go and find the nurse - see about getting that wheelchair, shall I?' he said, almost to himself, as he began to march out into the corridor.

Her phone pinged and she reached over to retrieve it from the bedside unit.

Mum:

I'm making lasagne for tea. Don't let Ian pick up fish and chips! Dad's coming too. And Sarah.'

Abbie smiled at her mother's kindness. She needed to find a way to be helpful, to show her love language and this was it: Acts of service.

Thanks, Mum. See you soon x

Abbie considered what Sarah had been doing since she left her this afternoon. Had she gone home or headed straight for mum and dads? Had she spoken to them about what she'd told her? Surely not in so much detail. Secrets weren't a good idea, but some things need not be said.

After Abbie had finished speaking, it was Sarah's turn to share. And Sarah's words had been shocking. Her admissions were unexpected and they left Abbie feeling concerned. But the act of talking had also released pressure from within them both. There was a weight lifted from knowing that others were going through shit too. Other people had secrets, dramas and horrors in their own lives. Things that they were trying to face alone. Things they didn't feel they could share with the world.

But Sarah *had* shared. And Abbie knew, as soon as the words left her mouth, that this would be the start of her getting some help. The start of things changing.

'So Katie told you then?' she'd said, as Abbie glanced down at her sister's stomach.

She hadn't meant to embarrass her, or to put her on the spot. Abbie had been vulnerable and she felt like they were connecting. This was her time to listen to Sarah now. To try and help.

She knew that Sarah didn't want children. They'd never been in her plan. She would be struggling with the dilemma she was facing. And she'd be going through it alone. *God knows Katie would have been no help.*

Abbie nodded at her sister.

'Last night, at the party. She was pretty drunk. She probably doesn't even remember.'

Sarah didn't speak. She seemed overwhelmed, confused, and lonely. She'd never really seen her sister like this before. She was always so sure; she held herself with an air of superiority - not an ego, but a confidence. She had her shit together.

Abbie continued to sit quietly. She'd done her talking. Now was the time for Sarah to share.

It was a while before Sarah spoke, but when she did, the words were both delicate and assured.

'People look at me and they think I have it all,' she started. 'I see the way strangers watch me. They see the makeup, the designer bags, the car, and they decide they hate me before they even know me.'

Abbie nodded. *People would definitely judge Sarah before they knew her.*

'The people that know me know I'm down to earth though, right? They see who I was before and how hard I've worked to get to where I am now.'

'Of course,' Abbie had replied. 'You're like a

Clydesdale when it comes to work, Sarah and you deserve everything you have.'

'But we all have secrets.'

Sarah looked over her shoulder and peeked her head through the privacy curtain, turning it both ways to inspect the room. Her stealthiness was almost amusing to Abbie and she had to restrain a giggle. *How serious could her secrets be?*

'When I was younger, I shrugged it off as a bad experience that I would learn from.'

Her voice was serious, shaking Abbie back into focus.

'I wasn't a girl who was desired by boys, by men. So when someone showed a flicker of interest, I was flattered.'

Abbie had no idea where Sarah was going. Sarah hadn't been a stereotypical beauty - a little overweight, slightly geekish - but she'd been popular. Maybe not in the traditional sense, but she'd had so many friends, she still did. Abbie envied her.

'But they weren't nice to me, Abbie.' Sarah averted her eyes, staring down at the stoney floor tiles. Her leg was twitching nervously.

'The boys who finally showed me interest. They weren't nice. They weren't gentle or kind. There was no romance.'

Abbie was beginning to understand what her sister was saying, but she had no clue how to react. *What was she supposed to say?* She stayed silent and still, listening hard and trying to absorb every word.

'Sometimes I tried to embrace it - dom sex or something - but that wasn't what it was.'

Sarah uncrossed her legs and crossed them over the other way, her other foot now twitching back and forth.

'I guess I learned that *that* was how I should be treated. Like I was unworthy or something.'

She glanced up at her sister, checking that she was with her, that her initial admissions hadn't scared her off or been too heavy. Abbie gave her the nod to continue.

So, I built myself up in other ways. I grew my business, I made money, I carved out my own success. And I tried to reinvent myself. No longer the chubby loser from school, but the intelligent professional, who could also be beautiful.'

Sarah paused at the sound of a nurse behind the screen. She waited until the patient's obs had been checked - at least a minute of silence - before the nurse shuffled away again and Sarah was able to continue.

'But something was broken within me. I think that deep down, I always felt unworthy, like I didn't deserve success or happiness. Like maybe I deserved to be treated badly, or to be made to feel shit.'

Abbie could not control the shaking of her head. *How on earth could her sister feel that way?*

'Of course, I had some lovely relationships, but I could never shake the feeling that something wasn't right, like maybe it was all too good to be true and that I didn't deserve them. So I ended up back with the bad guys. The ones who act loving and attentive in public, but behind closed doors.' She stopped. 'They're a different beast.'

Abbie was confused, now. Was she talking about Simon? About Tom?

'I've only ever wanted a husband, Abbie. A man to treat me right and to love me wholly. I never needed to be a mum or to have a house, or even money. I wanted someone who adored me and was besotted with me. Someone who would choose me, every time. And if the other stuff came along after, then great, but if it didn't, that would be okay too. Because we'd be together, a team, a unit. And that would be enough.'

Abbie thought back to Ian's words earlier in the day. *'We're a team'. How had she overlooked all that they had?*

'I can't keep this baby, Abbie.'

Sarah was staring straight at Abbie now, a desperation on her face, her eyes wide and her face sunken.

'Maybe if I had all those things, a baby would make sense and would slot into the dream. But I can't keep this baby,' she said again.

A flicker in Sarah's eye alerted Abbie to the truth, as if a switch had been turned on and suddenly the room was illuminated in facts. As if the foggy haze had lifted and a spotlight now shone on the clues that had previously been hidden.

Simon's jokes at Sarah's expense. His refusal to speak about his past. His constant appearance at her side.

'Simon's not a nice man, Abbie.' The words came out as a confident whisper. 'I don't think he even means it sometimes,' she continued. 'He's always remorseful.'

She sounded like she was about to defend him, until she stopped herself.

'But he isn't a nice man.'

'Sarah, why didn't you say anything?' Abbie urged gently.

'What would I say?' she questioned and Abbie understood. 'How do you just come out with the fact that someone is abusing you, Abbie? Do you say it over breakfast? Or in a text message, perhaps?'

Sarah's words were cutting, but she didn't mean offense or judgement. She was pouring out her truth and it was painful.

'I kept fooling myself, thinking: this too shall pass. Thinking that it wouldn't happen again. But it always did. It always does.'

Abbie didn't try to scan her brain for the right words to say. She knew there were no right words. Nothing could make it better. All she could be was authentic and present.

'I'm sorry I wasn't there for you Sarah.'

Sarah smiled, a warm and accepting smile. 'Ditto, sis.'

#

She heard Ian, before she saw him emerge round the corner. The wheels of the chair skidding noisily down the corridor. He smirked as he spun the wheelchair around the entrance and created a slalom weave from side to side as he drove it towards her.

'We can have some fun with this,' he joked. 'Races down the corridor?'

Abbie smiled and shrugged off his joke.

'Sarah will be at ours too.'

Ian nodded a casual approval.

'Her and Simon are over,' she added casually, sliding off the bed and into the chair.

'Oh right,' Ian paused in surprise at the comment.

'She's packing his things up, ready for him to collect them on Wednesday when he's back from this retreat.'

'Hmm,' Ian murmured, helping Abbie adjust into the seat and covering her with a blanket. 'I'll ask her if she needs a hand. I can be her muscle if she wants it.'

Abbie tilted an unexpecting look at her husband. 'That's nice of you,' she said sceptically.

'Well,' Ian said, spinning the wheelchair and turning her to face the exit route. 'I never liked him anyway. Always got the impression he was a bit of a cock to be honest.'

Male intuition? Abbie wondered. *Maybe it wasn't to be underestimated.*

'You ready?' he asked.

She took a deep breath. 'Ready as I'll ever be,' she replied.

Ian rode her out of the ward, down the lift, and out to the exit.

The doors slid open, releasing her back into reality - a reality that now felt a little more fragile, a little more precious.

BEFORE

CHAPTER 33

'Nice shot,' Ian called, watching the ball fly through the air.

Tom collected his tee and spun round to face Ian, smiling with confidence. 'Thanks mate, I've been practising.'

'I can see that! Not got another golf partner, I hope.'

'Well, you're not around much these days mate,' Tom jibed, finding a way to share his disappointment, while still hoping it didn't stab too hard.

'I know, mate.' Ian gathered his clubs and slung the bag over his shoulder, beginning the walk to the next hole. 'Things have been a little tricky at home, recently.'

Tom turned to face his best friend, concerned by his tone. They had never spoken much about their feelings, choosing to stick with friendly banter over deep chat. The only time Tom had seen Ian cry was when Lucy was born. Ian had only seen Tom shed a tear when his mother passed away from her long battle with cancer.

Tom arched his back slightly, preparing for an uncomfortable few moments.

Ian's feet scuffed over the blades of grass, leaving streaks of green against the polished white, as he walked on in silence. Tom knew better than to speak first. If Ian had an issue and needed to talk, he would wait it out and listen to him, no matter how uncomfortable it made them.

'It's Abbie,' he began, 'She's acting ...

irrationally.'

Tom went to throw out a humerus line about women acting irrationally, but stopped himself. Instead, he walked on slowly, side by side with Ian, both of them gazing ahead into the green hilly distance.

'The other week, I left for work, but as soon as I got in my car, I realised I'd left my phone behind.' He lifted his hat slightly, scratched at his head and readjusted the hat back into place. 'So, I come back in the house and Abbie is sitting cross legged on the floor, holding my phone.'

Tom inadvertently winced at the thought. He'd caught an ex or two in this predicament before and there was no getting out of it. Of course, his relationships were not a marriage. *Maybe it was different with a marriage; you can't just cut and run once the trust is gone.*

'I asked her what she was doing and she just burst into tears and ran upstairs.'

'Right,' Tom replied, waiting for more information that could make sense of the situation. *Surely Ian wasn't cheating. He was the most loyal man Tom knew. If Ian was having an affair, there would be no hope for the rest of them.*

'I followed her, of course and knocked on the door. But she wouldn't let me in. She just kept crying and saying that she should have known better.'

Tom could feel Ian watching him now as they continued to walk in step with one another, but he did not return the gaze.

'What did you do?' he questioned, hoping not to sound too judgemental.

'Well, what could I do? I was late for work! So I

told her I had to leave and then I went. But the weird thing was, as I got in my car I unlocked my phone to see what she'd been looking at.'

Tom chose this moment to turn and observe his best friend. He raised his eyebrows, to indicate that Ian should reveal the mystery.

'But it was just a text message chat with Lucy.'

Tom felt guilty at his disappointment. A little more drama wouldn't have gone a miss. 'Right, so why was she upset by that?'

'No idea,' Ian replied earnestly, kicking the grass with dejection. 'By the time I got home from work, she seemed fine, like she'd snapped out of the whole thing.'

Tom felt his friend's confusion. Women were confusing and they had never been able to figure them out. Not when they were teenagers and not now that they were adults.

'She's not been herself for a while now, and I'm not sure I know what to do about it. It's as if I'm not good enough, or something. I just feel like maybe she doesn't want to be with me any more, you know? Like maybe I'm not making her happy or something.'

Tom took a deep breath and considered his options: shrug it off and open up a chat about the footy, or try to engage in a difficult discussion which might make things better or might make things worse. He chose the latter.

'That's really shit, mate.' Tom said sympathetically. 'But there is no way that she doesn't want you any more. You guys are made for one another, the perfect couple that everyone else wants to be like.'

Ian shrugged off his compliments.

'It's true, Ian,' Tom continued. 'But sometimes things go awry a little. You need to reconnect and talk, try to understand what's making her feel this way and attempt to smooth things over.'

Ian nodded, shifting his clubs from one shoulder to the other as they walked round the next corner, seeing their balls come back into view.

'You're right,' Ian said sharply and Tom knew, from his tone, that the conversation was over. 'Okay you're on a par three so let's see what you can do from here.' He tilted his head, surveying the proposed shot past the row of trees.

Tom paused. 'Actually, mate, I wanted to let you know about something,' he started. 'Something I discovered recently.'

'Yes, mate,' Ian said, plonking his bag down and removing the driver with care.

'Well, you see, I was on a date the other night,' he started.

'Oh yeah? I thought you'd had enough of all that?' Ian questioned mockingly.

'I know, but this one was a woman I'd been speaking to for quite a while, so I thought I owed it to myself to meet her in person.'

Ian continued to fiddle with his club, not looking at Tom.

'Jasmine, her name was - she seemed nice. Well, as we got to talking, she mentioned her ex.

'Oh,' Ian winced, 'Red flag right?'

Tom chucked, 'Well, yes,' he said before regaining his composure. 'But, she said she'd been seeing this guy for a few months and things were moving quite quickly. He told her he'd inherited some money after his parents passed away - boat accident or something - and that he no longer needed to work.'

'Right...' Ian said slowly, rising from where he'd placed his tee, slanting his eyes towards Tom.

'So, she said he was acting as nice as pie and things were going well - he'd basically moved in - when one day his phone started ringing. He was in the shower, so she answered it and it was this crazy woman demanding her money back.'

Tom was speaking quickly now, his eyes widening with the urgency of his story.

'She dismissed it and hung up, but the calls kept coming through, day after day. She asked him who it was and he brushed it off as a crank call. So, one night, while he was sleeping, she took his phone and got the number of this *crank caller*, deciding she needed answers. She called the number and the same woman's voice was on the other end. She told her that this man was her ex too, but that he was a fraud! She explained how he had ciphered thousands of pounds from her before doing a runner.'

'Mad!' Said Ian.

'Indeed,' replied Tom. 'Then it all came out, about how his parents weren't actually dead. He'd just used it as a sob story to hook her in, before doing her over. How he'd turned violent when she confronted him and then just disappeared one day.'

'Shit, what did she do?'

'She said she called the police,' Tom announced, 'But when she got off the phone to them, he was there, behind the door. He'd heard her 999 call, packed up his things and was out of the house before she could figure out what was happening. Never to be seen again.'

'Jeez, that's the kind of thing you see on a TV

drama,' Ian spoke casually, teeing up his club with the ball and practising his swing, back and forth. 'Not what you expect to happen in real life.'

'That's what I thought,' Tom continued, 'And I almost dismissed her there and then, as a nutjob, inventing stories about exes for some attention or to prove that she was a hard-done-by victim. Until...' he stopped and reached out a hand to get Ian's attention.

Ian lowered his club and swiveled towards Tom.

'Until she told me his name,' Tom announced, 'It sounded familiar, but then I remembered you telling me about Sarah's new partner and how his name made him sound like a kid's TV presenter.'

'Simon Smith?' Ian questioned, a side eye fixed on his partner.

'Simon Smith!' he repeated back. 'Surely that's no coincidence?'

Ian stood still, the cogs in his brain moving too fast for his facial expressions to adjust. His eyes were flicking back and forth as he tried to consider the facts, before his face softened again.

'There's no way Sarah's boyfriend is a psychopathic liar and a thief!' he joked, but Tom's expression did not alter.

'Well, Saturday night will be interesting,' Tom announced. 'I'm looking forward to meeting the guy and asking him a thing or two, that's for sure.'

Tom removed his driver and ushered Ian forward. 'You first,' he said, continuing on with the game as if nothing had happened.

CHAPTER 34

By the time he had finished in the shower, she was gone. He knew it as soon as he stepped out, into the steam of the room. He could sense he was alone.

'Sarah?' he called out, hoping for silence to reply.

His heart was racing, a mixture of last night's whiskey and his desire to move quickly. He had been rumbled and he needed to get out, to make his escape before it was too late. It was only a matter of time before Tom spoke with Sarah - or maybe he already had. Would it have come up in front of Lucy? Or would he wait until the morning, find an excuse to get her alone and reveal his dirty secrets then?

The tennis retreat was his get out. He'd pack up his things - and a few of hers for good measure - and leave as if he were still heading up north for the week. But he wouldn't be back.

'Fucking twat!' he mumbled to himself, remembering Jasmine and her loose lips. He should have travelled further this time. It was his own fault for staying too local.

Last night's conversation was brief, but it was enough. The leer in Tom's eye as he spoke was clear, the cloak was lifting and he was uncovering the truth. He cast his mind back to the words Tom had spoken.

'Nice to meet you.' *Friendly enough. Casual but firm handshake. Tom was trying to assert his dominance, for sure.*

'I think we might have a mutual friend,' Tom had smirked.

No shit, Sherlock, Simon had thought, *We are at*

the same fucking party, you idiot. Instead he raised his eyebrows, feigning an interest

'She had some interesting stories to share, did Jasmine. Sweet girl really.'

Thank God for Katie's interruption. Katie, with her clumsy fucking drink and her drunken fucking mess of a life. The wine had spilled right over Tom's jeans - *what a shame* - and Simon had found his opportunity to escape amongst the chaos.

He snatched at his things: clothes, shoes, Xbox, shoving them into Sarah's favourite Michael Kors travel bag. He opened up the jewellery box and swiped out as much as he could gather, stumbling over his shoes as he hurried around the room.

He regained his balance and found himself face to face with the photo beside the bed: him and Sarah in Mexico earlier this year. His heart sank. *This isn't what he had wanted.* He truly believed that things could be different this time, that Sarah could be his forever person, the person who might even make him change. He'd even considered them starting a family, for God's sake. A real, proper family, with a baby and everything. This was supposed to be real. His real chance to move on and escape the demons from his past. But Tom had fucked it all up for him.

He grabbed his phone and unlocked it quickly, typing out his message with urgency. He'd have to take an Uber to the station and jump on the next train north. Hopefully he'd be far enough away before she came home.

He glanced out of the window and looked both ways, checking that she wasn't yet returning. He didn't know where she'd gone in such a hurry, but he hoped she'd be out for a while. It must have been pretty urgent if she left in such a rush - she'd still been in pyjamas when he'd left her to come upstairs.

He opened up the messaging app and typed quickly, the swoosh of the text ringing into the room as it was sent.

Mum, I'm coming home. x

TWO MONTHS LATER

CHAPTER 35
ABBIE

'Pass the gravy?'

Lucy obliged willingly and lent over to pass the steaming brown liquid to her brother.

Ian's wry smile was clocked by Judy and she chose the moment to pass comment.

'It's lovely to see you both getting on,' she commented, piling broccoli onto her plate before passing the bowl to Greg.

Greg eyed them suspiciously, placing a small floret onto his plate and holding the bowl out to the side, hoping that Lucy would relinquish them from him swiftly.

'Uh uh,' Judy interjected, grabbing the tongs and unloading another three onto his plate. 'If I'm eating healthily, we all are!'

Greg huffed dejectedly. 'This cancer is really starting to affect me!' he joked, surveying the room with his eyes to ensure it was willing to accept his sarcasm.

'Gregory!' Judy called. 'That is not appropriate humour in front of the children.'

Greg nudged his granddaughter with his knee, as she chuckled silently into her jumper.

'The doctor says that cruciferous vegetables and healthy carbs will speed up the healing process.'

Greg turned to Lucy and muttered into her ear. 'He must also have said that the removal of any taste or flavour helps.'

Lucy sniggered again, lifting her hand to her

mouth in an attempt to cover the laughter.

'When do you start radiotherapy, Judy?' Ian asked loudly in an attempt to dispel the inappropriate humour.

'A week on Tuesday,' she replied quickly. 'Three weeks worth will take me to just before Christmas. Home in time for Santa,' she winked to George.

He beamed at the thought, before blurting out, 'Santa doesn't come to adults!'

'Indeed,' she replied. 'But I've been through a lot this year, so he may bring me a little something for being such a good girl.'

Judy's lighthearted childishness was refreshing. The lumpectomy was ten days ago and she was just beginning to gain her strength back. The radiotherapy would be difficult - they were all well aware of that - but Judy's positivity was infectious.

'Can I have a scooter this year?' George asked, as Abbie filled up his plate. 'And a phone.'

'There's no way he's getting a phone!' snapped Lucy, 'I didn't get one until I was eleven. He's not getting one at nine!'

George stuck his tongue out at his sister and she returned hers back, adding in a thumb to her nose and a wiggle of the fingers.

'No phone yet, George,' Abbie spoke calmly, 'But we can see if Santa might be able to do something about that scooter.' She looked over at Ian, who nodded in agreement.

Money was going to be tight moving forward and Abbie was extremely conscious of it. She'd tried to bring it up in conversation a few times, but Ian was always dismissive. 'It'll be fine,' or 'Nothing to panic over yet,' he'd reply, squashing the conversation before it really began.

'A week on Tuesday?' Ian said, diverting the conversation back to Judy. 'That's positive. The new year will come with a new start for you then, won't it? You'll be fit as a fiddle again and raring to leap into the new year with a fresh lease of life.'

Judy smiled obligingly, placing the dish of roasted carrots back onto the lazy susan. 'That's the plan. The world is our oyster and we plan on cracking it open and seeing what's inside.'

#

The table was almost clear, except for a few glasses which had been left strewn on the table for people's return once pudding was ready. Judy wiped her hand across its wooden surface, pushing some crumbs onto the floor, which Barney licked up gratefully, before scuffling back to his bed.

The men had retreated to the lounge to watch the football and George and Lucy had followed. From the kitchen, Judy could hear the jeers of the men, alongside the laughter from her grandchildren.

'They're getting on well,' smiled Judy.

Abbie instantly knew who she was referring to and a proud grin spread across her face. 'They are doing much better,' she said. Pausing momentarily before adding, 'We all are.'

'I can see that,' Judy replied, a delicate smile still arched across her face.

Judy noticed the softening of her daughter over the last two months and was buoyed by it. It wasn't just her features that had softened; her voice had softened too. Along with her mannerisms, her demeanor and her general aura. Judy had noticed that Abbie had been stressed in the past, but it wasn't until she let it all go that she saw her old daughter return, the one who had joy and optimism - humour even - within her.

'I'm so glad that you're doing better, Abbie.'

Abbie peered at her mother, a gleeful eye that welcomed her mother's pride, and Judy was hit by the realisation that she was still this woman's parent and parenting was an ongoing commitment - not a task that is achieved when your child becomes an adult, but a commitment for life. Perhaps she had forgotten that over time. *No matter how old your children become, you are still their parents, always.*

After a moment, Abbie shrugged off her mother's comments. 'You're the one we should be talking about, Mum. You're the one going through cancer, I just had a midlife crisis.'

Judy shook her head. 'No, no, don't do that. Don't minimise your feelings to deflect onto someone else. Everyone is going through their own shit, Abbie, and it is all real and it is all valid.'

Abbie chuckled. 'Those self help books helping you, Mum?'

Abbie was right, Judy had been reading self help books, and listening to podcasts and following life advisors on Instagram (Lucy had shown her!). She was embracing change and opening up to the world, in order to make the most of her life - however much of it she might have left. The cancer diagnosis had hit her like a bolt from the blue. She'd never really considered her own fatality before. She knew she was aging, of course - her mirror didn't allow her to escape *that* fact - but her mind was still aged twenty. *How do you convince your mind that you are in fact much older - a real life grown up - and hurtling your way towards your latter years at breakneck speed?*

'They are, in fact,' Judy said confidently. 'We only have one life, Abbie and we need to make the most of it.'

Even as she spoke, she was aware of her words being cliche, ironic, maybe even cringy, but she really meant them. This year had been a wake up call for her. No more fantasies about being somewhere else, with someone else or doing something else. This was her life - a good life - and she chose it. She needed to start enjoying it, really enjoying it and appreciating what she had.

'We all make mistakes in life, Abbie.' her mother continued. 'We get things wrong, we make bad choices, we say stupid things.'

Abbie raised an eyebrow, wondering where this was going.

'We are impacted by the way we were raised, and influenced by the people we have around us, so that affects how we act and how we raise our own children - the things we think are right or wrong, acceptable or not. God knows I made some mistakes.'

Abbie considered dismissing her comment and brushing her claims away. She didn't want her mother to feel guilty for the wrongdoings of her past - not at her age. But she stopped herself. She realised that now was the time for her mother to get some things off of her chest.

'I am sure I scarred you girls in more ways than one.'

Abbie couldn't control the shaking of her head, but her mother raised a hand out to stop her.

'The things I said and the ways I must have made you feel. The comments I made about weight and appearance. The judgements I passed onto you. But I just hope you understand, they came from a place of self-deprecation and self-consciousness. Because of the way *I* was raised and the comments bestowed on *me* when I was younger. It was never about you Abbie. I was probably just jealous.'

Abbie sat still, listening to her mother's words, breathing them in and trying to consider where they had appeared from and why now. She had long forgiven the comments from her youth, the remarks about weight. She had realised that they came from a place of envy - Abbie had never been fat - but they had been hurtful, nonetheless.

'It's ok, mum.' Abbie spoke honestly. 'We all say things we don't mean sometimes. I bet Lucy could tell you a story or two!'

Judy's face lifted and softened at Abbie's words, as if she'd been waiting twenty years for the guilt to be lifted and the forgiveness to be granted.

'It hasn't negatively impacted me mum. I'm ok,' she smiled.

And with those words, Judy's demeanour shifted suddenly back to normal as she scooped the last pieces of cutlery from the table and hurried them into the dishwasher.

'And yes, I am doing better now,' Abbie continued, allowing herself to be the centre of the conversation for once and to feel comfortable in that space. 'I knew that something needed to change in my life and we are all doing better as a result. It's just...'

Abbie paused, looked over the table at her mother for assurances that it was okay to keep talking. Judy sat patiently.

'I'm so much happier, Mum, and I feel a release

that's gone from me. A release that I didn't even really know I was holding onto until I let it go and felt how much lighter I was. But, I don't know what the future has in store for me, and that's a little scary.'

Judy nodded, but did not speak. She sat back in her chair, a signal to her daughter to continue talking. This was her space and she could say what she needed to say.

'I've been a teacher for so long; a wife and mother too. I've kept myself so busy and now that I have no job, I feel like maybe I have no purpose, or no real value - you know?'

Abbie's face squinted, in a desperate attempt at validation. *Did her mother understand what she meant at all?*

Judy continued to sit still, letting Abbie's words sink in for a moment, before replying. 'You know, Abbie, a person's worth is not judged by the number of plates they can spin. One is not more worthy because they are able to check more tasks off of their to-do list than their neighbour. A person's worth is judged on the way they think, the people they connect with, the feelings and memories they leave in their wake.'

Abbie was surprised by her mother's eloquence and philosophical change of tact, but more than surprised, she was impressed. Her mother had always been comfortable being the butt of a joke, the less educated of the family. She thrived in that space, perhaps she even enjoyed being the 'ditsy one'. There were only a handful of times in her life that Abbie had gone to her mother for advice or guidance, choosing her father instead, time after time.

Judy continued, 'Abbie, you are of value. You have value. Not because of what you achieve on a daily basis but because of the people who depend on you, who need you and who love you. That is all.'

Abbie smiled.

'You've always been a stubborn one, a confident woman who wants to have it all, but maybe 'having it all' is not quite what you think it is.'

Abbie was buoyed by her mother's comments, as a connection continued to grow between them.

'Yes,' she said, 'I *have* spent my life trying to have it all. But, how many years have women spent hoping to be considered equal to men? Striving to have a seat around the table or to finally have a voice that is heard?'

Abbie picked at her thumb, the skin beside the nail beginning to flake, exposing the redness beneath it. Judy noticed and as soon as Abbie noticed her mother watching, she stopped.

'I wanted to work,' Abbie continued, her hands placed firmly upon her thighs. 'I didn't want to sacrifice anything else. I still wanted to have children and be the best possible mother I could. I still wanted a husband, a house, a pension. I didn't want a cleaner - *I can clean my own house, thank you!*' Abbie's voice mocked at her own stubbornness. 'I didn't need a shoulder to cry on - *I didn't have time for crying.*' Her ironic voice attempted to bring humour to her rant. 'I waited until I had finally achieved it all, and then what did I go and do? I fell apart. All this time I've spent trying to prove to the world that I can do it all, and then I fail. All these years of women fighting for equal rights, for feminism and I'm just living proof that I, as a woman, was not good enough.'

Abbie's face was not emotional. She did not cry or look dejected or sullen. This was something she had been thinking and feeling for some time and she was finally letting out her honesty.

Judy considered her words carefully, before replying. She did not want to dismiss her daughter's feelings. It was important to hear her, to understand her, but she was also enraged at her daughter's misunderstandings.

Her voice was calm and monotone.

'Abbie, feminism isn't about having it all. It isn't about being a superhero. Feminism doesn't mean being the CEO of a company. And it certainly doesn't mean being the CEO of a company, while also being the perfect mother and wife.' Judy raised her hands as she airquoted the word 'perfect'.

'Feminism means having the option to choose what you want to be and being invited to work towards becoming that. It's about *choice*, and finding a pathway that invites you to *attempt* to be what you *want* to be. It's about having an awareness of the domination, oppression and exploitation of women that has been present for so many years, and wanting to make a stand for that. Abbie, you have the freedom to make choices, and the choices you make are yours and yours alone. Do not let them be governed, influenced or critiqued by anyone but yourself.'

Abbie's eyes were glassy as she sat, motionless in her seat. Judy was aware that Abbie had never thought much of her. She was just a housewife after all.

'Wow, Mum,' she said.

Judy stood up, scraping her chair against the floor as she moved. She winked at her daughter - a confident, supportive wink that said more than any more words could have done in that moment.

'You just do you, Abbie. And never, ever, feel like you are not good enough.' As she spoke, Judy flung her arms out wide. 'Just look around you, for goodness sake. Look at all you've achieved.'

Abbie scanned left and right, seeing her mother's kitchen, her mother's life, her mother's world and she realised that her mother was not just speaking to Abbie. Her mother was speaking to herself, to the world, to womanhood.

'Thanks, Mum,' Abbie whispered.

She was unaware if her mother had heard her, as her back was already turned and her head was poking out into the hallway.

'Pudding's ready!' she called.

CHAPTER 36
SARAH

The haziness in her head wobbled as she felt a wave of freedom wash over her. Her glass was still half full, but the first few sips had already hit her, the warmth rushing through her with ease. This was the first drink she'd had in a long time, and it felt good.

Around the room, an eclectic mix of people sat, immersed in their own worlds, completely unaware of each other's business.

The builder on his own at the bar, wobbling gently on the bar stool, unaware that his wonky glass was dripping beer onto his steel capped boots; too consumed with guilt and worry over how to tell his wife that he was 'let go' today. Agonising over how they would manage to make ends meet without his salary and with another baby on the way.

The couple in the corner, clinking their glasses of champagne, toasting to the exchange on their first house together. Making plans for the furniture they will purchase and the parties they will hold. Her smile shining brightly at the hope for what the future will hold, while his phone pings wildly in his pocket - desperate messages from his lover checking what time he'll be around later.

The four friends around the table - too old for the room - straining to hear each other above the music, leaning into each other's ears, a little too close for comfort. Their refusal to head across town to the quieter bar, being regretted secretly by each of them, but none of them brave enough to admit defeat. The youngest looking of the group, a man in his late fifties with an athletic figure and a healthy glow, choosing Diet Coke over the wine shared by the remaining three, completely unaware that tonight he would suffer a cardiac arrest and that, for him, tomorrow would never come.

The room held secrets. Each person had a history, a story to tell about their past and a vision of what their future was to hold. Each of them hurtling through life, feeling powerful and in control, but utterly defenseless to what life may throw their way.

Sarah stopped daydreaming and looked back across the table, where her partner sat. The silence that they held was comfortable and showed a level of security between them. They'd both always been people watchers, and they used to enjoy sitting at the bar, making up stories about the lives of the people who walked past the window.

She observed Tom's expression as he watched the young couple at the bar bicker over who was going to pay. His eyes were alight with humour as he realised the disagreement was over *wanting* to pay and he chuckled silently at how the world had changed since he began dating.

'I've missed this,' she said honestly, surprising herself at the truth in her words and the brashness of their arrival.

'Huh?' he replied, his attention focused back on her, leaning slightly in and resting his arm upon the table.

She shook her head dismissively and smiled. She would not repeat herself. *He knew.*

'So, what's the plan?' he asked.

'I'm happy here. Just a glass or two will be nice.

It's been a while since I've had a drink.'

Sarah had craved a glass of wine over the past few weeks, much to her surprise. She was never one to desire alcohol, but since Simon's departure, she'd felt a freedom lift within her. Dealing with the pregnancy had taken longer than she'd expected. She was not prepared for the pain, the blood, the feeling of emptiness that she would be left with. It had taken time, but as she began to heal and consider a life without his poison, she'd begun to feel more in control, more confident and more able to make decisions for herself again.

And, of course, there had been Tom.

Seeing him that night had been an eye opener, the way that sometimes in life, the stars align and things fall into place, when you're least expecting them to. The clarity she saw that weekend was glaring and transparent. The culmination of events, conversations and mishaps joined into one; and she could suddenly see that she did not need anyone to control or guide her. She could be her own shepherd and her own master.

Yet, there was something missing. Not someone to lead her or to nudge her along, not someone to steer her in certain directions or push her to be more or less of one thing or another. She simply needed a mate. Someone to share life with. Someone to speak to, who would truly listen. Someone to hold and be held by. Someone to love her and for her to love back.

And there Tom was.

'I don't mean tonight, Sarah. I mean what's the plan? What do you want to do next in life?'

Sarah coughed and considered the question carefully. It felt huge. *How was she to know what life had in store for her or even how much longer she had? She could not control her destiny, but she could control her choices.*

'Well,' she said slowly. 'I need to do some things for me.'

Tom nodded and placed the other arm upon the table top, crossing them and leaning forwards, facing her and listening carefully.

'I don't mean *for* me, I mean things that I've always wanted to do, but things that are done to help others.

'I'd like to do some charity work. There are amazing charities that campaign to end violence against women and girls. I've already reached out to a few and made some inquiries.'

'Wow, that sounds great. I think you'd be great at that, Sarah.'

'Yeah,' she replied, 'I think I would too. And I want to do something meaningful, you know? Help to give back. Be remembered. Leave a legacy.'

She paused to check that she wasn't getting too deep. Tom's nod was reassuring, so she continued.

'I've been thinking about that quite a bit recently: leaving a legacy. And I'm in a position where I can help others, so that's my next step. Abbie's all trained up now, so I can leave the business in good hands, while I take a little break.'

'She's a fast learner, that one,' Tom smiled, before adding tentatively, 'And, on the relationship front?'

This was not their first date since Simon had left. They'd seen each other several times. Sometimes at his house, sometimes at hers, once at a coffee shop. It felt natural and normal, like picking up from where they left off. She'd hidden nothing from him - being open about both Simon and the baby. Tom had been supportive. More than that. He'd been gentle and kind. When she had discovered the old newspaper article: *Heartless Man Steals Thousands from Suckered Widow* he was sympathetic and sensitive. She'd felt stupid and blindsided, but he'd reassured her with care and loyalty.

Sarah had a choice to make: she could either open herself up to the risk of getting hurt, or she could act just how she had done before: shutting things down and running away with self preservation at the thought of potentially losing him.

'I'd like a partner,' she started. 'Who *doesn't* want to share their journey with someone else? But I need to make sure that whoever I choose to do that with, understands what I am and what I am not able to offer.'

'And what is that, exactly?'

'Well,' she started, 'I don't necessarily want children.' She winced at the discomfort of the words. She'd always struggled to admit this fact, feeling that everyone else in the world believed it was her God-given duty to produce a child and that they had judged her for not wanting to do so. 'So I need someone who will be okay with that. I can't live my life feeling guilty that I've deprived someone else of that gift.'

She shifted uncomfortably in her chair, before stopping herself and sitting still, arching her back to be a little taller.

'I want to be someone's everything. I know it sounds a lot but I want my partner to choose me every time; to put me first and adore me, to have my back - even when I'm wrong - and to pick me up when I fall down. And I want to be able to be that for someone else. I want true transparency, vulnerability and connection.'

Her mouth felt dry. She'd blurted out the words too fast, afraid that if she didn't speak openly and honestly now, she would regret it for the rest of her life. Her words were a lot; she was a lot. But she had spent her whole life feeling like she wasn't good enough or worthy enough to have a man treat her properly. She wouldn't hold back any longer. She knew what she needed and she had to have the courage of her convictions. She reached for her glass and took another sip, the sharp liquid hitting her tongue and quenching her thirst.

Tom sat back in his chair and looked her square in the eye.

'Okay.'

Sarah waited for Tom to say more, but more words were not forthcoming.

'Okay?' she questioned back.

'Okay!' he repeated again.

The hum of their surroundings began to fade into the distance. She stared ahead at Tom, the man she'd once loved, maybe *always* loved, and saw deep into him. She held his gaze, soft and comforting, his face becoming clearer and sharper as the rest of the world faded away.

He reached across the table, without breaking his gaze, and collected her hands gently into his.

'Sarah,' he started, 'I have loved you since the first moment I set eyes on you. I loved you then, I loved you over time, and I still love you now.'

She felt her heart jump an irregular beat and her palms began to moisten.

'All I have ever wanted is to be your person. Nothing more and nothing less. What is love, if not the desire to better someone else's journey through life? I know you don't need anyone to *save* you or to *protect* you, but I'd really like it if you could let me be *with* you on your journey.'

'You've never said that before, Tom.' As she spoke, she felt her eyes begin to well and her stomach lurch heavily. She pushed the tears back down and drowned the butterflies.

'I was a fool, Sarah. And I know that now. I've spent a lot of time searching inside myself, trying to understand why I was never able to tell you before. I know that you needed that reassurance from me and I know that you couldn't be with someone who couldn't give you that promise.

'When I saw you that night at your father's birthday, I felt like a truck smacked me straight on, and suddenly it just hit me: I love you.'

She gulped in a breath, suddenly needing more oxygen to make sense of what he was saying and to prove to herself that this was real.

'It was like someone switched on a light and suddenly it was all so clear. Try as I might, I could not possibly understand why someone would ever refuse to tell someone else that they love them. Love is a word to be shouted from the rooftops and whispered in goodnights. Love is said at the start of cards and the end of phone calls. It's the start of forever and the end of everything. Why wouldn't you tell someone you loved them until they were sick of hearing it?'

'I want to make this work,' Sarah said, leaning in and squeezing Tom's hand.

'So do I, Sarah. That is, if you'll let me be part of

your journey again?'

His words hung in the air as she considered her choice: jump all in or run for the hills.

She had to be brave.

'Yes please,' she said humbly, 'I think that would be nice.'

Tom rose from the table and pulled her to her feet, engulfing her in to him and kissing her hard.

Onlookers in the bar had their attention stolen by the discreet couple who'd been sitting quietly all evening. Some were embarrassed at their public display of affection. Others felt joy at the confidence of their love.

Everyone wondered what their future had in store.

CHAPTER 37
ABBIE

'Morning sweetie.' Ian brushed past her, stopping briefly to plant his lips against her cheek, before continuing on into the kitchen. 'We've only got five minutes or so before we need to leave. You sure you want to come, too?'

Football was quickly becoming part of their weekend morning routine. George had finally made the under ten's first team and the commitment to coaching and matches had been more intense than any hobby she had been involved with before. The 8am Saturday starts were a shock to the system.

'Of course,' she yawned, unconvincingly. 'I wouldn't miss it.'

'Coach says he's starting up front today. That'll show Isaac!'

Abbie tutted at his competitiveness. 'Now, now,' she judged mildly.

Ian ignored her contempt and continued packing George's bag with protein snacks and drinks. Abbie was well aware that Ian was taking the football more seriously than her son was - but that was probably true of most of the dad's at the training club.

'And we will collect Lucy afterwards, yes?' he asked casually

Abbie was beginning to allow her daughter a little more freedom. Thirteen and a half was old enough to be left at home alone, she knew that, but it hadn't made it any easier to accept.

'Yep, around 11am,' she replied. 'She knows to

be packed and ready to go straight out after George has showered.'

Abbie was looking forward to the trip, it was just what they all needed. It had been a difficult decision to take the kids out of school for a week, but she was prepared to face the heat; the fine even. The thought would never have occurred to her before, but now that she was out of the system, she was able to think in a different way. School was important - of course it was - but it wasn't everything.

That's what she'd said when Joe had called her that evening, six weeks ago. He'd agreed to lift the suspension and had asked her to come back to work. But the decision had been made and she'd found confidence in her voice, telling him that she was no longer willing to give her everything to that job.

He'd been dumbfounded, expecting a different response, but she was certain and she had the backing of her loved ones. The course of her future was going to be different, from now on.

Three weeks later and he'd been gone too. A sudden removal from leadership - no explanation given. He hadn't been seen in school since. Abbie had known the truth - the rumour mill was rife, and stories were beginning to emerge.

At first, she found out about him and Katie - an affair that she discovered had been going on for months. Sarah hadn't even known about it! Then it came out about the others - members of staff, and even some parents!

There were reports of gross misconduct, then of inappropriate behaviour, and finally claims of sexual harassment.

She hadn't yet been asked to comment, there

did not appear to be a criminal case, but if one began, she would speak up. She had found her voice and she wasn't afraid to use it.

Katie had been distraught when she realised she wasn't the only one. He'd fed her a web of lies and promised her the world. In reality, he had delivered nothing.

Abbie was sure that Rob would leave, but the last she'd heard, they were starting marriage counselling. She hoped that they could fix things - she really did. Everyone makes mistakes. Some are just a little bigger than others.

Abbie considered the mistakes she'd made and, for a moment, her mind began to wander to the 'what if's. She shrugged the negativity away and glanced around the kitchen, choosing instead to remember all the seemingly simple, yet significant moments that had filled the room.

She remembered the games of Monopoly played at the kitchen table; Ian and Lucy bickering and battling over Park Lane and Mayfair.

She recalled the muddy wellies at the back door - a memory of their walks with Barney - everyone moaning about the prospect (too cold, too wet, too tired) but once the cobwebs were blown away, their loads were lifted.

Her mind jumped back to the evenings, standing over the stove at tea time, her feet throbbing from the day, stirring the pots and juggling the multiple meals to feed differing tastes. Turning at the sound of the front door beeping open and her husband returning from his day at work, appearing in the doorway exhausted, his tie dangling around his neck, top button undone and shirt hanging loose, searching for his slippers and grumbling about the mess on the floor.

And suddenly she was struck with an awareness that the mundane had been masquerading all this time as misery; fooling her into believing that the toing and froing of their lives, the monotonous activities and the tedious chores, was where the unhappiness lingered. But there was something to be said for the mundane. Mundane was life. Mundane was reality. Mundane was contentment.

Abbie looked over at her husband, noticing how his hair was beginning to fleck with the ashy signs of aging, his gut beginning to protrude over his waistline, his wrinkles around the eyes becoming more profound when he spoke. His face held a comforting familiarity along with an unknown newness. It was still the same shape that it had been all those years ago, although now his jaw line was hidden behind his stubble, whereas his face had once been smooth and polished.

She remembered his words the first time he'd opened up his heart to her: 'I'm falling in love with you,' and she recalled the same emotions she had felt in that moment. The gravity at this momentous moment, mixed with juvenile amusement at the adultness of the word. She wondered now if that word meant the same thing at age sixteen that it did at age thirty seven. The heaviness of the word was still as powerful, they had the ability to destroy worlds and break up families as well as the ability to join families together and ignite new worlds.

She had always been confused by the concept of love, often feeling that she could fall in love with someone new every day. Sometimes she fell in love with the postman who delivered her mail as he smiled at her convincingly. She fell in love with the stranger in the supermarket who she saw, aisle after aisle until they finally locked eyes. She fell in love with the actor on TV who played a role she connected with, knowing that she could marry that character if he existed in real life.

Yet none of those feelings were the same as how she felt for Ian. The love she had for him was deep, engrained and permanent. Not something that could be wiped away or chalked off with ease. Their love was built from a series of connections and shared experiences over time. They chose their home together and filled it with things they picked and wanted. They loved the same children.

Abbie thought back to the fears she'd had about Ian in the past. The times she'd assumed he wanted to leave her; to be with someone else. Now, they felt foolish. Ian had promised that there was no one else. He'd shown her the messages on his phone. He'd explained the exchange between him and Lucy, how he had neglected to save her new number in his phone. He defended himself and their marriage, he fought for them and owned his own mistakes, choosing to work together to regrow the love. And she'd chosen to believe him. It was a choice. She could have chosen not to believe him, but everything in life was a choice, and she didn't want to make any more mistakes. There were always reasons to leave; there were better reasons to stay.

'Have you packed the thermals?' Ian asked and Abbie was pleasantly reminded of the necessity of her place within this family.

'Yes,' she smiled, 'Everything is packed.'

The Lake District would be cold, but she was prepared for that: the thermals were already stowed deep inside the case and the logs for the fire were waiting patiently in the boot of the car.

Abbie grabbed for her laptop. 'I might do a bit of work while I'm there.'

Ian nodded. 'Sounds good. Just a little bit though, eh?' he smiled at Abbie and she knew exactly what he meant. The smile was a loving warning, a careful reminder to look after herself, not push herself too hard. But she was enjoying working with Sarah. The job was a change and she'd be lying if she didn't feel overwhelmed at first, learning a new trade was difficult. Especially after years of being institutionalised within the same sector. But it was refreshing too. Working from home was a novelty. She was taking toilet breaks whenever she wanted - something she'd not done at work for twenty years. On her first day, she'd called Sarah at 1pm, asking if she could take her lunch break now. Sarah had laughed. Not in a humiliating or a condescending way, she was just shocked. And it was then that Abbie understood the freedom she now had - she could have her lunch break whenever it worked best for her. She was an adult. She was trusted. She was respected.

'I was thinking of Italy for the summer.' Ian stuck his head out into the hallway and called up the stairs, 'George, it's time to go.'

'Italy sounds lovely. That's where mum and dad will be starting their trek at Easter.'

Ian raised an eyebrow, 'They've booked it then?'

'Booked it last night. She texted Sarah and I to let us know. Our dinner table chat must have spurred her on'

'Good on them,' he said earnestly.

It *was* good on them. Abbie was proud of her mother's resilience. She was proud of her new lease of life and she was proud of the choices she was making. For too long, the secrets had been sloshing about, hiding from view, lurking in the background of their lives. Abbie could see that her mother was making up for lost time. She was connecting, being present and choosing to live the life she was in, choosing to stay living in the moment and enjoying it wherever she could.

'Coats on,' Abbie instructed, as she flung George's raincoat over his shoulders and passed Ian his mack.

She ushered her boys out of the door and glanced back at Barney. 'We won't be long,' she promised. 'Bye Luce!' she yelled.

'Bye,' came the reply.

'See you in a few hours. Make sure you're ready.'

'Will do.'

The response was refreshing. No grunts. No silent ignoring. No sarky comments. She was sure that Lucy was still in bed and that's where she'd remain for at least another hour, but she was okay with that. This was progress and she was pleased with it.

'I love you,' she added.

'Love you too,' came the echo.

Abbie smiled and stepped over the threshold, looking out at the soft unbroken grey sky that cast a dull hue over her. The fine spray of misty rain floated in the air, leaving its glistening mark on the leaves that still clung heartily on to their branches. In the distance, car tyres swished gently through puddles on the rain-slicked roads and the wind whispered around her.

The world felt a little slower, a little quieter than it had ever done before, wrapped tightly within the gentle hush of falling drizzle.

She pulled the door firmly behind her with a thud and stepped her boot forward into nature's labyrinth.

She was going to be okay.

Printed in Dunstable, United Kingdom